TWISTED FLAMES

TWISTED INTENTIONS

SAVANNAH RYLAN

1

———

ANGEL

"Do you really think I'm an idiot, Dee?" I asked as I slid my shirt over my head.

"Depends on when you're acting like one," he said flatly.

I sighed as I ran my hands down the front of my shirt. "Tucked in or no?"

"Does it matter what I think?"

I rolled my eyes. "Either pull your head out of your ass and get with the program or go away. But this is a prime opportunity, and I'm not wasting it just because we can't get Cap on the phone right now."

"Then don't ask what I think."

I lobbed my head over to look at my partner. The man that had held me down at the DEA ever since I took the field agent job they offered me five years ago. One random drug bust as a police officer right in the heart of our country's capital, and the next second, I applied for a DEA job that they practically threw at me. For five years, Dee watched my back. Trained me up. Covered for me when I did stupid shit because he knew it was for the greater good.

So, why the fuck didn't he have my back now?

"I take it there's nothing I can say to stop you?" he asked.

I threw the car door open. "Unless you wanna tell me why you absolutely can't stand the fact that we're about to pick up a massive lead in a case Cap has yet to bust wide open."

He leaned toward me. "You mean, a case *you* have yet to bust wide open. You know this isn't an official case."

I snapped my stare toward him. "It's back out on the street. I saw the logo. You know that that means, don't you? It means—"

"Someone has come in to fill the hole and continued dispersing the drugs that killed your brother. Yes, Angel, I know," he said flatly.

I stood and ducked my head back into the car. "Then, put some respect in your voice when you're talking about it."

When he didn't respond, I gave him one last chance.

"Sure you don't wanna come in?" I asked as I shoved the car door open. "It'll probably be one of the only times you can have a drink while on the job."

Dee pointed at me. "That."

"What?"

"That right there is why I'm not going in with you. This isn't a case for you. Right now, you're not on the clock. You're chasing a vendetta, and you're going to get yourself killed."

I blinked. "So, you're going to sit in the car while I get killed then?"

He gnashed his teeth together. "Just don't do anything stupid, Angel. Last thing I need is to haul your ass back to Cap and tell him what you did."

"What *we* did."

"Oh, no, this isn't my idea."

I stood up straight out of the car and stretched my arms over my head. "And yet, you're here with me now. About to listen in on a conversation that could blow this case wide open."

He snickered. "Trust me, with how heavy handed you

always are? The only thing you're about to blow open is a hole in their roof."

I grinned as I closed the door, and I made my way inside. Dee called out something from the car, but I didn't give a damn what he said. For once, we had a leg-up on the competition. On the crew peddling the same drugs that got my brother addicted. The drugs that destroyed his life. That took away his soul. A crew that I had found digging of my own volition in the late hours of the evening in my own damn bed because I was apparently the only person that gave a damn about getting that shit off the street.

I buried my brother with their drugs in his system.

And now, it was time for payback.

The rush of wind that fluttered my hair as I pushed the set of double doors open made me draw in a deep breath. The smell of fresh deep fryer grease had nothing on the warm scent of tequila floating through the air. Someone kicked on a blender, whirring together a drink for one of the patrons that hung themselves over a sticky-looking table.

The place was a dive if I'd ever seen one.

"What'll it be?!" someone called out.

I followed the sound of the voice. The trail of dulcet notes it left in its wake tugged my head around until I found myself staring at a grinning bartender. His stature towered over the bar as he stood there, shining a massive glass with the rag in his hand. He kept his gaze fixated on me as he threaded the stem of the glass through a roof-mounted storage unit, then slapped that damp rag right over his shoulder. His jet-black hair contrasted with his pale skin, and the bright background only served to amplify the deep green of his eyes.

It pulled me right up to the bar, and I cocked my hip to raise myself up onto a stool in front of him.

"What is that heavenly smell?" I asked as I put on my best innocent voice.

He chuckled as his head tilted off to the side. "House special. Lemonade margarita."

I pointed. "I'll have one of those. It sounds delicious."

He turned his back toward the mirrored wall of liquors. "Our extra crispy fries go great with it."

"Sign me up then."

"Order up!" he bellowed. "One large order, extra crisp!"

"Coming right up!" a disembodied voice off to my left yelped.

"So," the bartender said as he reached for a glass above his head, "don't think I've seen you around here."

I slid my gaze down his body. His chiseled jawline matched the pulsing muscles that stretched against his crimson shirt. It was a great color on him despite his pale complexion, and I had an awful time pulling my eyes away. Had he already made me? No, there was no fucking way. My shirt was much too thick to showcase the microphone taped to my chest.

Say something, you look like an idiot. "Didn't know the view was this good on the other side of town."

He chuckled, and the sound warmed me over like rich hot chocolate. "A woman whose poison is tequila deserves a good view before she forgets her evening."

I couldn't help but giggle. "You make a fair point. Tequila is one of those liquors."

"That," he said as he poured my drink into the glass, "and gin."

"Ah, you're a gin man."

"I'm absolutely a gin man. Keeps the Christmas spirit alive all year round."

I smiled. Genuinely smiled. "Christmas is one of my favorite times of the year as well."

"Order up!" the random voice called out from my left.

The bartender slid the drink toward me. "That would be your fries. Enjoy the drink, and I'll be right back."

And as the man turned toward my left, I couldn't help but watch his perky little ass while he walked toward the kitchen window.

Good God, the man was sexy as hell.

"You done staring?" Dee asked.

His voice came alive in my earpiece. "Don't tell me you like the view, too."

He snickered. "I can tell by the way you're talking. Be careful, he's already got you dropping your defenses."

I rolled my eyes. "It's just a drink and some fries."

"Uh huh."

"Here we go," the bartender said when he got back. "One large order of extra crispy fries. You want anything to dip those in?"

I smiled. "What do you prefer to dip them in?"

He winked at me. "Got a nice little dip in the back. It's usually just for the workers, but I'll spare you some."

"Ah, my hero."

He chuckled. "You stay put. I'll be right back."

Mm, mm, mm. I didn't even care if the sauce was shit. Watching that man walk away for a second time was very much worth the wait. My head tilted off to the side as his long legs bled up into a rotund ass that my hands wanted to—

"I'm proud of you, you know," Dee said.

I adjusted my glasses that held the camera through which Dee was able to view everything. And just like that, it hit me.

That man watched me stare down some other dude's ass.

"What's so funny?" he asked sharply.

I covered my mouth. "I forgot there was a camera on these things."

"You… forgot? Seriously?"

I kept giggling into my palm. "Completely."

"And you want to try and convince me that you're not distracted?"

That stopped my giggle in its tracks. "I swear, you're no fun. Since when did you become no fun?"

"Did you even hear me tell you that I'm proud of you?"

I paused. "Yeah, I did."

"Well, I am. After everything that happened, I would've put money on the fact that you wouldn't come back to the DEA. Suffering a loss like you did is hard on anyone. And then you came walking through those doors and showed everyone why you're the best at what you do."

"Yet, you're still questioning my every move."

"You can't exactly say you're unbiased toward this situation."

The second I located the bartender, I cleared my throat. "Well, well, what do we have here?"

The man with the piercing green eyes set a small container of what looked like yellowish goop in front of me. "It tastes better than it looks."

"You sure about that?"

He planted his massive forearms onto the table so that his eyes were level with mine. "I'm positive. Go on, try a bit. See what you think."

I eyed the sauce carefully and tried to figure out what was in it. Why the hell did it look lumpy? Relish. It could be relish. But who put relish in mustard? I bent down and sniffed it. For all I knew, I had been had and that shit was poison.

Then, Dee came to my rescue.

"It's honey mustard, sweet relish, horseradish, and most likely a twinge of ketchup for a bit of sweetness. You're fine."

So, I picked up a fry, dunked it, and tossed the entire thing into my mouth.

"Well?" the man asked.

Flavors burst against my tongue, and I couldn't hold back the groan working its way up the back of my throat. The sound split my lips, permeating the air between us as I leaned back against the barstool. I chewed slowly, enjoying this newfound sensation of horseradish, mustard, and relish. Such an odd combination, and yet my body wondered why the hell I hadn't thought of it sooner.

"Wow," I murmured.

"Yeah?" the man asked as he raised up. "I figured you might like it. It's definitely not for the faint of heart."

I leaned back up and reached for another fry. "Could use some hot sauce, though. The tang of that horseradish would do well with it."

He chuckled. "I'll give that a go next time."

I reached for my drink and pulled it toward me as I thought about my next move. I'd spent a great deal of time backtracking the inner workings of how this drug specifically came into the States and how it disbursed. It didn't take me long to figure out where the main hub of the drug was, and that was how I ended up in that bar. I mean, come on. A motorcycle crew taking over important South Carolina docks that just so happened to be stationed painfully close to the epicenter of the distribution city where my brother's white powdered killer came from?

Come on, no one was that fucking stupid.

The goal? To figure out where in the absolute fuck this crew was stationed. Out of all the scouting work I had done from my desk in D.C. and all of the traffic camera reports I had pulled, I couldn't piece together a pathway between them and wherever their homebase was stationed. The only promising lead I had gotten was a local telling me that some of the stretches of beach along the South Carolina coast were privately owned, especially with regard to the docks. All I needed was to get a bit of confirmation from one of their mouths, and I'd have enough to raid every single private beach along the coastline.

Either way, I'd find their fucking clubhouse.

That was what they called it, you know.

A clubhouse.

Sounded like a child's treehouse, if anyone asked me about it.

"Man, you weren't kidding about this drink," I said as I took another long pull.

The bartender pulled glass-bottled beers from the refrigerator behind him. "Glad you like it. If you need anything else, just let me know."

"Actually," I said as I picked up another fry, "I could use some advice."

"Trust me, I'm not that kind of bartender."

"I'm actually looking for somewhere, but I can't seem to find it. I was hoping maybe a local could help?"

"Tread carefully," Dee muttered in my ear.

"Oh?" the man asked as he turned around and placed the open beers on a circular tray off to the side. "Where are you looking for?"

I had thought about this conversation for days, ever since I had gotten Cap to sign off on allowing me to explore things further. No contact, of course, but what crew was ever taken down without a bit of rule-breaking?

Besides, it wasn't like anyone had fired shots yet.

"I need some... help," I said cautiously.

The man tilted his head. "What kind of help?"

I sighed heavily. "I'm trying to find my brother."

"Angel," Dee warned.

I ignored him. "He was last seen in the area, but no one seems to know anything about him. Or even seen him."

"How do you know he was last seen in the area then?"

I shoved my hand into the pocket of my jeans and pulled out the small locket. I unraveled the chain and pried open the small heart, revealing my dead brother's face. I stared at the picture for a little while, running my thumb across his beautiful face. So full of life, he had been. Such a lovely laugh.

Whoever owned those drugs now would pay for what they took from me.

"Here," I said as I handed it to the bartender. "Have you seen him at all?"

The man studied the picture carefully, but eventually shook his head and handed the picture back. "Sorry, but I haven't seen him around."

I sighed heavily as I clasped the locket closed and slipped it back against my thigh pocket. "Thanks anyway."

I felt his gaze hot against my forehead as I took another sip of my drink. "I could call around to the other bars. See if they've seen anyone matching his description. Maybe someone else has set eyes on him?"

"Really?" I asked breathlessly.

"Boy, you know how to pour it on, don't you?" Dee asked with a chuckle.

"Sure, it's not a problem. I mean, I can't guarantee anything, but it won't hurt to place a few calls."

"Do you want to keep the locket?" I asked as I reached into my pocket again. "Maybe it'll help if—"

"Well, well, well," a booming voice said behind me, "what do we have here?"

"Nothing that concerns you," the bartender said curtly.

I craned my head over my shoulder and saw a stalwart, scar-faced man standing behind me. The salt in his beard and at his temples contrasted the playful brown of his eyes. But the kindness in the bartender's gaze wasn't present in his.

"Hello," I said as I turned back to the bar.

"Goodbye," the bartender said as he slapped his rag down against the bar.

The man behind me grunted before he shuffled away, and I had to admit, the rush it gave me was outstanding. I had to draw a deep breath in through my nose just to calm the adrenaline coursing its way through my veins. This was the shit I adored. Hanging on by a thread. Teetering on the edge. And as I sat there, watching the bartender eye everyone in the bar above my head, the smallest part of me wished I wasn't working.

Because dear God, I wanted a slice of him.

"Looks like someone is a bit possessive," I said as I reached for another fry.

The bartender picked the rag back up. "Can't have my men getting caught up with the undercover cop sitting at my bar. I'm sure you can understand."

Dee's voice came alive in my ear. "Her cover's been blown, everyone! Go! Go! Go!"

And as the doors to the bar crashed in with agents that I didn't even realize had been there all along with us, I stared that man down. I watched that playful, boyish grin on his face slip into the most unsavory frown on the planet. My heart stopped in my chest. Agents lined the walls of the bar as guns were drawn and cocked. But all I knew was his glare.

His angry, powerful, brutally beautiful stare.

2

CASH

Does she really think I'm an idiot?

She thought she was good at her job. That much was for certain when she stopped and stared right there at the entrance of my bar. Dear God, she couldn't have reeked more of "undercover cop" than if she would've tucked in her fucking shirt and put a pair of sunglasses on. But damn it, she had a rack on her, and I was a sucker for a good pair of tits. So, when she bellied up to my bar with those curious brown eyes of hers, I wondered how much fun she'd let me have before I showed my hand.

Because that bitch wasn't getting out of our bar without knowing exactly who she was dealing with.

"Take aim!" someone called out.

I watched all of the agents that framed the outside of the bar aim their guns down their sights and right at me. At least two dozen of them, all locked, loaded, and ready to go. I simply stood there, though. As that woman looked around the bar, she seemed more shocked than I was that agents had filled this place.

Did she not know they had been out there?

Such a bad girl, this one.

"Looks like someone's on a personal mission," I murmured.

She slowly peeked over her shoulder at me and that playful smile of hers slipped away from those apple-peaked cheeks. Hell, she even had that black hair of hers tied back into a tight ass little ponytail ripe for the pulling. And when I tossed her another wink, the grotesqueness of her scoff locked its way into the depths of my soul, forever to be replayed when I needed a little pick-me-up.

Women were so cute when they were disgusted.

Though, Baron was gonna ream me a new one for not pulling information from her when she had sat herself right into my lap.

"You! Behind the bar! Hands above your head!"

I watched as the woman in the seat in front of me slowly turned back toward her favorite view. I clasped my hands in front of me, staring her down as her gaze wandered along my body. She couldn't get enough of me. Not a first, but certainly not a last. I knew exactly what power I held over women who dared to scour me with their vision, and I let her. We had nothing to hide. Whatever the fuck she thought we had done, we hadn't, because we'd been above board for years after our old president almost got us thrown into fucking prison for some bullshit we didn't even know was happening behind our backs.

Wait, was something else happening behind our backs?

"Hey!" someone barked as they shoved the live end of their gun against my upper arm. "Hands in the air. Now!"

But the woman in front of me simply held up her hand. "How did you know?"

I tilted my head as I pinned her with a look. "A man never reveals his secrets."

"The fuck you assholes doing in my bar?"

Baron's bass-bumping voice rattled the floor at my feet as he stalked down the hallway from the kitchen. The door burst open, revealing the shadowed outline of a man who loomed high over all of us. Every single gun in the joint pivoted toward him as he walked out of the darkness and into the light. The gray at his temples shimmered like the icy blue of his eyes, and I swear, I heard every fucking agent in that joint draw in a collective breath.

And the second that undercover woman turned toward him, the way she paused damn near made me growl. I watched her shoulders pull taut. I watched her chest stop moving as she held her breath. The redness of her cheeks permeated down the nape of her neck, and even I could see her carotid right there on the side of her neck pumping with fury.

She was petrified.

At least she's got good survival instincts.

The woman moved, jamming her hand into her shirt, and pulled a leather flip-fold out of her bra. Not once did she take her gaze off Baron as she flipped it open and slid off the barstool, her small stature stalking toward a man who had at least a foot of height on her. And as she outstretched her arm, she held her credentials up to his face.

"I take it you're the president of the crew that runs this bar?" she asked.

Baron didn't bother looking at her badge. "And you are?"

She cleared her throat as she flipped her credentials closed and jammed them into her other back pocket.

Damn, she had a fine, juicy piece of ass on her.

"I'm Special Agent Lonna DeMarco. And you are?"

Baron drew in a deep, silent breath. "Whoever you're looking for, they aren't in this bar. So, why don't you show me the warrant that gives you the right to storm this place or see yourself out."

She didn't listen, though. All she did was snap her fingers before a spindly little person stepped out from a dark corner.

The person draped in all black with a gun strapped over his shoulder scurried to the small woman, dug into his pocket, and plopped something into the palm of her hand.

And the second I saw the light blue insignia, I froze.

It can't be. We wiped those drugs off the street.

"So," she said as he held up a little baggie with a light blue sun and moon logo stamped onto it, "if I were to ask you about this, you'd tell me you have no idea what I'm talking about? Because that's not what my files say back at my department in D.C.."

Baron flickered his gaze toward mine, and it was enough to know that we were royally fucked. How the hell was that stuff still on the fucking street?

I thought we had gotten rid of it all.

"Ah," she said as she peered over her shoulder at me. "So, you guys *do* recognize this symbol."

I reached for a glass to shine in order to give my hands something to do because the stone-cold look on Baron's face as he stared back down at that short spark of a woman told me everything I needed to know. I watched the way Baron clenched his fists at his side. White knuckled, and the next step was bloody if that woman didn't tread with ease. If I didn't do something soon, Baron would put his fucking fist through that woman's face without a second thought for even daring to show us the drugs that damn near took this crew under because of our former president's addiction.

I had to diffuse things, and quickly. Otherwise, we were all going to prison.

And not for drugs, either.

3

BARON

What a fucking night. Bunch of goddamn idiots.

There I was, sitting in my back office dealing with stupid refill orders when I heard it.

The crash.

"Hands above your head! Now!"

I didn't have to look over at the bar to feel Cash staring a hole into the side of my head. Four more. I had four more fucking orders to fill, and then it was time to go home. Relax. Have a fucking beer, turn on the television, and catch the tail end of whatever terrible sports game our prospect had on the big screen in the basement.

"I said, now!" the DEA agent in front of me bellowed.

"You really should do what he says," the woman with the grin on her face said.

My gaze slowly panned down to her. Those sultry eyes of hers sat against a face etched with a tan. Her black hair poured down her back in a ponytail clinging to the back of her head, and despite the fact that she barely came up to my chest, her presence filled the room. I saw why Cash had been taken with her. After all, I watched the cameras whenever I was in my office. I saw them schmoozing. I saw Cash flirting with her like he always did when he saw a nice rack he wanted to face-plant into.

Then, she held up that little packet and dangled it in front of my face.

"See this?" she asked.

I nodded, but it was still hard to process. I thought we had wiped those motherfuckers off the face of the planet. I thought we had stained enough of our sand in their blood to hold Hell itself at bay at least until we were all dead. We had kicked them out. Dumped their stash into the harbor. We made sure it was never in circulation again. Not after our own president damn near took us down because of it.

How the fuck was it back?

We didn't get it all?

The woman let out a piercing whistle through her teeth and two men decked out in all black came and stood beside her. With a crook of her finger, they lifted their guns, pointing them at my chest as a devilish smile crossed her face. She thought she was in control, and I understood. I got it. Everyone with guns always thought that they had the upper hand.

No one had the upper hand in my bars, though.

"I take it you think we're doing this?" I asked as I stared the woman down.

"I don't know," she said as she slid the packet into her back pocket, "you tell me. Are *you* doing this?"

"No," I said plainly.

"Then, I suppose you and I are going to have a problem."

I raked my stare back down her form. "You look a little young to be a special agent."

Her gaze stayed connected to mine as she pointed to her temple, wiggling her finger around as if I were a fucking moron.

"And that gray in your hair tells me you're a bit too old to be riding bikes with friends."

Someone in the background barked with laughter, but I kept my stare level with hers. The trick was to never blink. It was one of those psychological tricks Cash had passed on to me once I stepped into the role of President of The Death Cheaters.

And the longer I stared at her, my body completely unwavering, the more her nose wrinkled.

"Well," the woman said as she cleared her throat, "you guys can either start talking to me now, or I can haul you back to the station downtown and you can talk to one of my guys there. Either way, I'm getting the answers I came looking for."

I didn't like taking orders. But if those assholes thought they were busting out cuffs for me and my crew, they had another fucking think coming.

I'd slaughter them all before we let that cold, hard metal touch our skin.

"Our old president was wrapped up in that shit once," I said.

Her eye twitched. "And?"

"And...that was years ago."

"Well," she said as she turned toward her men and held out her arms, "dead men can't do drugs, then, am I right?"

Another agent somewhere in the darkened crowd chuckled, but I didn't move. Her pomp and circumstance didn't move me. She slowly turned back around with a proud smile on her face, and as she flopped her arms at her sides, I saw something flash behind her eyes.

Something feral.

Something angry.

"Those drugs took someone you loved, didn't it?" I asked.

Her back straightened. "Did you kill him?"

I blinked. "Kill who?"

"Your former president. Is he dead because of you?"

"What makes you think he's dead?"

"My files back at my office say he's been dead for three years."

I shrugged. "Then he's been dead for three years."

She took a step closer to me. "So, how did you do it?"

"Do what?"

"Kill him. You know, just between you and me."

She was cute, I'd give her that. But not that cute. "We didn't kill him."

Her eyebrows rose. "Oh? Because in my files—"

"I don't give a flying fuck about your files," I said as I kept my voice as even as possible. "What I'm saying is that we didn't kill him. He got himself killed with that shit when he overdosed. Shit we aren't peddling. Shit we never once peddled."

A grin slithered across her rosy, red cheeks. "Your former president did."

I nodded. "And just like you pointed out, he's dead. Has been for years. Which means we've washed our hands of that shit."

Her gaze hardened on mine, and I simply stood there. If she honestly thought some low-level posturing was going to scare us into giving her answers that weren't true just so she could fulfill her own narrative, she had another thing coming. I knew exactly why she was doing this. She was chasing down whoever was responsible for killing whoever she loved. My stare briefly swept over her left hand, tracing the base of her ring finger. No tan line. No indentation. So, she most likely wasn't avenging a dead spouse. I slid my stare along her midsection. Tight and trim with perky tits I'd love to get within the palms of my hands. Not a child, either, most likely. She had fight in her, though. That much was certain.

And I knew I'd fight like hell for my brothers.

"Sibling or friend?" I asked.

I broke the silence between us, and she froze. Even her breathing stopped.

"What?" she asked.

"The person you're avenging. Sibling or friend?"

She clicked her tongue as she slowly backed toward her agents. "I'm sure we'll be seeing one another soon, gentlemen. Don't wait up."

And as I watched her turn around, that juicy ass of hers taunted my cock already growing against my zipper.

Fucking hell, I understood why Cash had been so eager for her earlier.

"Boys!" she exclaimed as she twirled her finger in the air. "Let's go!"

Watching them exit was like listening to animals stampeding over a fucking field. The ground beneath our feet shook as the decked-out men grasped their guns and hightailed it out the double doors in their heavy boots. And as I watched that ponytail sway with every step she took, she peered over her shoulder at me one last time. So, I picked up my hand and wiggled my fingers at her.

And the scoff she let out before letting the door close behind her sounded all too wonderful.

"How fucked are we?" Cash asked.

I slid my tongue across my teeth as I ripped my cell out of my leather jacket pocket. I dialed the number two before pressing the call button and held the ringing phone up to my ear. One ring. Two rings. Three rings.

"Tuck your dick in and pick your phone up, Reid," I growled.

"Yeah, yeah," he said groggily when he finally picked up the fucking phone. "What is it, Baron?"

"Call the guys. Tell them to get to the clubhouse. We need an emergency church meeting."

"Why?" he asked as his voice perked right up.

I turned toward Cash. "Gather the men you've got on patrols. Cash and I will take care of the others. Church in thirty."

"What's going on, Baron?"

Cash typed away on his cell. "I'll send a mass text and get the bar closed down."

"Baron," Reid said curtly.

I pivoted on my feet and stormed back down the hallway. "The DEA just stormed the bar."

"What?! What for?"

I snarled into the phone. "Just do what I'm asking you to do and get ready for church."

And as I shouldered my way into my office, I slammed my thumb against the button that ended the phone call before I jammed it into my pocket.

I picked up my office chair and hurled it across the room.

4

ANGEL

"Well, that went swimmingly," Dee said as he climbed out of the car.

I shoved my hands against his chest, stumbling him in his tracks. "When the *fuck* did you call for backup?"

He held up his hands in mock surrender. "Whoa, whoa, whoa. Angel, what are you—"

I pulled his gun off his hip, cocked it, and held it to his head. "I won't ask you again."

"Angel! What the hell?!"

"When did you call for fucking backup, Dee!?"

"After you called me and told me we were doing a stakeout, Angel!"

My body vibrated with fury. It was supposed to be me and him. Nothing but a recon mission. Nothing but an undercover operation where I came away with whatever shred of information that big beluga whale back there spewed while staring at my tits. And he had the audacity to go behind my back?

"Angel, put the gun down," Dee said as his voice trembled.

"Ma'am?" one of the agents asked.

I uncocked the gun and shoved it back into Dee's hip holster. "Good to know I can trust my own partner."

He snickered. "Oh, come on, Angel. Did you really expect it to be just the two of us that showed up? You're running an official investigation. You're not hunting down cold cases like you were when you were on leave. There's protocol to—"

I took a step away from him. "I don't give a flying fuck about protocol. Cap didn't even give a flying hell when he put this team—"

Dee's face grew dark. "And what do you want me to do about it, huh? I'm not gonna let you die because you're letting some vendetta get in the way of your training."

I got in his face and gnashed my teeth together. I wouldn't let him intimidate me like that. "And I'm not gonna let some partner that wants to get in my pants override my command on my mission because he thinks I should be doing it differently."

I wasn't done with those men at the bar. Not by a fucking long shot. But I was done with Dee. I knew the crew was scrambling. I knew they'd call an emergency church meeting over the agents that stormed their bar. I had done my research before coming to South Carolina like a good little agent, so Dee could shove it about me being distraction. I was more focused than ever.

And I needed to know where that meeting was going down.

"Uh, Agent DeMarco?"

I drew in a deep breath and moved away from Dee. "What is it?"

"The lights in the bar. They've turned off."

I looked up at the neon sign for Roadhouse and, sure enough, it was no longer buzzing with yellows, oranges, and greens. It sat there, silent and unwavering, as the lights through the curtained windows of the bar shut off, one by one. A grin crawled across my cheeks. Hope blossomed in my gut. Crews like theirs were so fucking predictable, and I knew it was something I could capitalize on.

Alone.

"All right, let's get out of here," I said as I turned back toward the car.

"You sure about that?" Dee asked, ripping the car door open.

"Agents? You're dismissed. Dee?"

He flapped his arms out at his sides. "Yeah?"

I pointed up at him. "You'll need to catch a ride with one of them. I need the car."

He quickly stepped back out. "Oh, no you don't."

I shrugged. "I didn't ask you. Now, hand over the keys."

I held out my hand, but all he did was look down at it. "You're not going anywhere on your own. I know what you want to do. You want to tail those men and see where they go."

I lowered my voice to a hushed whisper and shot Dee a look that told him he needed to do the same, or else. "Yes, because the point of tonight was to find their clubhouse. I've got a second shot, and I'm not gonna let my partner who I can't trust any longer anywhere near it."

He wasn't an idiot. He lowered his voice, despite his arguing. "Oh, come on, Angel. Now you're just being petty."

"Give me the keys, or my next phone call is to Cap where I tell him that instead of being sick last month, you took off work so that you could get your dick wet in the Bahamas with some woman you shacked up with in a motel off Tinder two weeks beforehand."

I'd never heard grown adults try to stifle their laughter like that in all my life. All eyes were on Dee as his face slowly sank with the snickers and giggles that rose from the agents surrounding us. It would be a miracle if those assholes inside of the bar didn't know we were still outside. I couldn't let an opportunity go to waste, though, even if I didn't have much time. I had to do something.

And as if the heavens above finally had mercy on me, he tossed me the keys to the car.

"Don't call me if you end up in trouble," he said as he moved back toward the rest of the agents.

"Trust me, I won't," I said flatly as I stormed the driver's side. "Everyone? Go home. Your part in this miserable failure is over."

Getting myself situated behind the wheel of that car was nothing compared to the utter chaos everyone else created. I knew there was no way in hell those guys rode those bikes of theirs toward the front of the bar, so all I had was one opportunity to seek them out myself. I backed out of the parking space in the lone vehicle and almost mowed down a couple of agents who stood around gossiping and watching. Like we were in high school by the lockers on our free fucking period.

Sometimes, I really hated running ops with other people.

I was much more efficient by myself.

I inched my way by Dee, who stared me down the entire time. I made it a point not to look at him, though. He could try and convince Cap all day long that I was the one that blew the undercover investigation, but at the end of the day I had those men right where I wanted them before he took over. Before he made a call that blew our cover right out of the water. Did that bartender sniff me out? Sure. Could I have used that to my advantage, especially if he had decided to take me? Abso-fuck-ing-lutely. I never came unprepared, no matter what men around me thought.

But as I lazily drove around the bar, I saw nothing but darkness. Nothing but empty parking spaces, an overflowing green dumpster, and oil stains all over the gravel parking lot behind the shoddy brick building.

"Come on, think," I whispered to myself.

I laid my forehead against the warm steering wheel and closed my eyes. I had to be smart about things. If I had spooked them enough to close their bar early, then that most likely meant they were gathering for church. That meant the roar of bikes from a multitude of directions, depending on how many were patrolling routes.

Wait, that's it.

I yanked my head up and placed my head on a swivel. As I backed the car up and turned it around, my mind combed through the files on them that I had long since memorized. I was the queen of due diligence. My tracking skills were the stuff of legend back at the DEA. And if I was going to go after the fuckers that were responsible for flooding the East Coast with the drugs that killed my brother, then I had to do it right. Everything had to be clean, provable, and unsullied. An open and shut case. My brother deserved that much, and, quite frankly, so did my fucking sanity. So, while on extended bereavement leave, I set my sights on a personal goal that I knew would utilize all of my professional skills at once:

I was going to catch the son of a bitches responsible for those drugs.

When my hours upon hours of leads and investigative skills brought me to a small town being taken over by a motorcycle crew, I knew I'd found what I had been looking for. Cartels came and went. You chop off one head, two more emerged. But those heads always surrounded the South Carolina docks. And sure, some of the assumptions I made were hunches. Nothing but my gut screaming at me. So, I figured, why not? The worst that could happen was I chase my own tail and waste some time. No harm, no foul.

That was why I knew everything. I knew this crew's schedule and their delivery routes. I knew the businesses they had opened, and even some businesses they had failed at. I knew their names, their specialties, their routines, and their quirks. I knew their positions of power, how long they'd been with the crew, when they pledged, and why. I knew The Death Cheaters like the back of my fucking hand. And the more I uncovered, the more that I knew I was right. And when I beheld the look on those assholes faces when I brandished those drugs for them to see?

I knew all of my hard work was about to pay the fuck off.

That kind of deep dive was always necessary when bringing down crews and cartels that dealt with drugs. Information was always a sharp weapon to wield on the field, and I came armed to the teeth. I threw the energy of my grief into energy I needed to cull together the entire world these men dwelled in. Just so that I could pick it apart and find exactly what I needed to shutter them and those drugs away for good.

And when my mind finally settled on their patrol routes, I smiled.

"Gotta love those in-depth traffic cameras," I murmured as I eased myself back onto the road.

They weren't stupid enough to stick to their usual routes, so I took the long way. I weaved myself through back roads, keeping a close ear to the ground with the windows rolled all the way down. I kept my lights off so as to not draw attention. The salted ocean air filtered through the car, filling my nostrils with the scent of relaxation. Growls of what sounded like engines hummed in the distance, and part of me really wanted to know how in the fuck they got away from the bar without making a fucking sound.

My body wanted to sleep. My stomach wanted more food. My bladder needed a bathroom. My legs needed to stretch. But none of those were important.

Not as important as making sure my brother hadn't died in vain.

I drove for miles, following the routes that had been permanently carved out into my brain. I inched around curves and sat at stop signs for much too long. I took alternative routes that snaked parallel to the roads I had kept a fresh eye on for months via traffic cameras, and kept my stare focused on the edges of the road. I hoped to spot a headlight reflection. Or smell exhaust smoke. Or even hear the revving roar of an engine off in the distance. Anything to signal to me that those motherfuckers were on the road headed toward a specific destination.

There was nothing, though. Nothing determinate to my ears, anyway. There was so much nothing, in fact, that I lost my nerve. Maybe I had missed my chance. Maybe they had gotten the better of me in that moment. Maybe Dee really had spoiled my only solid chance of finding the information I required to move this case forward.

Then, I heard it.

Off in the distance.

So faint and so ethereal that, for the smallest moment, I wondered if I had actually heard it.

Until the squealing of tires sounded behind me.

"Oh, shit," I hissed as I tugged at the wheel of the car.

I did the only thing I knew I could do. I pulled my vehicle off to the side of the road and hunkered down. I unbuckled my seatbelt and tanked my seat backward. I held my breath, hoping that the shadows of the trees on those nasty backroads concealed me enough. The roar of the engine rushed toward me, rumbling the street and filling the air around me with that weirdly seductive exhaust odor. It reminded me of all the times my brother tried to get that hunk of junk he found on the side of the road up and running. Always cranking the engine. Always tinkering with the spark plugs. Always taking something off and tweaking it.

He would've been an incredible mechanic.

The motorcycles zoomed past me, and I quickly picked my head up. I caught the taillights of one of the bikes and my heart leapt into my throat. Holy fuck, they tried waiting us out. That was why I couldn't fucking find them. They turned off the lights and waited us the fuck out.

"Oh, hell yeah," I grinned as I quickly leaned my seat back up.

I kept my lights off and drew in a deep breath. I pulled back onto the road after waiting a few seconds, just to make sure no one else came through. Then, I stuck to the shadows, tailing the three bikes that were about to destroy things for their entire crew. My smile ached my cheeks. My heart refused to climb out of the back of my throat. Adrenaline coursed its way through my veins, curling my toes and shaking my muscles with the excess energy I'd need to keep me awake through the night.

It was officially stakeout time.

That back road seemed to go on forever. The further down the road we got, the more I wondered if someone was leading me into a trap. I'd driven for at least twenty minutes before that bike ever happened upon me in the first fucking place. For all I knew, they were already wise to my game. However, my mind went blank when the back road gave way to a clearing in front of me.

A sandy clearing lining the crashing waves of the ocean.

"What the hell?" I whispered to myself.

The thick trees and shrubbery that lined that back road suddenly stopped, and I came to a grinding halt. I turned my wheel sharply to the right to get my tires onto something that wasn't asphalt in case the tires squealed, and I was lucky that I got the car to stop before it kicked up anything else. Bike after bike poured into the sandy gravel parking lot across the road. The road we had been traveling dead-ended into a rickety, faded two-lane highway that looked like it hadn't been traversed by any decent vehicle in well over a decade. I held my breath as I snaked my way slowly into the darkness. I watched men of all shapes and sizes abandon their bikes in made-up parking spaces before they stormed up a set of beautiful white steps toward a house I would have expected The Joneses to own, not some pathetic old man bike crew.

And yet, as I parked my vehicle in the shadow of the trees across the street, the monumentally large house seemed like a small slice of heaven. Its outer coating, decadent in its white with ocean blue shutters lining the windows. The roof, a beautiful rich white, most likely to help keep the heat at bay during the hot Carolina summers. It sat right on the water's edge, or at least it seemed like it did, and the wraparound porch that lined the outside simply took my breath away.

"Holy shit," I whispered as I leaned forward. "I found it."

I found their fucking clubhouse.

5

———

REID

The second Baron hung up on me, I threw the covers off my body. I barely got my feet swung over the edge of the bed before I yanked my phone off the wireless charger next to it. The clubhouse was dead silent, save for the sound of the ocean waves filtering through a window I always kept cracked in my bedroom.

"Okay, Google. Call Pyre," I said as I dragged my ass into my bathroom.

"Calling Pyre," my phone said.

I pressed the speakerphone button before setting my phone on the bathroom counter.

"Yep?" he asked when he answered the phone.

The sound of wind whipping in the background made me jealous that he was out on patrol instead of me. "Turn around."

"What?"

"You heard me," I said as I turned on the sink. "Get the guys and turn around. Emergency church meeting."

"What for?"

I groaned as I splashed cold water in my face. "Just do it. Call Coal and Pitchfork. They're leading the other two patrols tonight. Everyone is due back at this clubhouse in twenty-eight minutes."

"Twenty-eight?"

"Yep."

"Any reason why that's so specific?"

"Because you're wasting some of the thirty minutes asking me asinine questions, that's why."

"Right," he said flatly.

I picked up the phone and reached for my hand towel. "Twenty-seven minutes. Don't let me down. And assume you're being watched at all times."

"Got it. See you soon."

"Yep."

I hung up the phone call and dabbed my face with the towel. The DEA? That could only mean one thing. There had only been one other time we'd ever had a run in with that particular alphabet institution, and it had been years since we'd even spoken of the debacle. I stared at my shadowed outline in the bathroom mirror, drawing in a deep breath to try and wake myself up. Jesus, were we really about to do this again? Were we really about to take on the DEA over some stupid shit someone was doing?

If any of my patrol guys had started this, their head would be mounted on my fucking wall.

"Let's go," I muttered before I headed for my closet.

I threw on some clothes and made my way downstairs. I greeted the first round of patrolmen that came storming in and listened out for the others. Three separate patrols had been sent out that night. One to comb the streets, one to keep an eye on the town, and another to watch the harbors. The last thing we needed was anyone or anything attempting to snake back into our turf. But if the DEA was in town, that meant someone already had.

The question was, who the fuck was it?

"Reid."

"Hey, Reid."

"We got any food in the kitchen ready, Reid?"

"Hey there, Reid."

"Reid."

"Get yourself any sleep, Reid?"

The men greeted me as they walked through the door, but I couldn't stop staring across the road. Someone was there. Lurking. Watching. Waiting. Every time a bike came down the road blaring its headlights, it glinted off of some sort of reflective surface right at the edge of the woods. I stood my ground, though. I stepped out onto the porch and received each and every one of the men that I had put out on the road that night. I shook their hands. Clapped their backs. Smiled at their stupid fucking jokes they always made whenever they were nervous. And the entire time, I stared directly toward the woods.

I wanted that asshole to know that I knew.

"Reid?" Cash asked. "You good?"

"Be careful," I said as I drew in a deep breath, "we're being watched."

Cash turned around and gazed across the road, and it didn't take him long before he heaved a heavy sigh. "Must be that woman from the bar."

That made me turn my head toward him. "What woman?"

He shook his head. "Some terrible undercover agent. I pegged her the minute she walked through the doors."

"Why are they always so terrible at that?"

He snickered. "Beats me."

I looked back across the street. "You think she's sitting alone in that car?"

"Why? You strike out tonight?"

I rolled my eyes. "Get inside and shut up."

He chuckled. "You'll get 'em next time, killer."

"Yeah, yeah," I murmured to myself.

Then, Baron's bike pulled up, our president. The one that had taken over the crew and singlehandedly pieced us back together after Whicker had been taken down. His face sat cold as stone while his eyes bubbled with the fury of lava. He balled up his fists at his side as he leapt up the porch steps, lunging past all of them before he soared through the door.

"Church. Now," he said curtly.

I grabbed his wrist and halted him in his tracks.

"It better be good," he growled as he yanked his arm from my grasp.

"You should know we're being watched," I said.

He peered across the street. "Figures. They'll probably be there all night, too."

"Why?"

"By the sounds of things, they've been trying to find this place for a while."

I shrugged. "You gonna really keep making me ask why?"

And when his stare connected with mine, he spoke those dreaded words.

"The sky is back."

I almost couldn't breathe. "But that's impossible. We—"

Baron snarled as he dropped his face to mine. "Church."

I didn't waste any time getting back inside. Holy fucking hell, it was so much worse than I could have ever imagined. I rushed inside before Baron slammed the door closed. I traipsed down the steps into the basement where we held all of our church meetings. Baron lumbered behind me, growling and grumbling something to himself that I couldn't make out. And still, part of me wondered if he had been seeing things. Maybe he'd had a nightmare that felt all too real, or maybe saw something he had mistaken for that shit.

My brain tried to rationalize it any way it could.

Yet, as Baron took his place at the head of the table, the sternness of his face made me sick to my stomach.

"Jesus, you're not kidding," I said breathlessly.

He stared me down as he backed up toward the wall. My eyes widened with every step he took, too. He flipped open the hidden panel next to the light switch, showcasing the big black "oh shit" button we had installed to trigger our basement's emergency mechanisms. He slammed his fist into it, and all the lights came on at once. I shielded my sleep-sensitive eyes as the sound of metal walls crawling out of the ceiling effortlessly slammed down against the floor. It kicked on signal jammers and canceled out the function of listening devices. It rendered whole pieces of technology useless at the drop of a hat. And as I stood there, watching his every move, I saw the pain behind his eyes.

He was tired.

We were all tired of this shit.

"All right, everyone," Baron said as he held up his hand. "It's safe for us to talk."

And as I watched him take a seat at the head of the table, that told me everything I needed to know. Sitting was never good. Not with Baron, anyway. He preferred to stay mobile. To always stay on his guard. The man never rested, never backed down, and he stayed chronically in survival mode for the sake of the safety of our crew. So, for him to be tired enough to sit when we had someone staking out the fucking clubhouse?

This was worse than I could have ever imagined.

"The sky is back," Baron said.

"What?!" Pitchfork exclaimed as he leapt to his feet.

"The hell are you talking about, Bossman?" Coal asked.

"I saw the package with my own eyes," Baron said.

"As did I," Cash said.

My eyebrows rose. "You really did?"

Cash nodded slowly. "That shit is back on the street. That's why the DEA is in town."

"Fucking Christ," Pyre murmured.

"Do they think we're peddling it?" I asked.

Cash shrugged. "Can you blame them for wondering?"

"Stupid motherfucking bitch," I hissed.

"My words exactly," Baron said flatly.

Of course, Whicker would screw us over, even from the fucking grave. "So, the sky is back, and the DEA believes we're peddling it."

"Seems to be the case," Cash said.

"This is some fucking bullshit!" Pitchfork exclaimed. "Why the hell are we letting some agent sit across the street and watch us when we know we aren't doing shit?!"

"I say we walk across the street and go have some words."

"I say we take out their tires and strand them there."

"I say we call 9-1-1 on their ass and make them think we don't know who the fuck it is."

Everyone talked at once, their voices growing louder by the second. I watched Baron's head fall back as he crossed his arms over his chest, and I waited for his signal. His eyes closed. His breathing evened out. I clocked the rise and fall of his chest. The way his eyes twitched, even when closed. He was furious. No, not furious. Livid.

Baron was fucking livid.

Then, as he slowly raised his head, his gaze found mine and he nodded.

So, I folded my tongue against my teeth and let out an ear-shattering whistle.

"Holy fucking shit!"

"Jesus Christ, Reid."

"Are you kidding me with that right now?"

"Enough," Baron said curtly.

That silenced all of them, and as they sat their asses back down into their seats, Baron closed his eyes again.

"If anyone has anything productive to say, now is the time to say it," he said.

Snake was the first to speak. "You don't really think we're doing that shit, do you?"

Baron shrugged. "The DEA never gets involved unless there's more than a hunch. They're here because they've got some sort of proof that we're putting this shit out on the streets. They wouldn't have stormed the bar otherwise. So, this is the one and only time to come clean with your life still intact by the end of your confession."

The guys all looked around at one another and I studied their faces. Their expressions. The little movements in their faces that they couldn't control no matter what they did. I tried to sniff out who it was that had betrayed us. Who it was that Baron had already condemned as guilty. But no one spoke up, and no one jumped out at me.

Which was odd.

"Has anyone heard anything on the streets lately?" I asked.

The guys turned their heads toward me, but they kept their mouths closed.

"No one is dying tonight if you're honest," I said as I placed my finger against the table in front of me. "So, I'll ask again: has anyone heard anything new on the streets here lately? Or heard about someone sketchy fucking around with people in town? Someone rattling other people's cages? Anything at all?"

The guys, yet again, looked around at one another. But it was Bic that drew in a deep breath through his nose.

"I didn't think it was anything when I first heard it, that's why I never said anything."

"But now?" Baron asked.

Bic peeked over at Baron, but I slammed my fist against the

table to keep his attention. "Don't look at Bossman; look at me. Talk to me, Bic. What did you hear?"

He leaned back in his chair and sighed heavily. "Couple weeks ago, Pitchfork and I were lunchin' at that new spot that's opened up. The one with the burgers."

"God, those damned things were so fucking good," Pitchfork said with a groan.

"Oh, what kinda burger did you get?" Cash asked.

Razor, our prospect, pointed at Bic. "Did you get one of those massive milkshakes that they do? I drove through and got one on my break the other day and I swear to hell on high, they had a slice of cake right on top of—"

I put my pinkies into the corners of my mouth and let out a whistle that rang my ears. But it got them to shut the fuck up.

"Get to the point," Baron said when the room quieted down.

"Right," Bic said flatly. "Anyway, we were eating and we had a couple of ladies behind us that were talking way too loudly."

"Way, *way* too loudly," Pitchfork said.

"What were they talking about, Bic, for crying out loud," Cash said.

Bic finally spat it out. "They were talking about some guy walking around their neighborhood and trying to talk to the kids."

My jaw about hit the fucking floor. "You never told me that."

Bic shrugged again. "Didn't think I needed to. The next part of that conversation was how all of the neighborhood moms came out with pots, pans, and bats and chased the fucker off. I figured it was just someone being an asshole or something."

I wanted to wring his neck, but we had more important things to do.

"What do you think, Bossman?" I asked as I looked across the table at Baron.

And without skipping a beat, he stood to his feet.

"I think we need to figure out who the fuck is pestering the kids of our town."

6

———

ANGEL

"Come on, where are you?"

I stretched my hand into the back seat and flung my fingers around. I knew it was down there somewhere. Dee never went anywhere without his rudimentary, virtually unhackable surveillance equipment. Grunts bubbled up the back of my throat as I shoved my legs forward for more leverage. I crooked my arm around the back of the passenger seat, determined to find the cold, hard, plastic handle attached to that black briefcase.

"Come on, you stupid fucking—"

Tink tink tink.

I froze at the sound of tapping glass. Jesus, had someone already found me? No, impossible. Concealment was one of my specialties. It was why Cap always picked me for—

Tink tink. "I can see you, even if you don't move."

I breathed an effortless sigh of relief and flopped back down into my seat. "Get in the car if you're gonna be here, Dee."

He reached down and played with the door handle. "You gotta press the little button to let me in."

I shot him a look before my hand crept to the buttons to my

left. I unlocked the door just as he galivanted around to the passenger's side. Two coffees donned his hands before he balanced one cup on top of the other, his gaze peeking over at the massive beach house extending along the stretch of private beach.

"Pretty nice for a clubhouse," he said as he opened the door.

"Get in and shut up," I said curtly.

"You really know how to greet a man," he said as he slid into the car and closed the door behind him. "Here."

I took the coffee from him. "So, how did you find me?"

He paused. "Are you really asking that question?"

I slowly looked over at him. "Is that supposed to be rhetorical?"

He cocked himself in his seat so that he fully faced me. "That's how I know you don't need to be alone right now."

"What?"

"The GPS, Angel. You didn't disable the GPS in the car first. I just had one of the guys track you so I could come meet you after your head climbed out of the clouds."

Shit. "Right."

"Are you okay? Honestly?"

I focused my gaze back out the windshield. "If you've given my cover away aga—"

Dee snickered. "No one gave away your cover. You're just not dealing with idiots. Now, drink your coffee, wake the fuck up, and let's do this stakeout the right way."

I took a long pull of the hot liquid and kept my gaze trained hard on the front door of that house. "Why are you here, Dee?"

"You mean, outside of the fact that you ran headfirst to the ends of the Earth when we were hunting down the woman who killed my cousin?"

"So, you're doing this as a favor."

"It's the least I can do after you followed me into hell to make her arrest happen."

God, what a fucking adventure that had been. "Ah, that's what partners are for."

"No, that's what friends are for."

I swallowed the knot in my throat. "Can you reach back there and find me that stupid satellite dish you always insist on using? I swear, it's like *Where's Waldo* in that back seat."

He chuckled as he reached behind his seat. "You mean, the sound amplifier? I just tucked it against the back of the seat. How hard is that to find?"

"Just get it for me and get it set up. I know they're having church in there. I want to know what they're saying."

"Got it," he grunted as he fumbled with the hard suitcase.

"Should we get closer?"

"No."

I scoffed. "Oh, come on. The shadows of this thick forestry extend for at least another twenty feet in front of us. There's no way they'd—"

"It's not safe," he said as he plopped the suitcase onto his lap. "We've got no backup this time around, either."

"Good, at least you're listening to me now."

He popped the top open. "We aren't getting closer. We're staying in this car just in case we need a quick getaway."

"No telling what kind of traps they've laid."

"Usually, people don't say that kind of sentence with a smile on their face."

"I'm not smiling."

"You're smiling from my angle."

I peeked over at him and grinned. "Maybe it's just the shadows playing with your imagination."

"Or," he said as he pulled out two sets of headphones, "maybe you're just crazy."

I tossed him a playful wink. "A girl can dream. You got that set up yet?"

He pressed a few buttons and the suitcase started to practically glow. "Here, put these on."

I took the headphones and slid them over my head. "All right, let's see what they're really up to in there."

"Just let me get it calibrated first. You know how these sound amplification things are. They can be finnicky if not set right. Let me know when you can hear voices."

The static sound zipping through the headphones made my eye twitch. It scratched a particular place in my brain that made my arms shiver, but as Dee held up the small, clear satellite dish stored within the cushioned compartments of the suitcase, voices started cropping up.

"Why?" a familiar gruff voice asked.

Baron.

"Can you hear any—"

"Shh, shh, shh, shh!" I said harshly. "Just put on your headphones and shut up."

"By the sounds of things, they've been trying to find this place for a while."

That was a voice I didn't recognize.

He chuckled. "So demanding."

"Shut up," I hissed, "they're talking."

He quickly slipped his headphones on and, for once, did exactly as I asked.

I wish he did that more often.

"You gonna really keep me asking why?"

And when Baron's voice spoke, it was like the heavens had decided to dump information right into my lap.

"The sky is back."

I couldn't help the smile that overtook my face. "I knew they knew about that shit."

"The sky?" Dee asked. "That's... actually pretty creative."

"Shh," I hissed.

"But that's impossible. We—"

Baron snarled, and for some reason it stopped my heart in my chest. "Church."

Hard footsteps complete with grumbles and groans were the only sounds to make their way to our headphones after that exchange. It wasn't much, but it was recorded, and I had proof that they had lied pretty much directly to our faces. First, they didn't want to ante up that they knew about this shit, and then they openly admitted that they knew exactly what we were dealing with.

The innocent had no reason to lie.

But the guilty?

"Jesus, you're not kidding," someone said breathlessly.

I pointed to Dee. "Turn it up, it's fading."

"Most likely because they've headed underground. Is there a basement in that place?"

"Just turn it up, Dee."

I watched him fiddle with the knobs and buttons, but the voices didn't get much clearer. I strained to hear anything through the static, any possible sound that might give something more away.

"If we could just get closer," I whispered.

"No, and stop asking," Dee said flatly.

I rolled my eyes. "Fine, whatever."

THUD!

The sound was so fucking loud that I tossed my headphones off the top of my head. My ears rang, causing me to stick my fingers in them and wiggle them around. Dee ripped his headphones off his head and massaged his temples, but it didn't take a genius to know what happened.

Especially once the static flitered back through the headphones.

"Those motherfuckers have a panic room," I whispered.

"Well," Dee said as the ringing in my ears subsided, "what do you wanna do now?"

"Oh, you care about my plans now?"

He shrugged. "It's your case that you're doing on the side. Your passion. So, obviously you're calling the shots."

"You didn't think that back when you decided to call for backup without my knowledge."

"And aren't you glad you had a partner that was able to sniff out what you needed without you having to tell me?"

I slowly panned my gaze toward him. I felt the tiny locket with my brother's picture in it burrowing a hole against my left thigh as it sat there, reminding me of him. My brother. The one those drugs had taken from me. The only person on the planet that understood what I went through as a kid. Who knew my memories. Who knew my heart. Who loved me uncondition-ally, no matter what. My brother was the only shred of family I had escaped with after all those years beneath the thumb of my parents. I was glad my testimony in court put them in prison. I was glad to finally rip their control away with nothing but my words. But putting them away brought my brother no peace, and I wanted the drugs that took him from me wiped off the street for good.

The drugs and the people who peddled them.

"Angel?" Dee asked.

I cleared my throat. "I should stay posted here to watch. You can radio one of the guys so you can head back and get some rest."

I saw him shake his head out of the corner of my eye. "I'm not leaving you here by yourself. That's a non-starter."

I shrugged. "Then take me back to the hotel to get my

vehicle and I'll come back on my own. But there's no point in both of us being here if they've got signal jammers in that place."

"I'm still not leaving you here by yourself like that."

"Then don't tell me I'm the one in charge. Now, let's go."

The truth of the matter was that we had nothing. After an entire evening of tracking them down, positioning ourselves right, and getting into the game, all we came away with was confirmation that they knew about the drug. Nothing about their operations or their delivery routes. Nothing about plans for locking down, or shutting down certain roadways for their nefarious pleasures. I had nothing, and if I was going to build a case against these assholes, I needed more than what I had.

And I wasn't gonna get it with Dee haunting my side.

Those victims deserve better than this.

And I was going to get them justice.

The kind of justice my brother deserved.

"Shit," I hissed as I cranked the car.

"What?" Dee asked.

As I threw the car into drive, I thought about the handful of paper pushers Cap had tossed my way. The bottom of the barrel. The newbies that were still training and ol' cronies that were on their last legs with the DEA. Cap had no faith in this operation, that much was for certain when he assembled me a team. But I couldn't betray them. I couldn't blow this op because I was angry.

Everyone that had been assigned to me deserved better than that.

"Where are we headed?" Dee asked as I eased out onto the back road.

"Back to the hotel."

"Where you're going to *tell* me you're going to bed and then ditch me to come back?"

"Dee?"

"Yeah?"

"Shut the fuck up and let me think."

He chuckled. "Suit yourself."

Someone had to keep an eye on these leather jacketed assholes. For all we knew, the entire town was beneath their thumb. I knew how crews like them worked. They networked themselves into the heart of whatever city they thought they owned, and then terrorized people until those same people finally caved. I'd seen the worst of the worst in some crews we had tracked down over the course of my short tenure at the DEA. Crews that bled small businesses dry through monthly protection payments all the while creating the scenarios they needed protecting from. Crews that made enough in the drug trade to pay off entire police stations filled with dirty cops who just wanted their slice of the monetary pie. I'd seen some scum of the Earth shit during my years with the DEA. And this crew was no different.

So, why couldn't I be the one to keep an eye on them?

"All right," Dee said as I parked the car in the hotel parking lot, "I'm going to head upstairs, take a shower, and act like you're settling in for the evening. Then, I'm gonna come around in a couple of hours when I can't sleep with food, and we're going to eat. Right?"

I shoved my way out of the car and tossed him the keys. "Sure."

"And we're going to eat together in a couple of hours, right?"

I slammed the car door closed. "Whatever you want."

"Good. Then, I'll see you in a couple of hours. Right?"

I started toward the entrance of the hotel and waved my hand over my head. "See you then."

"You're lying, aren't you?"

I flicked him off as the automatic double doors opened for

my presence. Dee cackled behind me like some fucking maniac, and I had to admit, it made me grin. I had been assigned to his side from day one. From the time the DEA handed me my badge until that moment, Dee had been my partner in chasing down everyone from every single case that had ever been put in front of us. He helped mold me into the cunning, conniving agent I had become. He helped sharpen my instincts and leadership skills. I wanted to do this with him. I wanted to take these assholes down together.

But if he thought for one second that we were doing this his way, he had another thing coming.

I showered the second I got into my hotel room. It was the quickest shower I had ever taken in my life, but it did the job. Then, I grabbed everything I needed. My phone charger. Drinks. Snacks. Another change of clothes. I shoved it all into a small backpack that I slung over my shoulders before shoving my hand in between the pillow and the pillowcase the hotel staff hadn't changed for me, per my instructions.

And when my hand graced the keys to the rundown rental car I had been smart enough to get for myself beforehand, I grinned.

"Gotcha."

At least I had one vehicle Dee didn't have access to all the damn time.

I'd sit there all fucking night if I had to. If that was what it took for me to get the information I needed, I'd sit there for the rest of the fucking case. I needed what they had. I knew they were peddling the shit. I knew it came from them. Because if there was one thing my brother taught me during his short years on this planet, it was that old habits never died that hard.

And the Death Cheaters would pay for what their drugs did to my brother.

7

———

CASH

The second church was over, I scrambled to get to my perch on the rooftop. I got up there with just enough time to bust out my rifle and scope before I pegged a very official-looking vehicle sitting across the way from the clubhouse. That same fucking woman from the bar was back, and I had to admit, I was impressed that she found us. Baron wouldn't be happy once I told him, though. I watch that same woman with a man who was so very obviously a Fed get into a very official-looking unmarked vehicle before heading off into the darkness.

And as I watched them drive off in my scope, I licked my lips.

They had been sitting there for a while. That much was obvious. Even my scope told me that the tire tracks I clocked in the dirt and sand across the road were pretty deep. My guess was they had been there at least through our church meeting, which again, would be something Baron wouldn't like. I knew someone would be back, though. My guess was that woman. She had a personal chip on her shoulder she was working out, and I knew what that kind of focus did to a person.

And now, they had found us.

I couldn't figure it out, though. As I sat there with my scoped rifle, I memorized the government plates on the back of that blacked-out vehicle. I watched as that woman from the bar and the nameless man moved off into the horizon. I kept my sights trained through the back windshield. Just in case. But when they completely fell away from my line of sight, I couldn't for the life of me pinpoint why the fuck the DEA was scoping us out without proof.

Well, obviously they have proof of something.

But what kind of proof? I had to find a way to get my hands on the information they had.

I thought back to my interactions with her at the bar. She was a pretty little thing, but not pretty enough to disarm me like that. Living the life we did required us to be on our guard all the time, especially after digging ourselves out of the trenches and trying to stay above board with our actions. Once the darkness had a taste of things, it always crept back. The temptation was always there, lapping our toes while files with our names and faces filled all sorts of alphabet offices.

Once you touched the darkness, there was no turning back time.

My earpiece came alive in my ear. "Anything?"

Baron's gruff voice made me tap my ear once so that it turned the volume down. "They've left, for now."

"Good. So, the guys can leave?"

"Yep, though I'd tell Reid to keep a station of them around the clubhouse. Just in case."

"Already on it," Reid said as his voice appeared from out of nowhere.

"You sure the coast is clear?" Baron asked.

I pulled my scope back up to my face and gazed around. "Yep. Positive. Get them out of here."

I watched as our men scattered. Their bikes struck up

before they blazed trails in all directions, making it harder for any one person to track us down if they were still around. I didn't like this. I didn't like having to pull out the old, "we're fucked, so what's next?" playbook. I watched their backs, though. I saddled a bullet into the chamber of my rifle and poised myself to shoot at whoever the fuck thought they could track my brothers down like dogs. And when everyone had dispersed, all was quiet on the beachfront.

Until the faintest noise caught my ear.

"Where are you?" I murmured as I scanned my scope around the woods.

I heard it. I knew I had. With my earpiece completely silent and the guys gone for the night, I strained to listen to the sounds around me. Soft footfalls of the patrol that had stayed behind at the clubhouse forced my teeth together. The clumping of their footfalls against the porch made me draw in a deep breath to steady myself. I had to focus. I had to think. I had to stay alert, otherwise the night would swallow me and my sanity whole.

Then, I heard it again.

Someone's back.

Even after the guys had changed positions and stopped moving, the smallest noise of brush wiggling around pulled my attention back to the woods across the street. The shrubbery sat still, barely moving in the soft breeze that kicked up from the ocean behind me. But I knew something was there.

"There," I whispered to myself.

It was the smallest movement. Barely discernible in the unforgiving darkness that had settled around us. But as I listened to twigs and leaves give way beneath something moving, I found it. The car. It had come from a different angle, nowhere near where it had once been perched. However, the minute I saw a bush's branches sink to the ground, the corner shadow of a tire led my scope all the way up to the windshield.

Where that pretty little woman sat behind the wheel.

"Night mode," I muttered as I pressed a button on top of my scope.

As the lens switched, she fully came into view. I watched her lean her seat back and pull out a bag of chips before she tossed one between the plump lips of hers. She looked freshly showered. Her hair, still dripping onto her shoulders as she kicked her knee up against the steering wheel. The thought of her being in a shower with water dripping over those toned curves of hers tugged at my cock. I felt it pressing tightly against my jeans, and with a quick snap of my scoped, I realized something.

She's alone.

A grin ticked my cheek. My tongue slid out over my lower lip as I ignored the growling of my gut. Could anyone have offered her up on a better platter than that? Alone and still wet from her shower?

"God, the things I'd do to you," I murmured.

"You see anything?" Baron asked from out of nowhere.

If I were a jumpy person, it probably would've sent me off the fucking roof. "She's back."

"That quick, huh?"

The grin on my face grew. "And she doesn't have her plus one this time around."

"Kinky," Reid said playfully.

I chuckled, but Baron wasn't having any of it. "What's our next move? She look aggressive?"

I tilted my head back and heard my neck pop, rushing relief down my spine. That was the thing about perches; make them too comfy and you were liable to fall asleep. But being uncomfortable meant inconveniences like my entire spine locking the fuck up because I refused to move.

"Cash?" Baron asked.

"Just had to pop my neck, give me a fucking second."

I placed my eye back against the scope and watched as that woman continued to toss chips into her mouth. I watched the way her jaw rolled, those silent chews flexing her facial muscles. Her legs kept slipping open the further she ducked down into her seat, and I swear every bone in my body was ready to fill hers to the brim.

"No," I said, "she's just hungry."

"I've got something for that," Reid said.

I snickered. "I bet you do."

"Guys, focus," Baron said.

"No, seriously," Reid said as I heard him pitter-pattering around in my earpiece, "I've actually got something for that. Where exactly is she?"

"If you come out onto the porch and turn three degrees to the right, she's straight ahead. Next to that bush we caught Pyre in one time taking a dump while piss drunk."

"Gimme fifteen minutes," Reid said.

I counted the seconds in my head like a fucking asshat. I couldn't help it, though. It was part of my training, after all. The seconds ticked by as the minutes crawled forth, and as minute one became minute twelve in my head, I saw Reid walking across the gravel parking lot in front of the clubhouse.

"Three minutes early, go him," I murmured.

"Don't take your eyes off him," Baron commanded.

"Not a fucking chance," I said.

I watched Reid ease himself across the street, and if the woman had seen him, she gave no indication that she had. She dug around behind her in the backseat, looking for something at the most inopportune time. Is this what the DEA employed now? Subpar agents with a bone to pick? She'd be easy to take down. Easy to break in.

Just like she was easy on the eyes.

"Knock, knock," Reid said as he approached her window.

The woman froze, but she didn't flinch. Hell, even after she settled back into her seat and peered out the window at Reid, she didn't look panicked. I was impressed, honestly. Her stoic face glared at him as she inched her window down, and I readied my trigger finger to fire off a warning shot right through her windshield.

"Figured you could use some food for your stakeout," Reid said.

I did my best to bury my chuckle as he held the plate of steaming hot food up to the crack in her window.

"Here, take it," Reid urged.

I watched her roll down the window a bit more, allowing Reid to slip the paper plate through. She took it before he brandished a soda from behind his back, and I was shocked when she freely took that as well. She kept staring at Reid with those narrowed eyes of hers. Eyes that sparkled, even through the night vision of my scope. It was clear that she didn't know what to make of things, and she was right to choose the route of silence.

Especially in the presence of someone with Reid's particular...skillset.

"So," Reid said as he leaned against the car, "I'm just gonna go out on a limb and say that you've got questions to ask?"

The woman nodded, but still refused to use her voice.

"Well," he said as he straightened his back, "why don't you come inside and ask them then?"

"Baron?" I asked quickly.

"Yep, setting shit up now," he said.

I paused. "So, we're just gonna roll with this?"

"Reid knows what he's doing. Get inside."

And while I was happy to stand and shake the numbness from my legs, I wasn't the least bit happy at having to entertain a fucking DEA agent. Especially since it was clear that she had a vendetta driving her actions.

After all, it was the only reason I could come up with for ditching her partner just to come back.

8

ANGEL

"Well," the tall, lean man with the hazel eyes said as he straightened his back, "why don't you come inside and ask them, then?"

I couldn't stop staring at him. Even as the warm food in my hand enticed me, I couldn't pull my eyes away. Jesus Christ, he was gorgeous as hell. His t-shirt sat snug against his body, showcasing the taut muscles pulled tightly over his bones. His disheveled blond hair swayed softly in the salted breeze that kicked up, and I swear there was a boyish grin playing over those languid, glistening lips of his. They were all sexy as fuck, to be honest. Every single one of them, in their own way. And as I swallowed the knot that had somehow worked its way back into my throat, I nodded my head.

"I suppose that's the efficient way to do it," I finally said.

The man smiled, and it lit up his hazel stare. "So, she's got a voice."

I snickered. "Yeah, something like that."

The man reached down and tried opening my door. "Are you going to unlock it and let me be a gentleman? Or are you going to insist on doing everything yourself?"

"Gentleman? Really? That's what you guys are?"

He didn't flinch. "Why don't you come inside and find out?"

I stared at him through the partially rolled-down window as my finger hovered over the unlock button. I couldn't let them have the upper hand. Giving something like that to a man—any man—always ended in heartache and sorrow. Men didn't know how to take control without mucking things up, so I moved my finger away from the unlock button and tugged hard on the door handle.

"Here," I said as I handed the plate of food back to him, "not the biggest fan of bacon."

He chuckled as he scooped the plate out of my grasp. "Duly noted. Follow me."

I scooped up my small backpack and tossed it over my shoulder. "I know where the front door is. I can make it myself."

"I'm sure you can."

I stood tall and proud as I clutched the leather strap of my backpack. I had a hell of a lot of questions that I required answers to, and if they were willing to sit down and hear me out, then I had no choice but to give them the benefit of the doubt. Anger bubbled beneath my skin. The darkness in my soul hissed in my ear, trying to convince me to lash out.

We had to do this the right way, though.

Otherwise, my brother would never get the justice he deserved.

"Here," the man said as he reached around my body, "let me get the—"

I reached for the doorknob and quickly tossed the door open. "I said I've got it."

The second I stepped into that clubhouse, my gaze went straight to the vaulted ceiling. Fucking hell, they had a foyer. Who the hell had a grand foyer nowadays? The beautiful white-and-black granite floors matched the white walls with black accents. They matched, for crying out loud. It didn't look like a frat house like I had imagined. There weren't broken beer bottles everywhere or soda cans overfilling trash bags abandoned in random corners. There weren't boxer briefs with skid marks littering the floors. In fact, it barely looked like the place was used.

I couldn't stop staring at how gorgeous it all was.

"You aren't helping her with her shit?"

That gruff voice snapped me out of my trance long enough to see the lumbering behemoth trudge down a hallway in front of me.

"What?" I asked as I found my voice again.

"Not my fault if she's stubborn," the man behind me said.

Their president grumbled something underneath his breath as he walked up to me. He ripped my backpack off my shoulder and slung it over his. My jaw hit the floor as he pivoted quite smoothly on his feet, and his heavy footfalls started back toward the hallway that had just given birth to his dark presence.

"You coming or what?" he asked.

The man behind me brushed by. "Come on, kitchen's this way. You can eat at the table."

A movement out of the corner of my eye caught my attention and my head whipped to the left. There he was. The bartender. The one with the playful eyes and careful stare. How long had he been standing there? Had he been there the entire time?

"You coming?" I asked as I pointed down the hallway.

But all he did was nod.

"Right," I said before clearing my throat once more.

Somehow, I managed to put one foot in front of the other. One step, then another, until my body finally got the picture. We were doing this, no matter how many times my heart tried to bottom out through my asshole. I'd ask my questions, and I'd get to look straight into their faces in order to figure out whether or not they were lying to me.

And I'd know if they were lying to me.

"Here," the man with my food said as he pulled out a chair, "you can sit here. Your back will be to the wall, so you won't have to worry about anyone creeping up on you."

I quirked an eyebrow. "Is that something I should be worried about?"

"Reid always takes that shit into account," Cash said as he walked up behind me.

"Reid?" I asked.

The man nodded before he motioned to my seat. Those hazel eyes of his sparkled as Baron dropped my backpack next to the chair. Cash brushed behind me, no doubt taking up space in yet another corner where he could watch me like a hawk. Still, I managed to find the courage to sit in front of the still-hot plate of food and soda that Reid had brought out to my rental vehicle.

And it wasn't until I looked down at the table and focused on it that I realized a meal had been prepared.

"Are we...all having dinner together, then?" I asked.

The men sat down at place settings I hadn't even clocked before they reached for food. They dipped up luscious amounts of meat and vegetables. Steaming spicy rice with peas inside looked heavenly as Reid pried the lid off the pot. The sound of soda hissing open tickled my ears as I picked up my fork, and I found the pot roast calling to the tip of my tongue.

But I didn't even get through my first juicy, awe-inducing bite before Cash spoke up.

"So, you think we're selling drugs. Is that it?"

"Jesus, Cash. You can't let the woman eat?" Baron asked.

"This shouldn't shock you," Reid said as he dipped into his rice. "He's always been a steamroller."

I did my best not to moan at how delightful the food was as I chewed and swallowed. "You're the only crew with a history of this junk, and now it's back on the street. Don't tell me that's a coincidence."

Baron stabbed his pot roast. "Hate to break it to you, but."

My gaze locked with his forehead. "I don't believe in coincidences. You guys have something to do with this."

Reid chuckled. "Got anything that isn't circumstantial or coincidental then?"

Ah, that was what they wanted. They wanted to see if they could dig around in my head and figure out what kind of proof I had of their escapades. I wasn't that stupid, though. Maybe some of my actions were misguided, but it had gotten me right where I wanted to be.

Sitting down with all three of them so I could look them in the eyes and ask my questions.

"I'm not that stupid, Reid. The second I tell you what I've got, your plan is to go find it and destroy it, kill it, or burn it. Then, I'm right back at square one where I started."

"Yeah, *Reid*," Cash said.

Baron shoveled rice into his face and damn near swallowed without chewing. "You're not very good at this job, are you?"

I crossed my arms over my chest. "About as good as you are at covering your tracks. Or do you think we forgot about what you did to Whicker?"

To say that stopped the conversation was an understatement. Baron held his fork halfway to his mouth before allowing the food to slip off its tip. Cash shoved his plate away out of the corner of my eye, and even the playful grin on Reid's face melted into a frown that could have killed had I looked him dead in his face. I held my breath as Baron stood. His shadow, looming over me as his eyes boiled with fury.

"You better choose your next set of words very carefully, Angel."

It shouldn't have shocked me that he knew my nickname, but it did.

"Baron, take a breath," Reid said.

"Sit down," Cash said.

I loved that I had gotten a rise out of him, though. Maybe he'd be more willing to cooperate if he knew that Whicker's death hadn't gone unnoticed.

"I mean, let's face it," I said as I stood to my feet, matching energy for energy, "killing your own president and pinning it on your rival crew is gutsy, to say the least. And efficient."

Baron's voice dropped through the fucking floor. "Do you know why we did it?"

"Baron," Reid hissed.

I tilted my head. "Are you admitting that you did it then?"

Baron leaned forward and planted his hands into the table, causing it to creak with his weight. "All I'm saying is what if I had done it? If I had taken that fucker out, do you know what my motive behind it would have been?"

I matched his movements, making sure he understood that he couldn't intimidate me. I'd seen the worst of what life had to offer. I'd been smacked around by my own father, thrown into the basement and concussed by my own mother, and watched as those drugs slowly ripped the life from my brother's chest.

Some bullshit bike-riding grandpa didn't scare me.

I leaned in so close that I felt his breath pulsing against my lips. "So, tell me, Baron: why would you have done something like that?"

He didn't hesitate either. "Because the Black Diamonds were the ones peddling that shit. Not us."

I held his icy blue gaze with mine as moonlight softly poured through the kitchen window behind him. The soft glow enhanced the white coming in at his temples, and somehow it served to make him even more brutally delectable than he already was. His attractiveness didn't stop me from wondering, though.

It didn't stop me from wondering if there was any truth to his words.

I knew of the Black Diamonds. Whenever one researched motorcycle crews, the first thing to be established was rival crews. People we might encounter that may be hostile toward us being on their turf or possibly even willing to help, given the right price. The Black Diamonds were ruthless motherfuckers, according to the slim file we had on them back in my hotel room. We didn't know much, but we knew enough to stay out of their path, no matter what it took.

Still, I wasn't sure the tension between the two crews was enough for me to believe that the Death Cheaters were as innocent as they came.

But I also committed his words to memory, just in case.

"So, Baron," I said as I sat back down in my chair, "ever talk to those foster parents of yours?"

He growled. "Why you stupid little—"

"Oh, no you don't," Cash said as he leapt up and grabbed one arm.

"Calm down, Baron. She's trying to get underneath your skin," Reid said as he lunged for his president and grabbed his other arm.

"You have no right!" Baron exclaimed.

I took a bite of my vegetables. "Could use a bit more garlic."

"Who the fuck do you think you are, coming after us like this?!" the behemoth bellowed.

I picked up my napkin and dabbed it against the corner of my mouth. I raised my hands above my head, cracking my spine back into place before I stood once more to my feet. I slipped out from behind the table, moving away from the wall they had attempted to trap me against. No risk for anyone sneaking up on me. How stupid did they think I was?

"Hey," I said as I picked up my backpack, "I'm not the one who invited me inside. Maybe you should talk to your men about that."

"You're never going to get away with this," Baron growled.

A shiver worked its way down my spine as I turned toward the hallway. "I'm sure we'll be seeing one another soon. Enjoy your evening, gentleman."

As the gruff anger of the mountainous man behind me followed me toward the front door, my chest swelled with pride. Hopefully, that gave them a little taste of what I already knew about them. Hopefully, that put them in their place. Their dossiers were thick where I came from. They were well known within the ranks of the DEA.

Which meant they needed to tread carefully if they wanted to get out of all this alive.

"Toodleloo!" I chirped as I made my way out the front door.

And oh, the angry roar that came from Baron's gut made every single bit of my difficult evening worth it.

9

———

BARON

My fists clenched at my side as my voice echoed back at me, as if
I were stuck in a hellish chamber that forced me to relive the
worst moments of my life.

"Fuck! Reid!?"

The wind that whipped with the movement of his body
brushed past me. "On it."

I raked my hands through my hair. "Cash!"

"Want me to go with him?" the man asked as he loomed in
the corner, perched as always.

I whipped toward him. "We need this place on lockdown.
She's looking into us. She's looking into our histories. We need
to know exactly what she knows."

Cash pushed off the wall. "I can work with that."

Reid, my Road Captain, and Cash, my Enforcer, both raced
out the door as I stood there in the empty kitchen. The food
continued sizzling behind me, fresh out of the stove and still
smelling fantastic. I turned back toward it, gazing down at the
peaceful offering we had set out for her. Peace. That was what
the club had worked ages to obtain. Money, peace, and sanity.

The shit Whicker had gotten us into damn near killed us all. It damn near pulled the crew apart at the seams.

How the fuck had it come back to haunt us?

How the hell was this happening again?

"God fucking damn it!" I roared.

My callused, scarred hands gripped the edge of the table, and my arms came up. Every muscle in my body flexed as the legs of the table came off the ground. With a whip of my hands, they launched over my head, sending the food soaring to the ceiling as plates and glasses shattered on the floor. Meat flew through the air and vegetables scattered at my feet. Drinks slammed into the wall, dripping down the white plaster Cash had just repainted not too long ago. And as I stood there, panting, nothing could have prepared me for what came next.

"Tsk, tsk," she said as her voice flitted through the air, "what a mess. And such good food, too."

My back stiffened. The hairs on the nape of my neck stood on end. It wasn't very often that someone got the better of me. That someone was genuinely, truly able to shock me. But when I heard her voice… When I heard it behind me, as I stared down the hallway she had just stormed down…

I had to admit, I was impressed. "How the fuck did you—"

She snickered. "You genuinely believe your rival crew is doing this, don't you?"

I turned to face her, my fists still balled up at my sides. I rolled my shoulders back and stood tall, keeping my head level on my shoulders. She was a formidable opponent; I'd give her that. Sneaky and stealthy in a way that Reid would have adored.

Too bad she caught me instead.

"You can look at me like that all you want," she said as she leaned against the doorway between the kitchen and the useless dining room we never fucking used. "You wouldn't be the first man to do it. So, when you're ready, you can answer my question."

I drew in a deep breath through my nose. "How long have you been working this on your own time?"

She grinned. "My boss knows I'm running this case."

My stare slithered down her body before I took a step toward her. "Not very often a special agent runs their entire case."

She shrugged. "This one is a bit personal. Cap's doing me a solid."

"Why?"

She kept that plastered grin on her face, but I watched her gaze focus on me. With every step that I took, something else girded itself. First, her back. It straightened with the first step that I took. Then, her forehead. Her eyebrows rose, pulling her entire head taut, even as she tried to keep her composure. I took another step, and her legs locked out. A terrible decision, if you asked me. You never locked your legs out, anyone knew that. And when I hovered over her, cloaking her in my shadow, she tilted her head back as her shoulders rolled.

Fucking hell, she smelled nice.

"Is this the part where you try to fuck me into submission?" Angel asked.

I smirked. "Why? Care to try it out?"

Her gaze dropped to my mouth. "That tactic never works with me."

"So, someone's already tried it then."

"Awww, sad you're not the first? I could've *sworn* you weren't that kind of asshole. Not with all of those lovely things that happened during your foster care years."

My hand darted out without a second thought. I pinned her to the doorframe, listening to her gasp as my fingers closed around her throat. Her eyes widened as I shoved my knee between her legs, feeling the heat of her juicy pussy battering down against my jeans. I slid my hand upward, forcing her head to tilt back as her tanned skin gave way to those forest-colored eyes of hers. And as I ground my knee against her tender folds, I watched it happen. I watched her eyes flutter closed.

And that brought my lips down to her ear as a growl escaped them.

"No real man ever wants a woman that doesn't know shit about what she's doing."

The second I crushed my lips to hers, I knew I was a goner. Whether or not I wore down her defenses didn't mean shit to me, although I hoped that it might help. All I wanted was to taste those sarcastic little lips of hers. I wanted to remind her that, at the end of the day, I could make her scream. Or cry. Or come. Anything I wanted was mine to bestow upon her. Maybe if she knew who she was fucking with, she'd enjoy who she was fucking.

And as our tongues collided, her hands coiled into my t-shirt.

"Fuck," she groaned.

"That's it," I grunted as my hand fell away from her neck, "take it like a woman."

"Oh, shit," she whimpered as my hand slid down her body and I cupped her clothed breast.

"Goddamn it, you smell amazing," I hissed.

"We can't do this."

"Just close your eyes and—"

"We can't do this, Baron. It isn't right."

I bent down and cupped her ample ass with my palms. Her excess filled the slats of my fingertips as I hoisted her against me, feeling her curves blanketing my muscles. She squealed when I walked her into the kitchen. Her body jiggled as I sat her on the kitchen countertop. With her legs dangling on either side of my body and those wide doe eyes of hers staring back at me, my head tilted to the side.

Then, she closed her eyes and leaned her head back against the cabinets.

"Perfect," I grumbled.

I leaned forward and sank my teeth into her neck. She groaned as her body jumped, and I wrapped my arm behind her lower back to keep her heated pussy pressed against me. I lapped my tongue along her flittering pulse point, relishing the height of her heart beating. She gasped and groaned, her hands gripping my leather jacket as she trembled in my grasp.

"Baron," she moaned.

"Mmmm," I hummed and slid my tongue down the length of her neck, "that's it."

"Baron, please."

I pulled back, gripped her cheeks, and forced her to look at me. "Please, what?"

Her eyes danced between mine. "I—"

I leaned forward, feathering my lips against hers. "Please, what, Angel?"

If she really wanted me to stop, I'd stop. I sure as fuck wasn't about to rape a goddamn DEA agent. But I saw how puckered her peaks were behind that filthy bra of hers. I felt the heat battering from between her legs like a ram, waiting for my cock to fill her. She wanted it. She wanted me. And maybe, in the process, I'd get a few fucking answers out of her.

Hell, maybe even an ally to get us out of this if I could convince her that I was telling the truth.

"Angel," I said curtly.

She blinked. "Don't hurt me."

My brow ticked. "What?"

She looked dead into my eyes. "Don't hurt me."

I grinned. "Ah, sweet girl, pain is only enjoyed when both parties want it."

10

___

ANGEL

The second his mouth collided back with mine, I was transported. His kiss tasted divine. His tongue danced along the roof of my mouth, shivering me to my core as his fingers slid away from my cheeks. I wrapped my arms around his neck. I pulled him as close as I could get him. His muscles made me feel safe. His kiss made me feel beautiful. And as his hands ran up my clothed thighs, for the smallest of moments, I forgot how angry I was at the world.

"Fuck," I whispered as my head fell back.

"Mmmmm, I can't wait to taste that pussy of yours."

With a flick of his fingers, he undid the button of my jeans. The zipper popped open, sliding down as if a dam had burst and it was running for its life. He scooped me against him, my ass cheeks barely teetering on the edge of the countertop as he shoved his hand into my pants. And when I gazed into his eyes, with nowhere else to go, his thick, callused fingers found my sensitive nub.

And oh, how beautifully he caressed it.

"There she is," he growled.

"Oh, shit," I whimpered.

"That's it," he groaned as he popped a finger into my entrance.

"Fuck," I hissed.

"So tight for me. So wet."

"Baron," I said breathlessly.

He grabbed my hair and pulled my head back. "You're going to come for me, and you're going to like it. Understood?"

I nodded quickly. "Y-y-yes, I understand."

"You're going to cry out my name for the world to hear. Understood?"

My legs jumped with every soft stroke of his finger against my clit. "Yes. Yes. I understand. I get it."

"And one more thing," he said, bringing my head back up to face him.

"Yeah?"

He grinned as he slipped another finger into my pussy. "You're going to keep your eyes on me until you unravel. Understood?"

I swallowed hard. "Yes."

"Good girl."

His fingertips moved like lightning, zipping over the tip of my clit as his thick, callused digits curled against the walls of my pussy. I braced myself against the edge of the countertop, my fingers curling around the squared-off edges as I bucked against his hand. My eyes threatened to close. Threatened to flutter shut as ecstasy coursed through my veins. His fingers teased my swollen nub, swirling and undulating as my thighs quivered.

"That's it, let it pour over you," Baron said slowly.

"Oh, God. This—I—I can't," I grunted as my eyes almost closed.

His grip on my hair tightened. "Don't you fucking dare. Keep your eyes on me."

"Baron," I whimpered.

"Come for me."

My toes curled. "Baron, please. Don't stop."

"Not until you unravel for me, sweet girl."

"Baron, yes! So close!"

"Come for me," he growled.

He crooked his fingers against my clit, and the second his finger slid across the top, I was a goner. My body unraveled, expanding and contracting as my head fell back into the palm of his hand. I couldn't keep my eyes open a second longer. They squeezed shut as fireworks burst behind my eyelids. He cupped my pussy, holding me within the palm of his hand as my juices flooded his palm. I shivered from head to toe. Lightning streaked through my veins, igniting my bone marrow in a sizzling debate between coming alive and staying dead. It had been years since I'd felt any kind of joy. Or pleasure. Or happiness.

I wanted more of him. All of him. I had to feel him. It was all my body knew. All my body wanted.

Despite the guilt coursing its way through my veins.

"More," Baron growled.

"Oh, yes" I moaned breathlessly.

In one fell swoop, my pants were off my body. Gone were my shoes. Gone was my dignity. And in its place, a monstrous man with a brutal stare clasped my bare hips in his gigantic hands. He teetered me on the edge of the kitchen countertop, fiddling with something that clinked and clanked around. And when I finally managed to find enough bodily autonomy to look down in between our bodies, I saw the thickest cock I'd ever laid eyes on.

Veins, throbbing just beneath the skin.

Jesus, he was going to make that fit?

Baron chuckled. "Eyes on me, sweet girl."

I slowly raised my gaze to his. I couldn't speak. I couldn't breathe. All I could do was grip his shirt to hold myself up as my legs wrapped around his waist. His lips fell to the crook of my neck. His tongue lapped against my pulse point. And as arousal flooded my pussy, his dick pressed in between my folds.

Before sinking inside of me, inch by fucking inch.

"Oooooh, my Gooooood," I groaned out.

He nipped at the shell of my ear. "You know Baron's just fine, right?"

The instant his fingertips curled against my bare hips, I was transported. I didn't even give a shit about that comment of his. My body jumped against his, helpless to his assault as my wet sounds filled the spaces between us. I wrapped my arms around his neck. I buried my face against his shoulder. His muscles swallowed my groans and grunts as he stuffed me full, over and over again. His cock dragged along my helpless walls. He touched every part of me at once, it seemed. Electricity shot its way through my veins and blood rushed through my ears, drowning out the world and everything in it.

Except the feeling of Baron filling me up.

"Baron. Baron. Baron," I chanted.

"That's it," he growled.

My nails raked down the back of his shirt. "Baron, please."

He slammed me down his dick, staking me on his length. "Goddamn it, Angel."

"Baron," I choked out as my head fell back.

His hands splayed across my back, holding me to him as I succumbed to my second orgasm. My body unraveled for him, shivering and shaking as goosebumps fled across my skin. My jaw unhinged in silent pleasure as his cock twitched. His movements stuttered as he pounded against me, his fingertips curling so deeply into my hips that I just knew he'd leave his fingerprints behind.

Euphoria held me hostage, like a hand around my throat, as Baron's cock filled me to the brim.

"Fucking hell," he growled as his hips finally ceased their movements.

And as my body collapsed against his, tears sprang in my eyes.

"My God," I whispered.

He chuckled. "Like I said, Baron will do just fine."

I blinked away my tears and picked my head up from his shoulder long enough to watch pull away from him. The sight alone puckered my nipples against my sports bra, and they ached to be touched. I watched his tongue dart across his lips, his eyes casing me as I sat there on the kitchen countertop. Perched, and dripping with the evidence of our debauchery.

Part of me wondered what his tongue had the capability of doing in between my legs. But the other part of me swam in guilt for sleeping with the enemy. I fucked one of the men responsible for peddling the fucking drugs that killed my brother.

And the thought made my head buzz with nausea as his eyes met mine.

"What's wrong?" Baron asked.

His heated voice ripped me out of my trance. "Huh?"

His hands dropped away from my body before he stuffed his dick back into his pants. "Your eyes are red. What's wrong?"

Shit. "I, uh…"

He pinned me with a look as he zipped up his jeans. "I won't ask again, Angel. What's. Wrong?"

VROOM! VROOM VROOM!

Saved by the bike. "Your guys are coming back. I should probably get decent."

His head slowly tilted to the side as his hands planted themselves against the kitchen countertop. They sat on either side of my legs, effectively blocking me in as I sat there, half naked, on the cold, hard surface.

His stare robbed me of my breath. "Tell me what's wrong. Now."

I didn't know why I listened, but I did. Tears continued to crest my eyes and I continued blinking them away, as if my body were battling itself.

Then, I got the tears to settle down and I cleared my throat. "It's just...been a long time since I've felt anything but anger. That's all."

The sound grew closer. The bikes drew near, and I watched Baron tense. He peered over his shoulder as he rolled them back. He cracked his neck before turning back to me, and to my surprise, he offered me his hands. One of them, still glistening with my mark, and the other still heated from the skin of my neck. *Do I take them? Do I allow this man to help me? Do I give him that kind of upper hand?*

"I'm just helping you down; stop analyzing it," he spat.

So, I took his hands. "Thanks."

"Get your clothes right."

I didn't like the sound of his voice. "What's wrong?"

He charged toward the hallway. "Just do it."

I quickly zipped up my pants and redid the button of my jeans. "Baron, talk to me."

He shook his head. "Those aren't my guys. You need to get out of here. Now."

"Wait, what?"

He turned toward me and charged forth. "You can head out the same way you got back in. Out the back door, around the side of the house. Make sure no one sees you."

"Baron, wait a second. How do you know if—"

He grabbed my arm and tugged me into the defunct dining room. "I'm the president of this crew. I know exactly what my guys' bikes sound like. Now, get the fuck out."

He shoved me toward the door, but I whipped back around

on him. "I'm not leaving you. If you're about to be in trouble, the best person to be with is an agent that can do something about it."

Both of his hands darted out at that moment. He grabbed my shirt, heaved me up to his face, and held me there as my toes barely danced along the beautiful granite flooring.

"Baron," I choked out.

"This isn't a fairytale," he snarled as his breath pulsed against my face. "This isn't something you can fix with your pathetic little case. These are our lives you're fucking with. Our reputation. Our livelihoods. Our families. And if you don't get out of here now, you may not get out at all. Now, get the fuck out, Angel."

He shoved me so hard that I fell to the ground. I slid toward the back door, hearing it creak open as I watched Baron pivot on his feet. He stormed away, blazing a trail through the kitchen as the sounds of those engines crept closer. His lumbering footsteps scattered throughout the clubhouse, darting this way and that way as doors were thrown open and guns were cocked. My eyes widened at the sound. Jesus Christ, what the hell was about to happen? And how the hell was I supposed to leave him to defend himself like that?

I needed to know who was rolling up on them.

So, I scrambled to my feet and silenced my footsteps as I darted through the kitchen.

Baron grumbled to himself as he passed by me. I pressed myself into the darkened corner of what looked like a library, of all things, though the bookshelves didn't have much on them. No pictures. Barely any books. A few balled-up pieces of paper, maybe. I heard him talking to himself, but I couldn't decipher it because of the mounting sound of the engines that kept getting steadily closer.

Then, I heard his footsteps above me.

"The stairs," I whispered.

Baron moved like thunder, but I soared like lightning. I made a break for the steps, scaling them two at a time as the grand foyer fell behind me. I heard him to my right, so I took an immediate left and made my way down the first hallway that I found. His boot-falls echoed along the cavernous upper level. I heard him cock just about every single gun on the fucking planet. And as I heard him coming my way, I eased my way into a darkened room.

He soared by with a shotgun in his grasp. "This room is perfect. Shoot those fuckers before they even see me."

Dear God, he was placing a readied weapon in every single room.

Which meant—

Shit.

I looked around, trying to find somewhere to duck for cover. There wasn't much, though. A bay window that looked out over the beach. A couple of doors, most likely closets, but that was a terrible bet because most people kept their guns in closets. His footsteps came closer. My hands began sweating. And as his shadow tickled the door, I did the only thing that came to mind.

I scrambled to get underneath the bed.

I held my breath as the dull roar of engines came to a grinding halt. I watched Baron's steel-toed boots from beneath the bed as I saw him march to the first door I had considered throwing open. He threw it open before he murmured something to himself, then headed toward the other door and tossed that open as well.

"Gotcha," he muttered.

I watched him pull a semi-auto from the closet. My eyes widened as the barrel alone could have poked someone's eye out from across a fucking room. I heard him piddling around before he placed something back into the closet, but what he placed, I couldn't see. And after he closed both of the doors, I heard him load up the semi-automatic in his hands.

He exited the bedroom and closed the door with a thud behind him.

I released the breath I held and laid there for a moment, trying to get my bearings. What the hell was I doing? God, if Dee had been with me, he'd be bitching up a storm. Well, more than that; he would have absolutely called Cap over the decisions I had made.

Fuck, who was I kidding? If Dee had been with me, I would've never gotten back into the house a second fucking time.

"Let's make the trip worth it," I grunted as I slid out from beneath the bed.

I raced toward the bay window, wondering what I would see from my position. I didn't find the side of the house like I figured I would, however. Instead, I found myself staring right down at the heads of at least a dozen men straddling bikes while wrapped up in pitch black leather jackets. And stitched on the upper arms of their jackets in bright white stitching was nothing other than a diamond.

"The Black Diamonds," I whispered to myself.

Holy fuck, maybe Baron was telling the truth.

A door opened in the distance and I watched every single man out there on a bike cross their arms over their chests. My heart leapt into my throat as I saw Baron step out onto the porch. With that semi-automatic slung over his shoulder and a shotgun in his left hand, he stood there, facing off with at least a dozen men who looked like they had walked through Hell just to get to his front door. Men like that didn't have much to lose, and that put Baron in a precarious position.

I found myself worried for him.

Well, that's not good.

Lips moved, but I couldn't hear voices. Fucking hell, what I wouldn't have given for my listening equipment. I couldn't hear a fucking word they said over the roar of those bike engines, but maybe if I removed barriers, I'd be able to hear better. I scoured the window until I found a crank toward the bottom. Pretty old school, if anyone asked me, but it made things easier since I wouldn't have to move around as much. I grasped the cold, unforgiving metal against my palm. I leaned my body weight against it, hoping to jar the damned thing around so that I could crank the window open.

Until a gun cocked behind me.

"I'm unarmed," I said as I eased my knees beneath me and slipped my hands into the air. "I mean no harm."

"Turn the fuck around, Angel."

The familiar voice caused me to whip around with the force of a tornado. "Cash?"

He quickly decocked his gun and holstered it. "What the fuck are you doing here?"

I furrowed my brow. "Where the hell did you come from? I thought you and Reid—"

"You're not the only one with tricks."

I stood to my feet. "Baron's down there. Does someone have eyes on him?"

His stare slid down my body. "Yes."

"Up here, Money Man."

He chuckled as his stare slowly slid back up my body. "Fair enough."

"Why are they here?"

He shrugged. "Don't know. Wanna listen in?"

I blinked. "You've got surveillance equipment set up? Where?"

He stuck his hand into the pocket of his crimson leather jacket. "We've got something better."

And when he handed me that earpiece, I couldn't get it into my ear quickly enough. Because when I did, Baron's voice came alive. That brutal, gravelly tone of voice that sent shivers down the back of my spine.

"Now," Cash said as he guided me back toward the window, "don't move a muscle and just listen."

The vinyl paneling of the outside of the house pressed against my back as I stood there with my pistol against my cheek. I closed my eyes, allowing the cool metal of the gun to center me as I listened to Baron and that motherfucker at the head of the line talk. I'd never liked the President of the Black Diamonds. He had always seemed like a shifty fucking character to me. Even before the debacle with Whicker, he always seemed off. Like not every peg had a hole. And when me and my team rode by those assholes on the road, I knew exactly where they had been headed. So, for the first time since Whicker's betrayal, I sent out the emergency warning signal.

Beckoning every single guy back to the clubhouse.

"Abandoning bikes for the woods," Pyre said.

"Hm-hm," I softly hummed twice.

"Organizing ourselves on the railings now," Bic said.

I eased over toward the railing of our wraparound porch and stared down the cliff face. I watched Team B line themselves along sturdy metal railings we had embedded into the rocky lining ourselves for stealth positions that concealed our big boys perfectly. I drew in a deep breath as I slowly moved back toward the side of the house. With my back flush against the vinyl, I scooted toward the corner of the house.

If I could just get a bit closer...

"Watch it, Reid," Pitchfork said as his voice bombarded my ear.

"Hm," I hummed once.

Razor snickered. "You know that man doesn't like being told what to do. Now hush so we can all hear."

"They haven't started talking yet," Coal said softly. "They're just staring at each other."

"A pissing contest, that's what this is," Snake grumbled.

"I'm unarmed. I mean no harm."

I paused at the sound of her voice. "Cash?"

"Who the fuck was that?" Pyre asked.

"Cash," I hissed.

"Turn the fuck around, Angel," he said curtly.

"Who the hell is that, Reid?" Snake asked flatly.

What in the absolute fuck was she still doing in the clubhouse?! While we sat outside waiting for round two with these Black Diamond fucks, Cash was inside with the DEA agent? Hadn't Baron already taken care of her? Something didn't add up.

"Shut up," I whispered as I peeked my eyes around the corner of the house.

"Cash?" she asked.

"What the fuck are you doing here?" Cash asked abruptly.

"Where the hell did you come from? I thought you and Reid—"

"You're not the only one with tricks."

"Baron's down there," she said with a twinge of worry in her voice. "Does someone have eyes on him?"

And when I clocked how relaxed Baron's body was in the face of imminent death, I knew what had happened.

Holy hell, they fucked.

Cash paused. "Yes."

"Up here, Money Man."

I bet he got the best eye full. "Fair enough."

Jesus Christ, I bet she's a good fuck.

"Are they kidding us right now?" Bic asked.

Angel's voice came alive as I ducked back around the corner of the house to conceal myself. "Why are they here?"

Cash didn't hesitate. "Don't know. Wanna listen in?"

"He fucked her, didn't he?" Pitchfork asked.

"Shut up or you'll be thrown to the dogs," I glowered.

Angel's voice sounded shocked. "You've got surveillance equipment set up? Where?"

I grinned as Cash spoke. "We've got something better."

"Well, then," Jagger, the President of the Black Diamonds said, "who's gonna break the ice?"

Baron cocked his gun in front of God and all those assholes. "Seems like you just did."

"Now," Cash said as he lowered his voice, "don't move a muscle and just listen."

"Stay alert, everyone," I muttered.

"Then, I'll get straight to the point," Jagger said as he planted both of his feet into the gravel of the parking lot, his legs still straddling his bike. "Why the fuck is the DEA in town?"

Baron snickered. "Funny, I was hoping you could answer that question for me. You know, since you guys are responsible for peddling that shit in the first place."

"Allegedly."

"There's nothing allegedly about it. You hooked our former president onto your cheap ass drugs, trying to take us down because he wouldn't let you sell in our territory."

I expected Jagger to respond, but he didn't, and that made me nervous.

"So tell me, Jagoff," Baron said, "are you here to try and sell us out again? Because I won't be as easy to kill."

I heard a sound that I couldn't place, and I kept my voice quiet. "Pitchfork, talk to us. You're on the roof?"

"He's getting off his bike, guys. Stay ready, because he's walking right up to Baron."

"On my mark," I whispered as I pulled the gun away from my cheek and held it out in front of me.

Then, Jagger's voice came alive. "I don't care what the fuck you're talking about, old man. So, give me the answers that I want. Why the fuck did you call the DEA into town?"

"Why would you think we called them?"

"Because there's no other reason why they'd be here."

"You mean, other than you guys trying to push your drugs into our territory?"

"I don't give a flying fuck about your stupid, useless territory!"

Baron chuckled. "Then you shouldn't give a shit about selling in it. And yet, you're on my doorstep, wondering about the DEA because they're most likely tracking you, right?"

Then, I heard it. I heard Baron's steel-toed boots scramble against the concrete of the porch. And it didn't take a genius to figure out what had happened.

"He's shoved Baron," Pitchfork said.

"Now!" I commanded.

I leapt away from the side of the house as Baron and Jagger crashed through the door of the clubhouse. Bullets rained down from above as Pitchfork let out a piercing war cry that damn near rang my fucking ears. I popped two men in the sides, watching them fall off their bikes before I ducked back against the comfort of the siding of the house.

"Now, Cash!" I exclaimed. "Make it rain for 'em!"

All at once, doors flew open, and windows raced upward. A

cacophony of sound rumbled the ground beneath us as Cash and a few of the guys inside leaned out of the clubhouse, emptying their rounds into bodies that wore those bullshit black leather jackets. Baron and Jagger tussled inside as glass broke, picture frames shattered, and plaster on the walls gave way to fists. They were fighting. No, they were brawling. But I kept shooting. My men and I kept pursuing those motherfuckers as they struck up their engines and peeled away from the clubhouse.

"Pussies!" Pitchfork called from the porch.

"Take out their tires if you can!" I bellowed.

"Upstairs is on lockdown," Cash said, "for obvious reasons."

"Guys!" I exclaimed as I whipped around.

I watched them peek their heads just above the cliff face.

"Get up here and empty your weapons. I don't want a single magazine left filled."

Those who chose to fight ended up with bullets in their legs. No one had to die today, but they sure as fuck needed to know that we weren't fucking around with this. We wouldn't get pulled back into their nonsense just because they were hooked on their own drugs and needed money to fuel their own desires. They could do it somewhere else.

But they sure as fuck weren't doing it in Barbeau.

"And stay out!" Baron bellowed as Jagger's body flew through the front door.

I had to take a step back in order to make sure I didn't get clocked by his body as he soared through the air. The Black Diamond's president hit the gravel ground with a thud, gasping for air as his hand outstretched toward his bike handles. Someone came up behind me and sat the barrel of their shotgun on my shoulder. I stood there, tall and proud, as yet another one of my men settled their rifle's barrel on top of my other shoulder. And as we stood there, with the entire crew surrounding our home, Jagger finally managed to pull himself upright and catch his breath.

"When we come back, all of you are dead. Do you hear me? You'll all be fucking slaughtered like the pigs you are!"

"Good luck," Baron said as he stood in the doorway of the front door, clutching his semi-automatic in his hands.

We stood there, a united front as those remaining assholes peeled out of the parking lot. Blood splatter dripped in between the rocks of the gravel lot, and I couldn't help but wonder if it did, indeed, foreshadow events to come. The world faded out of view. Everything around me muted. Nothing was heard, not even the ocean waves lapping against the cliffside below us.

But when I turned and found Baron with a black eye and his nose dripping blood, everything came crashing back all at once.

"Hey, you good?" I asked as I decocked and holstered my gun.

Baron shrugged. "I've dealt with worse."

I shoved my hand into my pocket. "Here, I've got a—"

"No."

Pitchfork came up from behind. "Bossman, you good? He clocked you pretty decently before you tumbled through the door."

Baron slowly turned to face him. "I'm fine."

Pitchfork quirked an eyebrow. "I don't think your swollen eye would agree."

Baron grumbled beneath his breath as he stormed past Pitchfork. "We need a church meeting. Now. Where's Cash and the girl? Cash?"

"Oh, my God," he said breathlessly.

Fear crept up the backs of my legs. "Cash, talk to us. Where are you?"

"Guys?" he asked.

His voice didn't just appear in our earpieces, it sounded behind us. And when we all turned toward the staircase, all I saw was blood dripping from a body in his hands.

"I'm calling Doc," I said as I jammed my hand into my phone.

Baron took off, leaping up the stairs before he scooped her body from his arms. "What happened?"

"She's—she's been hit," Cash said.

"I know that, Cash. Look at me," Baron said. "What happened?"

I dialed Doc's number as I pointed at Bic. "Get the surgery room ready. Take a team with you."

"On it," Bic said as he tapped Pitchfork and Razor on the shoulders.

"She's been hit," Cash said. "She's—she's been hit. We—we need Doc because she's been hit."

"Cash, go help them prepare the surgery room," Baron said.

"She's been—"

"Now!" Baron roared.

That seemed to snap Cash out of his trance long enough to stumble down the stairs before heading toward the back of the clubhouse. But it was Doc's voice that commanded my attention as I held my phone to my ear.

"Reid?" Doc asked. "What's wrong?"

"We have a bullet wound that we can't patch. How fast can you get here?"

"How bad is it?"

I looked over my shoulder at Baron and found his hands, arms, and legs coated with blood.

"Bad," I said.

I heard him scrambling over the phone. "Give me ten minutes."

"I don't know if she's got ten minutes."

He paused. "She?"

"What can we do to help stop the bleeding until you get here?"

"Where's the wound?"

I quickly approached Baron as he stood at the bottom of the steps, unmoving and unwavering.

I'd never seen him like that in all the years that I'd known him.

"Her side, and it's bleeding pretty well."

"Through and through, or trapped?"

"There an exit wound that you can feel, Baron?"

His eyes stayed forward, locked on the front door. "No."

"No exit wound."

"Perfect," Doc said as I heard a door slam in the background, "pack the wound, put as much pressure on it as you can, and if it's nicked an artery and it doesn't stop bleeding after that, someone's gonna have to jam a finger into the hole and plug up the breach until I can get there."

"Just get here soon," I said as I hung up the phone.

But when I turned back toward Baron to tell him about the instructions, all I caught was his leather jacket wafting behind him with the urgency of his movements.

He turned the corner down the hallway and headed straight for the surgery room at the back of our clubhouse.

"Get down!" I roared as I shoved Angel out of the way.

I shot the window out before hanging my torso out of the hole in the glass. I nailed two of those motherfuckers in the neck before they looked up and found me. I ducked down as bullets flew in all directions. Pitchfork let out an ear-shattering war cry that damn near made me rip my fucking earpiece out of my ear. But when I looked over at Angel, who was trying to peek back out the window, she hadn't even flinched.

"Don't you know the meaning of get down?" I asked as I poised myself for another shot.

I quickly pulled the trigger and nailed one of those assholes in their knee.

"You got a gun I can borrow?" she asked.

I scoffed as I pressed my back to the adjacent wall, watching a bullet fly through the room before embedding itself into the crown molding. "What kind of cop comes to a stakeout without a weapon?"

God, I worked hard on that crown molding, too.

"I've got a weapon, Cash," she said flatly. "It's just in my car."

I raced back to the window and leaned out the hole once more. "Lot of good that does you."

"Well? You got one you can hand me?"

"Not on your life," I said as I pulled the trigger, trying my best to nail Jagger. "Shit."

"Miss?"

I shot her a look. "Just stay down. I don't have a gun for you."

She grinned. "Not even the gun on your ankle?"

A bullet whizzed by my head and I ducked down, but it didn't alter her facial expression one bit. I had to admit, it was hot as fuck that she was crouched there with me, ready to peg these motherfuckers at my side. She had balls, I'd give her that. Most police officers and the like were cowards, at best.

Maybe that was why I ended up taking the small pistol off my ankle and handing it to her.

"You get down when I say down, understood?"

She nodded as she checked the chambers and smiled. "You lead, I follow. Got it."

"Good."

I launched myself back toward the window with Angel in tow, and the smell of her deodorant filled my nostrils. Or maybe it was her shampoo. She didn't strike me as a perfume kind of woman, but god damn it, the scent fit her perfectly. Subtle, yet present. It snuck up on you and surprised you, just like she did with us. And as we both leaned out the window, popping off bullets down below at the cowardly boys in black leather jackets, I could've sworn I heard her giggling.

"Up there! The window!" someone shouted.

"Get down!"

I grabbed Angel's shirt and pulled her to the ground with me. She hit the floor with a thud, grunting before gasping for air.

I hated that sensation, when you fell on your back just right and you couldn't fucking breathe.

"Work through it and relax. You're all right up here with me."

But when I went to settle my hand on her back to rub it, something wet greeted me instead.

"Cash," she groaned.

"What the—"

I brought my hand back in front of my face and it was covered in red. My skin dripped with the viscous liquid as it slid down my wrist. Down my arm.

"Cash," she whispered. "I've—I've been hit."

"Fuck," I growled as I scrambled to get to my feet.

Bullets pierced through what was left of the windowpane glass, littering the opposing wall of the room with lead. Pieces of white plaster chipped off, spraying the room with paint and insulation as I grabbed Angel's arm. I pulled her into a corner that had been left untouched by their bullet sprays. The streak of blood that her body left behind captured my attention as it marred the black carpet we had chosen for the rooms.

The floor was fucking black, and I still saw her blood glistening at me.

"All right, you're okay. You're good," I said as I dropped to my knees at her side.

The firefight, as well as my men's voices, faded into the background as I slipped off my leather jacket.

"Is—has anyone else been—been shot?" she choked out.

"Shh, shh, shh, shh, shh," I said softly as I ripped my t-shirt over my head. "You're bleeding badly. Save your strength."

"Cash."

"I'm right here, Angel."

I couldn't look at her. I couldn't look at those tears as they streaked down her face. So, instead, I occupied myself with ripping my shirt up one side and wrapping it around her body. She had been shot in such a precarious position—her side. I was pretty damn sure an artery had been nicked. I rolled her over, laying the t-shirt down onto the floor where her back had been and tried to ignore how quickly my shirt soaked up her blood from the carpet.

Then, I laid her back down on it and tied a knot right up against her bullet wound.

"Oh, my God!" she cried out.

"I know, I know. It hurts, but it'll keep you alive until we can get you somewhere."

Her unfocused gaze lobbed itself in my general direction. "Cash?"

I undid the knot and tugged it tighter. "Yep?"

She grunted with pain. "Christ, are—are all of you so—so—"

I sat that knot against her wound and prayed that it held. "So, what, Angel? So, what? Come on, keep talking to me. Keep your eyes open."

They fluttered closed, so I patted her cheek.

"Stay with me, Angel."

Her eyes bounced open. "Are all of you so fucking hot?"

I couldn't help but smile. "Stay alive long enough and you may just find out. Now, stay here, all right? And don't move a fucking muscle."

She peeked over at the knot against her bullet wound. "Yeah, not going anywhere, anyway. Ugh."

Shirtless and with a vendetta as large as God's own fucking ego, I raced back to the window. I leaned out the hole and popped two men in the sides as recompense for what they put Angel through. They dropped to the ground, crying out for help as their blood spilled onto the gravel. And then, from out of nowhere, Jagger flew through the air. He dropped to the gravel, gasping for air as he reached up toward the sky. I watched as his men rushed toward him. I watched with my gun leveled with their fucking heads as Jagger rolled over and outstretched his fingers for his bike handles. And as our men surrounded him, Jagger needed the help of four fucking men to get back onto his bike.

"When we come back, all of you are dead. Do you hear me? You'll all be fucking slaughtered like the pigs you are!"

"Good luck," I heard Baron say.

A smile crossed my face when those assholes hopped back onto their bikes. They raced off in all directions, skidding their tires along the asphalt and leaving their DNA behind in our gravel parking lot. Victory tasted so sweet. We had defended our territory in front of a DEA agent, no less.

There was no way in hell she'd think we were lying now.

"Angel, we did it," I said as I holstered my weapon. "They're gone, see?"

She didn't respond to me, though.

"Angel?" I asked as I turned around. "Sound off for me."

Still, nothing but silence.

"Angel, this isn't funny," I said as I raced back to the corner where I had left her.

And when I found her slouched against the wall, sitting in a pool of her own blood, my breath froze in my chest.

"Cash!" Reid barked.

I jumped at the sound of his voice. "Huh? What?"

Baron slid his face into view from the side. "Put your finger in her motherfucking wound and help us. Doc is still three minutes out."

I looked down at her body, laying there on the sterile surgical table we had in the back of the clubhouse, coated in her own blood. Stained gauze had been scattered everywhere, and some of it even sat against the toe of my boots. Gone was Angel's tan skin. Gone was the light in her eyes. All she did was lay there, staring up at the ceiling as life drained from her body.

"Cash!" Baron bellowed.

That leapt me into action, and I quickly jammed my finger in the hole.

"Oh, God," Angel groaned.

"Can you feel it?" Reid asked.

"Come on, Cash, you can do this," Baron said.

"You guys need anything else in there?!" Pitchfork called from the hallway.

"Just shut up and give us a second!" Reid yelled.

Then, I felt it. The artery pulsed with life before something wafted against my finger.

"Just a little bit more," I muttered.

"Jesus Christ," Angel choked out.

"There," I said as I shoved my finger into the hole, "got it. How far out is he?"

Reid checked his watch. "He should be coming through the door any—"

"Someone call for a doctor?" he asked as he strolled through the sterilized entryway.

Fucking hell, I'd never been so happy to see that man in all the years he had worked with our crew.

13

BARON

"Coal! Take Razor and soak up that blood outside. Pyre! Get your ass upstairs with Bic and clean up the glass from all those busted windows. We'll have to fix that shit up before the storms this weekend. Pitch!"

"Yeah, Bossman?" he asked.

I pointed at him. "Take Snake and do a lap. I want to make sure there are no fuckers lying in wait."

"And if there are?" Snake asked as he looked up from the carving he was whittling in his hand.

In the middle of the fucking hallway.

"Kill 'em," I glowered.

Snake grinned as he flipped his blade closed. "You heard the man. Let's get on it."

Then, I turned to find my Enforcer staring blankly at the closed surgical door.

With Angel's blood still coating his body.

"Cash," I said as I walked up to him.

He didn't so much as budge.

"Cash," I said curtly as I stood beside him, staring at the profile of his face.

His ear twitched, but that was the only life sign that he gave me.

So, I lowered my voice. "Go get cleaned up; you look like hell."

And I sure as fuck didn't have to tell him twice.

"Reid!" I bellowed as Cash brushed past me.

"He's pacing!" someone called out.

"In the kitchen!" someone else yelled.

"Ah, fuck," I muttered as I turned around on the heels of my boots.

Reid pacing was never a good look for him.

As I charged toward the kitchen, I heard his footsteps before I heard his mutterings. His lips flew a million miles a second as he whipped around, his hands flailing in the air as if he were drowning right before my very eyes. The conversation he was having with himself must've been some argument, because the redder his face became, the quicker his legs moved.

"Reid."

His whisperings grew closer with every step that I took.

"Reid."

His hands and fingers continued twisting and turning about, as if explaining to the gods why we deserved to get out of all this alive.

"Reid, we have to focus."

And it wasn't until I snatched his wrist out of thin air that he finally paused.

"What?" he snapped.

I held him in place. "She's in capable hands, and we have bigger fish to fry. Stay focused with me, all right?"

He scoffed. "What could be bigger than a DEA agent shot on our watch?"

I shook my head. "This isn't an official case yet?"

That got him to turn his head in my direction. "What?"

I released his wrist. "While you guys were gone, she told me that this is a personal case she's working. Her boss knows, yeah, but it's not official. She's running on hunches. That means she won't tell anyone what's really happened to her because that'll mean her badge in the process."

"Not to mention, they'll most likely throw out her case."

"Yep."

He drew in a deep breath through his nose. "We need a plan."

"Yeah, we fucking do. Everyone!"

Reid let out one of his high-pitched whistles. "Everyone who's in this clubhouse, kitchen! Now!"

The throng of skittering boot-falls that sounded all around us rattled the foundation of our clubhouse. The behemoth men that had all pledged their unfailing loyalty to The Death Cheaters soared into the kitchen, guns at the ready and gazes focused and unmoving. I hadn't seen my men this engaged since the last time we had to wipe the sky from our territory, but the worry in their faces didn't go unnoticed.

"All right," I said as the men left gathered around me, "we need to know every single movement the Black Diamonds make."

Reid nodded as he pivoted with his words, staring down all of the men at once. "Their drugs are back on the street, that much we know for certain."

"And," I said as I stretched my arms over my head, "it seems as if they're making another run for our town."

"That shit won't stand."

"We drove them out once, and we can do it again. But this time, it has to be well-timed. Well-coordinated. They've been doing this much underneath our noses, so God only fucking knows how much they've really accomplished."

"That's why we have to catch up," Reid said as he stared hard down the hallway, "and quickly."

I followed his gaze and found Cash standing at the end of it, all fresh and clean.

"You good?" I asked.

Cash nodded as he started toward us. "Everyone who's supposed to be on patrol now, with me."

Reid let out his whistle again. "Bic, Razor, Pyre, that's you guys. Everyone else, hang back."

They fell in line with Cash as they headed toward the front door, and I hoped the man could keep his shit together long enough to give me a picture of how far along in their plans the Black Diamonds were. My guess was they were headed to the docks first, but there was never any way to be certain with Cash. He had always been the wildcard bet of our group.

But he was nothing, if not efficient.

"The rest of you?" I asked as I held my hand in the air to command their attention. "Formation: Defense Alpha. I want us all on our guard while we gather intel."

Reid clapped his hands and rubbed them together. "All right, assholes. You know what that means. Bodyguard Team One, you have the outside of the clubhouse. Team Two, you've got the inside. I want quarterly patrols of every single floor of this place while that woman is in surgery, and on the half hour once she's out."

"Need anything else?" I leaned over and muttered into his ear.

He shook his head. "The rest of you?! Come with me. We're headed to the docks. We have to figure out what the fuck has been happening beneath our noses all this time and why the fuck we didn't know about it sooner. Any questions?"

The guys all shook their heads as various shades of devious smirks crossed their faces.

"Then, let's get the fuck out of here," Reid said as he blazed a trail for the front door.

And as I stood there, staring off toward the side of the house where the agent was currently getting worked on by Doc, I found myself at a loss for words.

14

ANGEL

Brrrt, brrt brrt, brrrrt.

"Hmm?"

Brrrt, brrt brrt, brrrrt.

I grunted as I tried moving my hand.

Brrrt, brrt brrt, brrrrt.

My phone was buzzing. I heard it somewhere. I knew that buzz anywhere.

Brrrt, brrt brrt, brrrrt.

But when I tried unsticking my tongue from the roof of my mouth to ask for it, nothing happened.

Brrrt, brrt brrt, brrrrt.

Until I felt the cold, vibrating plastic cover touch down against my palm.

"Thank you," I managed to choke out.

Though, I wasn't sure who I thanked.

Brrrt, brrt brrt, brrrrt.

I grunted as I answered the call and lifted the phone to my ear. "What do you want, Dee?"

"Jesus Christ, finally. Guys! I got her!"

I winced. "Can you keep it down? Geez, you can shout."

"What the hell are you going on about? Why the fuck haven't you been picking up your phone? It's ten in the morning!"

I squinted my eyes in an attempt to clear the haziness from them. Was it really the next morning?

"Angel!"

His voice yanked me back from my trance. "I'm going to hang up on you if you yell at me like that again. What do you want?"

"Can you not hear me at your door right now? I've been knocking for fucking ages. Open up and let me in; I've brought breakfast."

I finally stretched my neck enough to turn my head, and I found that bartender standing in the corner, staring at me. Just... staring.

And it all came rushing back at once.

The glass shattering. The piercing heat of the bullet. The cold, unforgiving corner I had been slumped in as my life force drained from me. Watching Cash lean out that hole in the window and shoot down at those motherfuckers had been the weirdest thing I'd ever see in my life.

Weirdly sexy, anyway.

But as I craned my neck up long enough to look down at the rest of my body, I found myself topless. Save for something covering my tits and the tight gauze bandage around my waist.

"Earth to Angel," Dee said as his hard knocking sounded on the other end of the line. "Are you gonna open this fucking door or am I—"

Then, Cash pushed off the corner of the wall. "I gotta call you back."

Dee groaned. "Cap wants us to come back to headquarters.

We've got an urgent case. That's why your ass needs to be out of bed."

Cash moved out of my field of vision, and I slid my free arm beneath me. Where did he go? What was he doing?

My questions were answered when I felt his palms slip beneath my back.

"I've got too much to do here," I said with a grunt as he lifted me upright.

"Angel, are we seriously gonna talk on cell phones when there's a perfectly good door you could open so we can talk face to face?"

And as Cash raised me up, helping me to sit upright on the edge of the hospital bed, it took a second for the room to stop spinning.

"I'm not in my room, Dee," I said flatly.

He paused. "Don't tell me you're still on that fucking stakeout."

I rolled my eyes. "I fell asleep, so sue me."

"Angel," he said as his voice lowered, "you have got to get back to this hotel. It's time for us to go. We've done as much as we can here. Let's take everything back to Cap and—"

I shook my head. "I've got a lot of stuff to sift through for this case. I can't go. Not yet."

"There isn't a case," Dee said. "Just a hunch and some circumstantial evidence."

I grinned as Cash came into view in front of me. "What if I told you it's not all circumstantial now?"

His stare hardened on me as my partner spoke. "It's boss's orders, Angel. We have to come in. Our plane leaves for D.C. in two hours."

"I won't be on that plane, Dee."

"Apparently you can't hear me, but you don't have a choice."

"Look, I'll come back when the case is wrapped up. Even if I have to do it myself."

He scoffed. "I can't cover for you any longer on this. We've already taken too much time as it is. Just come to the plane and we can talk about it while we—"

I knew he'd never understand. Even with all of the time I bought him so that we could chase his cousin's killer down, he still had the audacity to convince me this wasn't worth it. I scoffed as I hung up the phone. I didn't have the energy to spend hashing basic shit out with him. Too much had gone down and there were still too many questions that I needed answered.

It didn't shock me when Dee called back, though.

"You should pick it up," Cash said as his unwavering stare somehow grew hotter against my skin.

I ignored the phone call and turned my cell off. "That should do it."

"Angel."

"Hmmm?"

"Is that really your name?"

My gaze met his stare. "It's my nickname, yes."

Cash's gaze slowly raked down my body. "More than circumstantial?"

My back straightened. "You mean to tell me that innocent crews go around shooting up other crews just for funsies?"

The shadow of a grin ticked his cheek. "You make some valid points."

I held out my hand. "I've been known to do that. Now, help me down. I have to get to work."

But instead of taking my hand, he placed his hands on my shoulders. "You're not going anywhere until you rest."

"Seriously? You, too?"

"You'll be down at least a week while you heal through the worst of things, and bullet wounds to the torso are no joke."

"Not my first rodeo," I murmured.

His grip grew more tense against my shoulders. "Doc left some pain medication to help get you through the worst of it, and after he comes back around in a week he will—"

I shrugged off his touch. "I don't have a week to spare. I need to get to work now."

"You're already going to miss your plane, so as far as I'm concerned, you're the only one in charge of your schedule."

"That's right. So, stop forcing me to sit here and help me down."

He held up his hands in mock surrender and I took that as my cue. Fine. If he didn't want to help me down, I'd get down myself. I placed my hands on the edge of the cold, unforgiving hospital bed they had tossed me into, and I slid myself down to my feet. I didn't hop. I didn't jostle. I didn't move anything that didn't warrant a need to be moved at that moment.

And yet, my legs still caved beneath me the second I tried putting all my weight down onto the floor.

"Cash!"

I yelped his name before I could do anything else, and before I knew it, a pair of long, strong arms blanketed themselves around me. My body dangled there, my knees inches from the ground as I dug my nails into any surface on his body I could find. His muscles bulged, as if to give me something to cling to while my body hung there like a damp fucking rag.

My God, he was so warm.

"If I didn't know any better," he murmured as he hoisted me back onto the hospital bed.

And yet again, before I caught the words coming out of my mouth...

"Then, don't know better."

Even I was shocked at my words. My head flew upward, and I found his hungry stare glaring back at me. His pupils, blown wide open as the brightness of his emerald eyes disappeared before me. His raven black hair shimmered in the harsh fluorescent lighting beating against us from the ceiling. Hell, the slope of his jawline could have sliced me back open, if necessary. But it was the pout of his lower lip that my mouth was hungry for. That luscious, pink pout that had enticed me the other evening during my failed undercover sting. Though, as he laid me back down onto the hospital bed with his strong arms, I wasn't sure I categorized any of it as a failure.

Not with him hovering over me like he was.

No words were exchanged as his fingertips slid along the bare skin of my torso. I shivered at his touch, my legs spreading for him as his gaze held mine hostage. His nostrils flared. His other hand slid through my hair, softly working out the knots as he cupped my gowned pussy. A shot of air hissed through my teeth, puckering my tits against the cloth covering that bound my breasts to my body.

"It's going to hurt..." Cash said before trailing off.

My lower lip quivered as he slid his hand up my leg beneath the hospital gown I found myself wearing. "It already hurts."

I felt him dancing his other hand around before warmth flooded my system. I sighed with relief as the pain washed away, and the room tilted around me as if I were on a circus ride. A lopsided smile crossed my face. The pain melted away with ease as I laid there, staring up at the ceiling.

"Are we still in the clubhouse?" I asked.

Cash's chuckle sounded like something from the heavens. "We are. You're just in a rest room next to the surgical room we've got back here."

I lobbed my head over toward him and smiled. "Hi."

He chuckled again and tossed me a wink. "Feeling better?"

I wiggled my eyebrows. "I'd feel better if you were closer."

His eyes darkened. "You've been shot, Angel."

I walked my fingertips toward his hand. "And I hear you've got the healing touch that I need."

"You just got shot up with pain killers. That's why you're feeling so good right now."

I grabbed his hand and placed it against my cheek. I needed his warmth. I needed his comfort. Blame it on the drugs for all I cared, but the way he looked down at me while I laid there in that recovery bed tugged at something deep within me. Something carnal. Something attached to a baser instinct. His hand sat there, cupping the inside of my thigh as his emerald stare drilled a hole into my face. And as his face bent down toward me, his nose gently nuzzled mine.

Which sent goosebumps parading around my body.

"Angel," he whispered as he kissed the tip of my nose.

I gasped softly as his fingers caressed my hip bones and traced the hem of my cotton panties. He caressed my skin and traced the hem of my cotton panties. My toes curled against the soles of what felt like grippy socks, anticipating the searing imprint of his touch against my throbbing clit.

"Cash," I whispered as I reached down for his hand.

He placed the softest kiss against my cheek, not allowing my touch to impede his movements. "So impatient for me."

I snickered. "Can you blame me?"

He kissed the shell of my ear. "Yes."

My eyes fluttered closed. "We don't have to do much. I just—"

Goddamn it, his touch was so close to where I wanted him.

"You just want to forget?" he murmured against my ear.

Before I could even respond, his fingers slipped between my pussy folds. It unleashed a flood of juices that leaked down my slit, coating my ass crack as his fingers found my pulsing entrance. I tilted my head back, exposing my neck to him as his thumb traced my swollen mound. His nose traced my pulse point as the heat of his breath taunted my skin. His touches were so light. So skittish. Barely there, and yet overwhelming. I'd never experienced anything like it in my life. And the instant he sank his teeth into the crook of my neck, his fingers filled my body.

Before his thumb tickled the tip of my clit at lightning speed.

"Oh—my fucking—God," I managed to choke out.

And the pain that zoomed through my body, despite the pain medication they had me on, muted itself entirely.

Halting at Cash's soft, intentional thrusts.

15
———

CASH

Her juices coated my hand as her walls clamped down around my fingers. My tongue flicked across her skin, and feeling her jump stoked the fire at the base of my cock. I pinned her down, stilling her fragile body as her feet dangled off the edges of the bed. I couldn't get enough of her. She laid there, spread for me, helpless toward my soft assault as I rose up from her neck and studied her presence. I'd never seen a more beautiful woman. A healthier woman. A stronger woman. Her skin flushed itself with a robust shade of red, reminding me that her heart was still beating. That blood still coursed its way through her veins. Her cute little pants as her chest rose and fell with her breathing stiffened my dick as her clit grew with every stroke of my thumb. Her hips lifted. Her body rolled. Where she found the strength to fight the pain, I didn't know. But as I stared down at her pleasure-ridden face, I memorized each and every move-ment of her perfect features.

Like the way her nose wrinkled as her legs quivered.

Or the way her cheek dimples puckered every time she gritted her teeth.

Or the way her eyes glistened with delight every time she parted her lips to speak.

I dipped my lips to the shell of her ear. "Mmmm, you like that, don't you, princess?"

She swallowed hard. "Yes. Yes, Cash, it's—so good."

I chuckled before nibbling at her earlobe. "I see why Baron's a fan."

She gasped. "What? H-H-H—How—How did you—"

I rose up and caught her widened gaze. "I smell him on you."

The mixture of terror and ecstasy behind her eyes rattled the beast inside me.

"But you're not upset?" she asked breathlessly.

She was the strongest woman I had ever come across. Lying there, on a surgical table where she had almost lost her life, with her legs spread and her body wantonly spread out for a man she didn't know. For the second time. All in an effort to gain answers for a mystery she needed solved. That took gumption. It took guts. It took so many things that only a hard, sinful life carved into another human being. If anything, she *deserved* the pleasure. The ecstasy. The rush.

And it was an honor to watch it wash across her face as my fingers teased her.

"Oh, my God," she groaned as her eyes fluttered closed.

"There it is," I growled.

"Shit, shit, shit, shit," she hissed as she bucked against my hand.

Then, she pawed at my jeans. "Gimme."

I moved my thumb quicker against her clit. "Come for me."

She somehow managed to rip my button open. "Pull that dick out or I swear to hell on high, I won't come for you just to piss you off."

I tilted my head. "Is that a threat?"

She looked up at me and did her best to hold it together. I crooked my fingers inside of her body, watching her struggle as she put on a good face. A strong face. One that almost didn't move. That almost didn't flinch. That almost didn't cave.

Almost, anyway.

"Mm, mm, mm, stubborn as ever," I said as I reached into my pants with my free hand and pulled out my dick. "I can't wait to break you the way you truly deserve."

"Oh, fuck," she choked out as she wrapped her trembling hand around my cock.

I grunted at the feel of her skin. Veins bulged from my girth as I slammed my hand down onto the other side of her head on the bed. I glared down at her, working that tight cunt of hers as her walls crumbled around me. Her hand stroked my dick, clamping and pulsing. Twisting and stroking. I thrusted against the softness of her palm. She fucked my fingers and swiveled her hips, coating my hands in her mark.

"Goddamn it, princess."

"Come for me, Cash," she whispered with quivering lips.

That was when I bent forward and hovered my lips over hers as I stared her down. "Ladies first."

Her eyes rolled into the back of her head as her body locked out. I filled her with my fingers, splaying my palm against her drenched pussy as she rocked her aching clit against my callused hand. She thrusted hard against me, feeling her grip tighten as she chased her high. She used my body however she needed to climb to the top of her mountain. Her muscles quivered against the hospital bed. My balls pulled into my body. I ground my teeth together, staving off the inevitable as something squirted against my skin. I watched her unravel, perched above her as ecstasy washed over her features.

And as Angel unraveled, she finally managed to say my name.

"Fucking hell, Cash. Oh, my God."

I couldn't stand it. I ripped my hand out from between her thighs and leapt onto the hard surface with her. I placed my hands on either side of her head, listening to her pant for air as my hardened cock fell between her thighs. She groaned softly, feeling it slap against her skin as my balls gravitated out of my body. And as I lined myself up at her entrance, I heard her breathless pleas.

"Please, Cash. Oh, shit."

Sure as fuck didn't have to tell me twice.

The second I sank into her, my eyes rolled back. Her pussy was so tight. Wet and warm. And oh, the sounds that fell from her lips. She gasped and groaned. Her walls quivered around me as I sank to the hilt, seating our hips together. Her thighs molded to me. Her curves shivered for my viewing pleasure. I already felt her juices dripping down my balls, teasing me and taunting me as her skin flushed from head to toe.

Then, her eyes met mine, and the fire behind them spurred me on.

"Oh, shit," she whimpered as I pulled my dick out.

I thrusted forward quickly, snapping back against her.

"Cash," she groaned as her back arched.

"Son of a bitch," I hissed as I pulled my cock back out of her body.

Every time her body jumped for me, her walls quivered. Milking me, as if it were their life's only purpose. I ground my teeth together as grunts fell from my lips. Our bodies became one, melding together as her hips raised to meet mine, thrust for thrust. Her hands wrapped around my forearms. Her nails, raking against my skin as she panted and moaned.

"Right there. Oh, God. That's the spot. Cash. Cash. Cash. Cash."

I snarled as I bent down to her ear. "Be a good little princess and come for me."

Her arms blanketed my back. She clawed at my leather cut, raking her nails against the worn leather as I chased my high against her body. The sounds of wet skin slapping wet skin filled the space around us, and the smell of her womanhood wrapped me up in a high that I couldn't explain. Silver stars burst in my vision, overtaking the sweet contortion of her face as my balls pulled back into my body. I growled, snapping my hips against hers as she pulled me down on top of her. I held myself up, relishing her warmth as her muscles pulsed and ground against me.

Then, I heard that sweet, luscious voice right against my ear.

"I'm gonna come. I'm gonna come. I—I'm—"

The second her pussy collapsed around me, it was game fucking over. Her walls clenched and my pelvis stilled. She lost herself in her orgasm, shaking and quivering as her walls collapsed around me. My eyes bulged as her body pulled thread after thread of hot arousal from the tip of my cock, and I watched as she fucked herself against my girth. I filled her up, feeling our intermingled juices spilling from her sweet, swollen pussy. And as I watched her pant for air, flushed from head to toe, I managed to hold myself up on shaking arms as my dick was pushed out from between her legs.

"Holy hell," Angel breathlessly whispered.

I'd never forget her sounds so long as I lived. "How are you feeling?"

Her cockeyed smile filled me with pride as she reached up and patted my chest. "Not an ounce of pain in sight."

"Good," I growled as sat back on my haunches and tucked myself back into my pants. "Now, come here, you."

One quick zip of my jeans, and my arms were free to scoop her up. She needed a bed that was more comfortable than the one she had been given. She needed fresh sheets, fresh air, and plenty of time to rest. So, I hoisted her into the air and cradled her against my body as I moved her out of the recovery room we had in our private surgical wing and headed for the upper levels of the clubhouse.

But not before Doc caught me at the top of the steps. "I take it you don't need the rundown?"

I chuckled as I peered down at him from above. "Not my first rodeo with a gunshot wound. We've got her, Doc. Thank you."

He tipped his hat. "Not a problem. I'll be back in about a week to assess how she's doing. Keep that pain medication in her, all right? A pain like that gets out of control and we—"

I nodded. "Yeah, yeah, we won't be able to get it back under control. I know, Doc."

He smiled as he turned away from us. "Just making sure."

"You'll see payment in your account by the end of the day."

"I have no doubt about that!"

"And Doc?"

He paused at the front door and peered over his shoulder. "Yeah?"

"Thanks."

He unlocked the door. "One week. Put it on your calendars!"

I couldn't help but grin. "Will do."

As I turned away from the man who saved her life, I ventured down to the right. I wanted her as far away from the room where she had been shot as possible. I wanted her to have peace while she recuperated. Down to the right was a hallway that cut straight up the middle of the clubhouse, dead ending into a staircase that went up one more level. I stopped just shy of that staircase, however. I turned to the right, bumping the door open with my shoulder as soft snores fell from Angel's lips against my chest.

I couldn't help but smile as I settled her down in bed. As I pulled the comforter over her body and watched her nestle into the plump, soft pillows that lined the headboard of the bed. She looked so peaceful like that. Flushed with life and smelling of sin.

It wouldn't be the last time I'd have her like that.

"Get some rest," I murmured as I leaned down and placed a kiss on her forehead.

"Mmmm," was all she managed to hum.

I wanted to crawl into bed with her. I wanted to hold her close and make sure that those stitches stayed exactly where they needed to stay. But there were things to do and shit to clean up.

Me claiming her body again would have to wait.

Reid's voice, however, ruined the moment the second I stepped out into the hallway and closed her bedroom door behind me.

"Awwww, how sweet."

"Fuck you," I grumbled beneath my breath.

He snickered as he nodded to the closed bedroom door. "How is she?"

I drew in a deep breath. "Stubborn as a motherfuck with an agenda she's playing out."

"Any idea what kind of agenda?"

"If I had to take a guess?" I asked with a shrug. "Those drugs killed someone she loved."

That gave the two of us pause. But Baron doesn't let that shit stand for long.

"Don't you guys have shit to do?!" he asked as his voice barreled down the hallway.

Reid patted my shoulder. "Come on, we got work to do."

Like putting a bullet in the motherfucker that shot her. "Let's go before he has a stroke."

And I couldn't help myself as I peered over my shoulder one last time, staring at that closed bedroom door.

Jesus, I hoped she got the rest she needed.

It was the only thing that would get her through the nightmarish few days she was in for.

16

—————

ANGEL

"Jon Jon! Look! I did it!"

I slapped the top branch of the tree and peered down at my brother. He clapped his hands over his head with that big, goofy smile on his face. The wind whipped through the trees, swaying the branch and spreading red leaves everywhere as the cool autumn breeze wiped the sweat off my forehead.

Then, I heard it.

The sound of a crashing glass.

"What the fuck do you think I work 70 hours a week for, huh?! So you can blow all our money on fucking clothes!?"

"For the kids, Daniel!" Mom screamed. "They can't just wear clothes that are too small to school!"

Through the kitchen window from my vantage point, I watched Dad cock his hand back. I braced myself, even though I was nowhere near him. Even though I wouldn't feel the sting, the movement was automatic. And as I watched his hand crack against Mom's face, I shimmied down that rope faster than I ever had in my entire eleven years of living.

"My turn, my turn!" Jon Jon exclaimed as he clenched the climbing rope in his hand.

But the growing sounds of Mom and Dad arguing meant we needed to be elsewhere.

"How about we go get a snack first, yeah?" I asked.

My brother's eyes lit up. "You mean, Dad's gonna let us go to the gas station?"

I peeked over my shoulder and saw their shadows tussling around in the kitchen. "Oh, yeah. Just this once. Now, let's get going before he changes his mind."

"All right!"

"No, Daddy! Stop it!"

"Daniel, get off your son!"

"Dad, please," my brother said through his tears. "I didn't mean to. It was an accident."

"Boy, you don't spill shit on my new pants on accident," Dad growled. "Now, hold still and take your punishment like a man."

"Daniel!" Mom shrieked.

"No!" I yelped.

Before I knew what I had done, I dove in front of him. I spread my body and turned my back, wrapping my arms around my little brother as his tears flooded my shirt. The leather belt came down against my back, searing with the heat of a thousand suns. The sound of the instrument whipping through the air shivered me to my core as the belt caught my shoulder blade, and I bit through my lip to keep my screams to myself.

I'd never let that man hear me scream so long as he lived.

"Don't. You. Ever. Spill. Shit. In. My. Lap."

"Nooooo," Jon Jon wailed against my chest.

Tears flooded my cheeks as Mom raced into the room. "Get off of my children or I'm calling the police!"

And when the belt stopped, I knew Mom was in trouble.

"Run!" I cried out.

"Jon Jon, nooooooooooo!"

Time stopped the second I inched his door open. Jon Jon always locked his door. My brother always locked his door. Privacy was paramount to him. It was to all of us, but especially him. We had seen too much. Endured too much. I knew it was his way of blocking out the world. Of making sure it couldn't get to him ever again. His car had been out front. The lights in the house were on. But when I found his bedroom door cracked open, I knew it was bad.

"Oh, my Gooooood!"

I dove toward his body on the floor and turned him over. His lifeless eyes stared up at the ceiling as chunks of vomit clung to his cheek. My nose wrinkled with the smell. It turned my stomach, threatening to force up my breakfast as I checked for a pulse.

But there was nothing.

"Oh, no you don't. You're not leaving me alone like this. Come on!"

I threaded my fingers together and placed them against his heart. One, two, three, four, five. I bent forward and tipped his head back, trying to check and see if his airway was blocked. I wiped the vomit from his mouth and placed my lips to his, breathing life into his lungs as his chest rose. Thank fuck. No obstruction. So, I placed my hands back on his heart and counted.

"One, two, three, four, five," I whispered.

Another puff, another rise of his chest, and yet he didn't come back to me.

"Come on," I grunted. "One, two, three, four, five."

As I leaned down to breathe my life into his lungs, something small and blue caught the corner of my eye. I breathed into his *body, praying it would undo the damage that had already been done. But the ice cold nature of his skin told me everything I already needed to know. I pumped my hands against his chest until I felt all of his ribs crack. I breathed into his lungs until the taste of his vomit had buried itself into my own lungs. And all the while, I stared at that little baggie.*

At that light blue Ziploc bag with a sun and moon logo on it.

"The hell is all this, girl?" Dad glowered from behind me.

And as he yanked my head back, I gasped.

"No, please," I said breathlessly.

"You have to take it, but you can go back to sleep after."

I blinked a few times. "Reid?"

He paused. "Yeah?"

I squinted my eyes until he came into focus. "Oh, God. It's you."

He narrowed his eyes. "Who did you think it was?"

I swallowed hard, and I swore I still tasted that vomit on the tip of my tongue. "What am I taking?"

"You okay?"

I ignored his question. "What's going on? Is everything okay?"

"Everything's fine," he said as something pressed against my lips. "It's just time for some pain meds. I've got some water you can chase it with."

I cleared my throat. "Pain meds?"

"It'll help you feel better, Angel. Just take it."

I tucked my chin toward my body as the small pill came into view. It didn't seem out of place or out of the ordinary, so I parted my lips and allowed Reid to plop it against my tongue. I groaned as I eased my way back into the comfort of the bed with a straw following my every movement. My mouth still felt like a dried-out cotton ball, so I wrapped my lips around the small plastic implement and chugged as much as I could. Down went the pill, hopefully to put me out of my hellish misery so that sleep was actually productive.

But I couldn't shake the feeling that we weren't alone.

"So, you're Reid," I said after I stopped chugging.

He placed the cup out of sight. "And you're Angel."

"Mhm," I said as I pushed myself upright.

"Here, let me help," he said as he scrambled to get his arms beneath mine.

"Lean up," Baron said, even though I couldn't see him.

"Ah, Baron. Is the one with the pretty eyes here, too?"

"That's a new one," Cash said with a snicker.

"Well," Reid said as he placed a pillow behind my head, "I guess that means formal introductions aren't necessary."

"What do people usually recognize on you?" I asked as I gazed across the room at him.

His smirk answered me before he did. "Are we talking about everyone? Or just women?"

I rolled my eyes, even though everything about my body was on high alert. The hairs on my arms stood on end. The nape of my neck prickled. As those three men surrounded the edge of my bed—Reid to my left, Cash to my right, and Baron at the foot of it—I couldn't help but clock everything in that room that I could use as a weapon. Entry points. Exit points. Vulnerability points.

There weren't many, however.

"So, your brother," Baron said.

I watched him cross his arms over his gargantuan chest as all of the blood rushed from my face.

I wasn't gonna let these men get a leg-up on me just because I had gotten shot.

"So, your former president," I said in stride.

Baron glowered at me. "Don't speak of things you don't understand."

"Takes one to know one."

Cash shook his head in the corner of my vision. "Not much to understand. Abusive father. A mother who wasn't protective enough."

I snapped my vision toward him. "Shut up."

"A brother who got hooked on drugs."

"I said, *shut up*, Cash."

"Which, ironically enough, are the same drugs that—"

I pulled out the big guns for him. "Rocky."

In an instant, Cash lunged toward me with anger so fierce in his gaze that he could have burned hotter than the fires of hell.

"Whoa, whoa, whoa," Baron said as he leapt in front of the man.

"Don't you dare fucking say that name in my presence," Cash growled.

Terror took hold of my heart, but I held my head high with pride. Never show fear, that was what living with my father taught me.

"It must've hurt, didn't it?" I asked as I tilted my head. "Watching Rocky succumb to—"

Cash damn nearly broke out of Baron's grasp. "I said, shut the fuck up."

I tossed him a cheeky wink. "No, you didn't. Not like that, anyway."

Cash shoved Baron with such a force that he almost fell to the floor. In a flash, his hand wrapped its way around my throat, squeezing as I struggled to breathe. Reid cried out his name as he jumped over the bed with one spring of his long, strong legs. Cash's fingernails carved crescents against my skin as Reid tackled the man with the angry green eyes to the floor. And as Baron picked himself up, he finally started asking smart questions.

While I did my best to not give an audible sound to catching my breath.

"How long have you been digging into us?" Baron demanded to know.

I drew in a sobering breath. "Much longer than you've been digging into me."

"And that means?" Reid asked curtly.

I shrugged. "It means I know everything there is to know about you. About this crew. About your men, and how you guys got yourselves here in the first place."

I figured Baron would answer me. I figured he would've been the one to rebuttal. But it was Reid's voice that garnered my attention next.

"So, you just thought you were gonna come in here and fuck the answers out of us?"

I couldn't help my giggle. "Nah, the fucking's just for fun. Though, not as good as I figured it might be."

That was when Baron answered. "Not judging by the way you sounded."

I tossed him a playful wink. "Women get good at faking things. It's sort of our specialty."

The room fell silent with my words. The three of them stared me down as the rays of the setting sun streamed through the windows of the bedroom. It illuminated them from behind, somehow making them seem more brutal than ever. Yet, as they stared me down, I refused to move my gaze from Baron's.

He hadn't looked away yet, so neither did I.

He was the one that I had to control. He was the one that I had to keep beneath my thumb. Otherwise, I was a dead woman walking. The giant looked me up and down. He studied my bed before reaching down and tucking the comforter in at the foot of the bed. He brushed his hands off and nodded his head, as if he were having a conversation with himself.

Then, he walked over to the bedroom door and whipped it open. "Reid?"

"Yeah, Bossman?"

"Post two guards here at all times. She goes nowhere without our permission."

I blinked. "Excuse me? You're what now?"

Reid crossed my field of vision and shrugged. "Sucks to suck, I guess."

"You're what now?" I asked a bit louder.

Cash made his way out of the room next. "And here I thought you'd be a nice addition to our little family."

I scoffed. "I would rather die."

He peered at me over his shoulder. "Say his name again, and you just might get your wish."

I watched him disappear before Baron slid out into the hallway himself. "Enjoy your nap."

As he closed the door behind him, I found myself shivering beneath the covers. Shadows moved beyond the frame of the door, with footsteps lumbering up and down the hallway. Floorboards creaked as the room tilted onto itself. My head grew heavy on my shoulders before it flopped back against the pillows. The pain medication took hold, causing my eyelids to droop as the shivering died down and the panic subsided. And from out of nowhere, a stupendous dose of guilt dropped right onto my shoulders. The pain in their eyes, I caused that. The anger in their voices. I caused that, too. Just like Dad. Just like Mom. Just like JonJon.

And as a tear rushed down my cheek, only one thought crossed my mind.

Holy fuck, what have I gotten myself into?

17

REID

"Fucking bitch," Baron glowered as he bumbled down the stairs.

"It was a shit decision, thinking she'd work with us," Cash practically spat.

I eased myself down onto the third step from the bottom. I knew they were fuming, but they had to stay focused. Her comments had done exactly what she had intended for them to do: they had thrown us off. We had to stay focused.

"Look, guys—"

"Who the fuck does she think she is, anyway?" Cash asked.

"Fucking beats me, but I'm ready to put a damn sock down her fucking throat," Baron said.

"I say we take her and the shit she's got on us to her boss at the DEA. Fuck her over the way she wants to fuck us over."

"I've got something better," Baron said as he charged down the hallway toward the kitchen, "I say we—"

"Stay focused?" I asked as I picked my head up.

Cash pinned me with a look. "Don't think for one second she doesn't have shit on you."

"Oh, I'm sure she does. But look at you two, turning your-selves around in knots because of stuff she knows about us. We know shit about her, too. You see her getting all flustered like that?"

That shut the both of them up.

"Look," I said as I stood to my feet and came down the rest of the steps, "we've got a shot-up DEA agent upstairs, we've got our rival crew pushing those fucking drugs back into our territory, and once again, they're trying to make us the fall guys. We have got to stay focused."

"You're right," Baron said as he came out of the kitchen.

I looked down at his hand. "There a reason you've got a carving knife?"

He looked up the stairs. "Might need it."

I snatched it out of his hand and held it up to Cash's neck. "You listening?"

Cash's back stiffened. "Yep."

Baron came over and placed his hand on my wrist, lowering the knife. "You've made your point."

I shot him a look. "Good, because the one thing we do have going for us is the fact that we already know what the Black Diamonds are going to do. This is right out of their former president's playbook."

Baron took the knife from me. "Explain."

I shrugged. "Just look at what's happened. What was one of the first things those motherfucks did the first time around when they were trying to pin all this shit on us?"

Cash nodded. "They rolled up on our turf."

I pointed at him. "Bingo. They rolled up on the clubhouse."

"Just like they did last night," Baron said.

I slid my hands into the pockets of my jeans. "If they're running by that same playbook, or even a version of it, then they've already planned another shipment to come in and needed our attention diverted."

Baron's brain jumped into gear. "Reid, get your men down

to the docks with cameras. No firefights. We need hard proof before we make another move."

And right on time, Pyre walked in through the front door with Pitchfork and Bic right behind him.

"You three with me," I said as I parted them like the Red Sea. "Grab the surveillance equipment from our utility closet."

"Uh...yeah, sure," Pyre said, "but what for?"

"You're going to the docks to do some surveillance," Baron said.

"Oh, hell yeah," Pitchfork said as he grabbed Bic's wrist. "Come on, we got cameras for everyone to haul."

"Take the van; it'll be quieter," Cash said.

"Already on it," I said as I plucked the van's keys off the wall in the hallway.

I needed to get out of that clubhouse. Angel was more than capable, she was highly skilled, and the more time we spent around her, the more we risked her learning. For her sake, we needed to keep her out of the loop, especially if we had any hope of settling this without any sort of police intervention. We yanked the equipment out of the closet and packed up the van. With me behind the wheel and Pitchfork in the seat beside me, Bic climbed into the back to set up the cameras while we drove. The ride was silent. Thank fuck Cash had fixed that squeaky wheel bearing.

However, nothing could have prepared me for what we found when we set up shop down by the docks.

"We're too far away," Pitchfork said. "I can barely catch shit with these binoculars."

"I can zoom in pretty good with the camera," Bic said, "but he's right. If we want more angles, we need to be closer."

I put the van into neutral and let it roll along for half a block. "There, but that's all we can risk. Any further, and the moving brush gives us away."

Pitchfork groaned. "I still don't have a good angle. Bic?"

When he didn't answer, I reached behind my head and slid the little plastic window open.

"Bic, you got anything?"

Pitchfork craned his neck over his shoulder. "Are you gonna say some—"

"SSSSSSHHHH!" Bic hissed. "I swear to fuck, you guys are so fucking loud."

"What do you see?" I asked as I lowered my voice.

"You're never gonna fucking believe it."

"Believe what?" Pitchfork asked.

"Take out your cameras and point them toward the warehouse on the dock," Bic said.

"Why?" I asked.

He shifted around before his angry eyes peered at us through the pathetic slat called a window. "Just fucking do it."

"Fine, fine," Pitchfork murmured as he picked up his camera.

I did the same with mine, and it didn't take me long to hunt down what Bic had come across.

"Well, that explains a lot," Pitchfork said as he snapped pictures.

I pressed the record button on my camera and zoomed in as much as I could. "Is that—"

"Yep," Bic said, "it is."

"No wonder they're flying under the damn radar," Pitchfork said. "They've got local police helping them out this time around."

I watched as police officers in civilian clothing helped offload wooden crates with that fucking logo branded on every side of the crate. I kept the camera as steady as my hands would allow, even though anger rushed through my veins and threatened to tear my fucking world apart. Dirty cops. It was always dirty fucking cops that made this shit harder. And judging by the number of faces I recognized, they had at least a quarter of the local force helping them out.

Which was enough to sink us.

"Let's go, we've got enough," I said.

"You sure?" Bic asked. "I could try to get closer and—"

"No," I said as I ripped the gear stick into reserve, "just sit down and hang on until we get back to the clubhouse."

Backing out of that hiding hole took finesse. It seemed that every fucking stick on the planet had scooted itself beneath the wheels of the van, and we moved like molasses to get out of there without being seen. The second I hit the road, however, I shoved the gas pedal down. I took the back roads and the long ways, making sure to shake any tail that may have picked up our scent as we sat there. And when I was certain beyond a shadow of a doubt that we hadn't been followed, I sped back to the club-house, kicking up gravel and dust as I skidded to a stop near our shed.

"Take your equipment downstairs and put it all on the base-ment table," I said as I parked the van.

"On it," they both said in unison.

I unbuckled my seatbelt. "And keep your phones on you for your next commands. They'll come sooner than you want."

Somehow, I managed to gather Baron and Cash with me after getting myself inside. How I managed to do that, I wasn't sure. But as I hooked up our cameras to the projector system casting the images and video against the wall, I couldn't get the play button pressed before Baron recognized a face.

"Is that Officer Downs?" he asked.

I clicked my tongue. "Unfortunately."

Cash balked. "They've got a dirty cop helping them this time?"

I pressed play. "Not 'a.'"

And as the film reels played out before our very eyes, Baron slammed his fists so hard into the wooden table that I heard it crack.

"Fuck," Baron growled.

I sighed. "I counted at least six different faces that I recognized outside of the Black Diamonds."

"Fuck!" Baron exclaimed.

Cash pinched the bridge of his nose. "It'll be easier for them to pin it on us this time if they've got cops willing to forge paperwork."

"FUCK!" Baron bellowed as he raked his hands down his face.

"God, what I wouldn't give to put down every single one of them," Cash said flatly.

But I knew getting into a firefight with police would do nothing but wipe us out.

Unless...

"We could use her to our advantage now," I said, pointing to the ceiling.

"We could fucking *what?*" Baron asked as his voice dropped an octave.

I held up my hands. "Look, it makes me sick to even think about asking that woman upstairs for a favor."

"It boils my blood just thinking about it," Cash said as his nostrils flared.

That was never good. "But if we show her this...if we show an official agent actual footage of police officers helping to traffic drugs off the damn dock..."

I waited for their reasoning to kick in. Yeah, it was bad, but we still had an ace in the hole that they knew nothing about.

For all they knew, they had killed that woman.

"Fine," Baron said.

Cash scoffed. "You can't fucking be serious right now."

Baron waved his hand at me. "Go talk to her. Fill her in."

"Baron, come on!" Cash exclaimed.

"You got any better ideas!?" he roared.

And when Cash didn't answer, I thumbed over my shoulder. "Be back in a jiffy."

I sprinted up the steps toward Angel's bedroom.

Hopefully, those pain meds hadn't put her out completely.

18

ANGEL

I stared up at the popcorn ceilings and counted the dots above my head. Fifty. Sixty. One hundred. The dots melded together as the pain medication swept through my system, creating cartoons of little bunnies chewing on carrot tops and running through fields. Their entire life unfolded before my eyes upon that ceiling. Running about, free as birds, while the wind whipped through their silvery little furs.

There was no pain to be had. No ache to nourish. No more tears to cry. And yet, I couldn't make myself slip off to sleep.

It wasn't safe.

I'm not safe.

"I have to get out of here," I whispered to myself.

What the hell had I been thinking? I had no backup. No partner. For all I knew, I no longer had a fucking job, which meant no badge to help me out. How the hell had I allowed my obsession to spiral out of control?

JonJon deserves vengeance.

"No, he deserves justice," I said to myself.

Blood needs to spill.

"Justified blood."

All of their blood.

"No, that isn't how any of this is supposed to work."

You're his big sister. He was your responsibility.

I hated that voice inside of my head. "Of course, he was my responsibility. He will always be my responsibility. But he wouldn't want me ruining my life like this."

He deserves to be avenged.

My voice mounted. "He also deserves to rest in peace!"

The voice in my head tortured me. The more the pain medication relaxed me, the louder that voice in my head grew. Almost as if it were a person. Almost as if I could smell them right in front of me. The thing that killed me the most, however, was that it was right. The voice was right. My brother *deserved* to be avenged. He *deserved* for their blood to spill upon the ground, just like his had done. I was his older sister. The one who promised to take care of him throughout his entire life. I promised him that we'd get out. I promised him a better life than all of this. The drugs, the abuse, and the sleepless nights.

And instead, I ran off to play someone else's hero instead of being his.

You should be dead with him.

My lower lip quivered as the truth fell effortlessly from my lips. "I should be dead with him."

Footsteps pitter pattering softly down the hallway perked my ears. I bolted upright, swallowing the groan of pain that threatened to wash its way over my entire system. The room tilted on its axis, churning my stomach. The faint twitch of my stomach forced my eyes closed as I drew in deep breaths to keep the nausea at bay. I had to stay focused. I had to keep my wits about me. If they wanted to kill me, they already would have, which meant they still had a purpose for me.

And when a soft knock came at the door, I already knew who was there to greet me.

"Come on in, Reid," I said before he spoke.

He inched the door open. "Got a minute?"

Relief cascaded through my system. He was the least threatening of the three, and I found myself glad that he was the one that had shown up.

"Yeah, I do," I said as I propped myself up a bit more.

He slid inside and closed the door. "You look like hell."

I scoffed. "You really know how to flatter a woman."

When I looked over at him, it took me a second to remember how to breathe. Jesus, these men were so fucking sexy. He stood there, a solid six feet tall, with lightly tanned skin pulled over taut muscles that clung to his lean frame. His broad shoulders cast a shadow along my knees, cloaking me in his darkness before he ever reached my bedside. His hazel eyes spoke of kindness, not anger. His disheveled, dirty blond hair played against his forehead, reminding me of a time long since forgotten.

A time when things were innocent, beautiful, and full of life.

"Like what you see?" Reid asked with a playful wink.

I cleared my throat. "What is it that you need?"

Instead of answering me, however, he approached the edge of the bed. I couldn't help but scoot myself over, and yet in my drug-induced stupor it didn't occur to me that he'd take it as a sign to take a seat. The mattress shifted with the weight of his movement. He kicked his legs into bed, seated on top of the comforter while I sat nervously beneath it. He cocked his body toward me, his gaze lingering upon my face as he brought his hand up.

"What are you doing?" I asked as I leaned away a bit.

"You have a little... just... just come here."

"What?" I asked as my voice grew strained.

"A hair, Angel," he said as his gaze held mine and his voice held steady, "you have a stray hair flying around everywhere. Hold still."

Maybe it was the drugs, or the quiet, or the soft nature of his movements as he slid those fingertips of his along my cheekbone. Maybe it was the way his lips naturally crooked into a grin, or the way his hand felt caressing the shell of my ear as he swept that flyaway behind it.

But when he pulled away, I found myself wanting to grab him and keep him close.

"We need your help, Angel."

His words ushered me out of my trance. "What?"

"Your help. We need it."

My stare slowly focused on his. "I would rather die."

"You'd be that way if it wasn't for us."

I tilted my head. "According to the conversation we all just had not too long ago, I'm dead anyway."

Something moved beneath my left hand. My brow furrowed deeply as my gaze slid down, and I watched as Reid pulled a candlestick out from between the grasp of my hand and the mattress.

When the hell had I reached for a candlestick?

"The guys can be harsh sometimes," he said as he reached behind him and placed it on the bedside table. "But in their defense, you did sort of step in it with Cash."

Guilt overwhelmed me. "I can't imagine what he went through burying Rocky."

Anger flashed behind his hazel stare. "Seriously, don't mention his name to any of us. It'll always be a sore point."

I nodded softly and cleared my throat. "So, what do you need help with? Not that I'm helping. But you know. Curiosity, I suppose."

I didn't know what the hell happened. To this day, I was unsure of what took over. But, as I laid there, pressed against the pillows and snuggled beneath that comforter, a pain shot up my back. A pain so white hot and so electric that it stunned me in my spot.

"Angel?" Reid asked.

All I could do was take shallow breaths.

"Angel," Reid said curtly, "what's happening?"

I couldn't swallow. I couldn't speak. All that I could do was lean back. My breathing came in short bursts as darkness clouded my vision.

"S—sti—sti—"

"Stitches, yeah yeah, I hear you," Reid said as he scrambled to get onto his knees. At least, I thought that was what he was doing. I couldn't move, though. All I knew was the mattress giving way, over and over, before my back found its way to the mattress.

"Aaaaaall right, eeeeeeasy does it," Reid encouraged as his hand cupped the back of my head. "Can you look at me, Angel?"

I didn't dare move. "I—I-I-I—I, uh—"

"No, okay. Then, just hold as still as you can. This won't feel good initially, but then things will get better."

Tears streamed down my cheeks without halting. "Wha—what—what's—"

He hovered in my watery, dark vision. "I need you to focus on your breathing. You probably haven't popped a stitch, you're not bleeding. But a gunshot wound fucks up a lot."

I couldn't do anything but breathe shallowly. "M-m-m—Me—Medi—"

Reid eased me down onto my back and brushed more hair away from my sweating forehead.

Since when the fuck did my forehead start sweating?

"That's it, even breaths. As even as you can get them."

My lower lip quivered. "Shi-shi-shi—shit. This—mm—"

A smirk crawled across his face. "Guess you shouldn't have fucked Cash when you did. You've probably just strained a muscle that's tugging at your wound spot."

So many thoughts swirled through my head as my eyes widened.

"Don't panic," Reid said softly as he brushed his knuckles against my cheeks, "it was just a joke."

"H-h-h-he—he was—k-k-s-s—"

He quirked an eyebrow before he pulled the comforter up my body. "Soft?"

I nodded my head quickly. "Ye-ye—yeah."

"Shh, shh, shh," he said even softer. "Just keep taking those breaths for me."

I closed my eyes as more tears slid down my skin. Reid kept talking me through breathing, reminding me to take as deep of a breath as I could before holding it and letting it out. I did my best to do exactly as he asked, because anything was better than how I was feeling. There were no words for the pain. No jokes. No wise cracks. It felt like my body was being ripped to shreds by a woodchipper, and then there was Reid.

Stroking his fingers through my wet mess of hair.

"There we go, deeper breaths. See? It's already wearing off, isn't it?" he asked.

I had to admit, my lips stopped shivering. "M-my vision is—is c-coming back."

He paused. "You couldn't see me?"

I blinked a few times, trying to get the haziness to give way. And when it did, I saw Reid hovering in my vision again.

With a pill in one palm and a glass of water with a straw clasped in his other hand.

"Take this, if your vision is tunneling, you just need more meds."

I hated that I didn't want to take it. "I don't like how it makes me feel."

"I know, no one likes to feel helpless. But you don't have a choice right now."

I shook my head and buried the back of it deeper into the pillows. "It's okay, I'm okay. It's—it's settling down. See? I can even—even talk b-better."

Reid shot me a look that made me scoff.

"At least it's b-better than—than what it—it was."

He put the pill to my lips. "Take it."

"No."

"And why the fuck not?"

I couldn't help it, so I blurted it out. "Because the last time I spoke with any of you I got the distinct feeling that some of you wanted to kill me. Why the hell would I take anything around a bunch of men that want me dead?"

He stared down at me for a long time before he shifted. I watched him fade away from my vision and more tears brewed. Fuck. For all I knew he was about to reach for his knife. Or maybe a gun in the room that I didn't know about. For all I fucking knew, I had just signed my goddamn death warrant. My body shivered. My muscles tensed. The pain came rushing back to a point where I tried to pivot my head to find Reid. But all I heard after the mattress shifted beneath his weight was his voice at the door.

Jesus Christ, how did these men just move around like that without making any fucking noise?

"If you need it later, it's on your bedside table to your right."

I swallowed hard. "Reid, I-I-I—I'm—"

"Don't."

I managed to turn my head and saw the glass of ice water with the little blue straw dancing around the lip of the cup.

That white pill of serenity sat just in front of it, and I swear it was all that I could do to focus on the damned thing.

"Don't apologize," Reid said, his voice ripping through the pain wafting throughout my limbs again, "because you're right. Given the circumstances, you're making a good decision. I won't fight you on something that has solid ground. That's never been my M.O."

I lifted my tired, trembling arm and fumbled with the pill. "Okay, yeah."

"Do you need help?" he asked.

I shook my head as I lifted my hand. As I watched it float in the air. I slammed my palm down against the pill, almost as if I were playing a fucking claw game at a goddamn restaurant. I smiled as I raked the pill toward me. I closed my fingertips, feeling it press against the skin of my palm. God, it felt so good. I should've taken it when Reid offered. I shouldn't have been so fucking stubborn.

"Why are you always so goddamn stubborn, Angel?" I hissed at myself.

And when I pulled my hand closer to my face, I did the stupidest thing possible.

I knocked the fucking glass of ice water over.

"Ah!" I yelped as the ice-cold sensation splashed against my face.

All I felt was a rush of air before Reid appeared in my vision. "Here, I got it. Just let me help."

My brow furrowed. "Did—did you just—"

Did he just clear the fucking bed by jumping?

"Here, just stick your tongue out for me," he said.

His voice was so soft, and his hazel eyes were so comforting, and those boyish good looks of his were much too tantalizing. I didn't have the energy to fight. Not for my life, not for my sanity, not for anything else except pain relief. So, I did the only thing my body knew to do.

I did as he asked.

"Good girl," he said as he put the pill on my tongue, "now, slide it on, hold it there, and wash it over with water."

My brow ticked, but when he held the glass up, I saw that there was still half a glass of liquid left.

"Huh," I murmured as the pill melded to my tongue.

"Whenever you're ready," he said as he danced the straw along my lips.

And as I parted them, chugging down the sweet water he had held up for me, that pill slid effortlessly down the back of my throat.

"Oh, God, thank you," I murmured as I leaned back down against my pillow.

He smoothed my hair away from my forehead one last time. "I'll go refill your glass. You get some rest."

"Okay," I said groggily.

"And Angel?"

I closed my eyes. "Hmmm?"

"You had every right to feel the way you did," he said as I heard my bedroom door pop open, "so, don't feel bad about it."

But all I could do was nod before the pain pulled me under. A pain that I hoped would wash itself away with heavy narcotics and a little bit of sleep.

19

———

REID

The glass in my hand splintered as I made my way back downstairs. We had no hope or prayer of using her to our advantage, not in the condition she was in. She could barely keep her fucking head up. She was in so much pain that she was in self-preservation mode, denying herself things she fucking needed just so she could protect herself.

I wanted to throw that goddamn glass against the wall and listen to it shatter just to have anything else other than my thoughts racing through my head.

"So, did you show her?" Baron asked.

I scoffed as I tossed the glass into the sink. It shattered on impact against the stainless steel, and I watched as the little glass bits danced around.

Then, I heard kitchen chairs raking against the floor.

"I'm fine," I said as I placed my hands against the edge of the countertop.

"You sure about that?" Cash asked.

I hung my head, almost in shame. "She almost didn't take her pain medication."

"What?" Baron and Cash asked in unison.

"Why not?" Cash asked as he rushed to my side. "Is she bleeding? Did she pop a stitch?"

"Let the man speak," Baron commanded.

I shook my head before I turned to face my president. "She's scared we're gonna kill her, so she's not taking her pain medication."

That silenced the room, and I was glad for it, because just repeating it ripped the air out of my lungs. And when neither of them moved, spoke, or even fucking flinched, I whipped around and tore open the cabinet that housed our glasses.

"Should she be worried about shit like that?" I asked.

"Hell no," Cash spat.

But Baron didn't respond.

"You hear me?" I asked as I grabbed a glass and turned to face him.

"Yeah," he said flatly.

Cash snatched the cup out of my hand. "Water?"

I nodded my head, my gaze not wavering from Baron. "Yep."

Baron tilted his. "Does she even know about the footage? Were you able to show her?"

I shook my head. "I wasn't even able to have a conversation with her, Baron."

Cash filled up her ice water glass. "I can get her to take her meds. Just give me a bit to—"

I caught his arm as he moved past me, and it sloshed some of the water to Cash's feet.

"The fuck?" he asked as he shrugged me off.

I plucked the glass of water out of his grasp. "Part of the reason why she's in pain is because someone chose to fuck her right after her surgery."

Baron's eyes ignited as he whipped them to Cash. "What?"

Cash scoffed. "I was gentle, and she wanted it just as much as I did. She wasn't jostled."

"You did what?" Baron glowered as he took a step toward us.

I turned my body fully to him. "I'm not saying it's your fault, but I am saying that whatever muscle you aggravated, it's probably tugging at her wound. She's in a lot of pain right now."

"You what?!" Baron exclaimed as he charged Cash.

Cash's eyes widened. "What the fu—"

Baron slammed into him. I took a step back because, honestly? I was a tad bit shocked. And nothing shocked me. Not anymore. I knew my brothers like the back of my hand. They knew my struggles with my mother. How much it sucked to watch her dementia eat her alive, leaving her with nothing but memories to cry over. They knew everything, and I knew everything about them.

But watching Cash and Baron brawl it out in the kitchen wasn't something that I had expected.

"Enoooooough!" I bellowed.

It felt like the entire house had stopped. Their widened eyes whipped toward me before they leapt away from one another like two kids caught swinging punches after school in the back parking lot.

"You feel better?" I asked as my eyes darted between the two of them.

Cash walked toward me, his hand moving for the glass. "I got it. I'll take it to her. I need to—"

I held the glass away from him. "I've got it. I think you need to take a walk, though."

His eyes ignited. "Don't try me, Reid."

I grinned. "God, I really hope that's a promise."

"Cash," Baron growled as he stormed out of the kitchen, "with me. You need to help me put together a schedule."

Cash scoffed. "What schedule?"

Baron paused in the doorway of the kitchen. "A schedule to help take care of Angel. Keep her on her medication."

Hunter stuck his head in. "Can I get on that list?"

The three of us slowly panned our gazes toward him before he stepped into the kitchen.

"It just sort of sounds like she's giving you guys a run for your money," Hunter said with a shrug. "Might help to have more hands on deck."

I looked over at Baron and awaited his response, and yet again, was shocked when his head nodded.

"Anyone else wanna get in on this schedule?!" he bellowed across the clubhouse.

When our men came running, it was all I could do not to smile. Whatever Angel thought of us, she had certainly made an impression.

And not the kind of impression that got someone killed.

"All right," Baron said as he turned to face back down the hallway, "with me. We'll pound out this schedule before lunch time."

I held up the glass of water. "I'll get this back to Angel."

"Will you tell her I said hi?" Cash asked.

I walked past him and patted him on the shoulder. "Of course."

Then, while the rest of the crew funneled with Baron toward the back of the clubhouse, I made my way back upstairs.

Only to find Angel staring at the door as I ushered myself through.

"A schedule?" she asked as she stared at me from beneath the comforter.

I snickered as I eased her door closed behind me once more. "Baron's voice carries."

"So I've heard," she said flatly.

It honestly pulled a chuckle from between my lips as I walked her water toward her. "Would you like some more?"

She swallowed hard. "Yes, please."

I perched on the edge of the bed. "Can you reach for me?"

Her hand was shaky, but stable, so I held the glass in my hand while she wrapped her fingers around the other side. Her tips graced my skin. It shot heat all the way up to my shoulder. I gaze held hers as she pulled the water closer to her. Or was I pushing it closer to her?

"Reid?" she asked.

I cleared my throat. "Ready to take a sip?"

I found a grin on her face. "I can take it from here."

I looked down and saw that she had the glass propped against her breasts.

With my pinky shoved right into her cleavage.

"Right," I said as I cleared my throat and pulled my hand away.

She giggled as she wrapped those full lips of hers around the straw. Her throat bobbed with every chug, and it stiffened my cock. Her gaze held mine, and electric waves sizzled up and down my spine.

While part of me wanted to slug Cash for being so fucking reckless, I got it.

I understood why he felt the way he did.

"Like what you see?" she asked in a mocking voice before she tossed me a wink.

I snickered as I stood up from the bed. I needed to put space between us, otherwise I'd be no better than Cash.

"That supposed to be my voice?" I asked.

She giggled as she took another pull from the drink. "You do have a very distinctive voice."

God, what I wouldn't have given to replace that straw in her mouth.

How the hell was I jealous of a piece of fucking plastic?

"When you're feeling better," I said as I tried to steer the conversation back to its original intent, "I've got some footage I need to show you."

She paused. "Footage?"

I nodded. "Footage."

"Of what?"

"Of me and the guys."

She grinned again. "Kinky."

I audibly chuckled as I shook my head. "Not that kind of footage."

She playfully frowned. "A bit disappointing, but a girl can dream."

My cock jumped at the idea. What else did she dream about? The three of us taking her? The three of us having all of her holes at once while her muted sounds cried out?

I drew in a deep breath and focused on just her eyes. A set of eyes that I knew would morph the second I told her.

"It's footage of us at the docks, watching those who are responsible for those drugs you're chasing," I said.

She paused so long that the straw fell out of her mouth. "Wait, what?"

I clasped my hands behind my back. "When you're feeling up for it, we have footage of who's responsible for offloading those drugs into the area. We found them, Angel, and we took footage for you so that we could show you who you should really be chasing."

Her gaze danced in between my eyes. "Wh—when? When did you guys—what—"

I held up my hand. "You sleep and get better. When you no longer need the dependency of the drugs—"

"Let me see that footage."

"Angel, you aren't in any shape—"

She moved toward the edge of the bed. "I said, let me see that goddamn, motherfu—AH!"

She winced so hard that the glass of water she held fell from her hand. I moved as quick as lightening, catching her chest against my shoulder so that I could make sure she didn't tumble from the bed. My hand wrapped around the glass just before it crashed to the floor, and not a drop of water was spilled in the process.

And as I eased Angel back into bed with my shoulder, I held the straw back up to her lips.

"Please, let me see it," she whispered as tears trickled down her face.

"When you're better, you can see all you want. There's a lot of footage that we took. But can you honestly tell me that you're in a position to watch it and take it in while also not doing anything about it?"

Her watery gaze came back to mine. "It's not of you guys?"

I shook my head softly. "It's not of us. We told you we weren't the ones peddling those drugs, and we were serious. But we knew the only way to prove that to you was to get you proof that it wasn't us. So, we did."

She snickered before she took another long pull of her water. "Jesus, you guys are more efficient than my team."

That made me bark with laughter. Actual laughter. Laughter that I hadn't experienced in a very long time. And goddamn it, it felt good.

It felt so good to laugh with her.

"Well, it's true!" she said as her giggles started up.

I forced my laugh to come back down to a chuckle. "You know as well as I do that you're just like me: the second you see that footage, you're gonna want to be gone. You're gonna want to send everything you've got after them. Can you really tell me that you're capable of that right now?"

Her eyes sank with her sadness as she took a few more gulps. "No."

I set her glass of water off to the side. "Then, let's put a pin in that conversation until you can do something about it."

"But what about their shipment? Who's gonna—"

"Shh, shh, shh," I said softly as I brushed her hair back out of her face.

"Someone has to get those drugs off the street," she said as I placed my hands on her shoulders.

I eased her back down into bed. "Let us take care of all that for now. Baron isn't gonna let those drugs that almost dismantled this crew to sit on the streets for long. And when you're better? We can talk. But right now, your responsibility is to yourself. You can't help people if you also can't help yourself."

She smirked up at me. "Who knew you were the wise one of the group?"

I smirked as I stood. "Everyone. You're just slow on the uptick."

"Heeeeey."

I chuckled to myself as I made my way for the door. "The guys are coming up with a round robin schedule, so someone should be posted outside of your door at all times. If you need anything, just yell."

"Like this?!" she asked as she raised her voice.

I opened her bedroom door and found Hunter standing there.

"This is Hunter," I said as he stuck his head in.

"Hey there," he said with a soft wave.

Angel shot her hand up into the air and waved back. "Hello there."

I shook my head. "He'll be outside your door until..."

Hunter lowered his voice. "For the next four hours."

"For the next four hours," I repeated.

"I can hear him, you know," Angel said.

Hunter grinned. "She's feisty."

I shot him a look. "Down, boy."

Angel giggled. "Hunter?"

"Yep?" he called out around me.

She let out a bombastic yawn. "Get Reid out of here so I can sleep."

I scoffed as I shook my head, but it was Hunter that held his arm out, ushering me into the hallway.

"You heard the tired lady. Out," he said with a waggle of his eyebrows.

"Sleep well, Angel," I said as I stepped out into the hallway.

"Mmmmmhmm," she hummed softly.

And as Hunter closed the door, I put my finger in his face. "If you touch her without explicit permission from her first—"

He held up his hands in mock surrender. "No touchy unless she says so, got it."

My eye twitched. I didn't want any of these horny fucks putting their hands anywhere near her. But we didn't have a choice.

"Good," I grumbled as I made my way down the hallway, "and make sure you don't fucking forget it."

20

BARON

"Ah!"

I whipped my head up from my mug of coffee. "Did you hear that?"

Hunter cocked his head as he chugged his coffee down.

"Must've been my imagination," I muttered before taking another pull.

But the resounding boom that echoed over my head ripped me out of my chair.

"Angel!" I roared.

"I'm coming with you," Hunter said as he stood.

I whipped around and pointed at him. "Sit."

He eyed me carefully. "But what if you need—"

"I heard it, too. Angel!" Cash exclaimed as he sprinted through the kitchen.

"I'm headed up the stairs now!" Reid yelped.

I eyed Hunter until he sat down before I charged out of the kitchen. Scuffling and grunts blanketed the banging noise, and I swear to hell on high if there was someone in her room fucking with her, I'd rip their goddamn heads off myself.

"Cash, tell me something!" I bellowed up the steps.

"I got her!" Reid yelled back.

"No one's in the room!" Cash exclaimed.

Relief flooded my veins as a heave gave way to an episode. I heard her puking, absolute exorcist-style shit. My men went running past me, fear in their eyes and sweat on their brows. They damn near shoved me into the wall to get away, tracking puke and whatever the fuck else was on the bottoms of their boots.

"Get some shit and clean this mess up!" I ordered.

"Baron," Reid said as he stuck his head out the door, "she's asking for you."

And I sure as fuck didn't need to be prompted twice.

"I'm here," I said as I stormed through the entrance and tried to ignore the putrid smell of returned eggs. "What's going on?"

"I'm sorry," Angel said breathlessly as she shook her head. "I'm sorry, I don't know... what...mmph."

"Shh, shh, shh," Cash shushed softly as he tried getting her hair out of her face.

"She needs to get to the bathroom," Reid murmured.

"Ba—Baron?" Angel choked out.

I rushed to where she knelt on the carpeted floor, her face stuck into one of the many small trash cans we had floating around the clubhouse.

"I'm right here," I said as I brushed the sweat away from her forehead. "What is it? Did you eat something?"

She shook her head before she heaved. "N—no."

"She can't keep her pain pill down," Reid said.

She pointed at him, and I peered over my shoulder. "Why the fuck hasn't she taken it before now?"

"I—I-I-I—I di—mglborb."

I wrinkled my nose as the smell from the trashcan wafted up, slapping me straight in the face. "Cash."

"Yep?"

I replaced the hand holding back Angel's hair with mine. "Go downstairs and get some lukewarm water. We gotta make sure she can keep something down."

"Please, no more," Angel said breathlessly.

I dipped down into her vision, holding her hair off her neck while Reid exchanged places with Cash. He dashed out of the hallway, grumbling about the mess the guys had tracked off into the distance while Reid sat there blowing on the nape of her neck.

"If you can't keep anything down, we have to call Doc. Okay? It's just some water. It'll do you good to get that taste out of your mouth," I said.

Angel vomited again into the trashcan, and it caused Reid to snap.

"Cash! Where the fuck are you?!" he bellowed.

"Ugh, my head," Angel groaned.

"No more screaming," I said as I shot Reid a look.

Thank fuck, Cash barreled back in with a glass of water. "Here, try this. Hopefully, the straw will help with control."

He stood there with his hands on his hips like an old woman panicking over a small child. It made me grin as I shook my head and dipped the straw toward Angel's lips. She sat back, moving Reid with her as he continued blowing a continuous stream of cool air onto her sweating neck.

However, when I danced the straw against her lips, she shook her head. "Please, Baron. I can't."

"You have to try."

"I'm just going to throw it back up."

I peeked into the trashcan. "Not according to that in there."

"Baron—"

"No," I said curtly.

She furrowed her brow. "No... what?"

I scooted closer to her. "You're going to take a sip of water and swish it around, and then you're going to spit it back out into this trashcan. You're going to do that until that nasty taste in your mouth is gone, and then you're going to swallow for me."

She grinned. "Am I now?"

Cash chuckled. "Must be feeling better."

My frown only grew deeper, though. "Yes, you will, unless you want to end up in a hospital where we can't reach you."

She faltered at that statement. "What if I can't keep it down, Baron?"

She sounded so helpless. "Then, we'll go from there. But right now, we know nothing, and we won't until you do exactly as I say. Got it?"

And with that, she parted her dry lips and wrapped them around that little plastic straw. Even with her throwing up, it was a sight I could get used to. A memory that would haunt me in the thickest of dreams.

How the hell is she so fucking sexy even after puking?

She swished and spit. Swished and spit. She repeated the pattern until the glass was damn near drained of all the liquid. I eyed her hotly. If she thought she was gonna get out of this, she had another thing coming.

Then, she took a large gulp and didn't spit it back out.

"Now," I said as I reached over her shoulder and placed the glass on her bedside table, "we wait."

Reid stopped blowing against her neck. Cash stopped hovering as he perched himself on the edge of the bed, his burner phone out and ready to call whoever we needed. I watched as her cheeks flushed. As her eyes bulged. She gagged once. Twice. Three times.

But she didn't throw up.

"There we go," I said as she smiled up at me with those bloodshot brown eyes of hers, "see? Not that hard."

Her face fell flat. "Ha. Ha. Ha."

"Think you can stand?" Reid asked.

Angel sniffed the air. "Jesus, I need a shower."

Cash leapt into action. "I'll go get the water started."

Reid got up from his perched position. "Cash she can't take a shower with the dressing on her wounds —"

"Guys?" Angel asked.

I already knew what she was gonna ask, even before she said it. But I gave her the floor. If she had enough energy to ask for what she needed, then I wasn't gonna get in her way.

"Who's supposed to be watching me right now?" she asked.

I peered over my shoulder as Cash and Reid looked at one another before their stares turned to me.

The man who had taken up her lunchtime post.

"Tell Hunter he'll be needed tonight before your shift, Reid," I said with a nod of my head.

"Can do," he said as he flittered out of the room.

But Cash hovered over me as he peered down at Angel. "You sure you don't need any help?"

Pain washed over Angel's face. "Once I can keep this medicine down, I'll be fine. I promise."

"Then, why don't you let me help with—"

"Cash," I said as I stood and turned to face him, "we've got it."

The worry was prevalent in his face. "If you need anything, you yell, okay?"

"Ugh, no more yelling," Angel muttered as she tried pulling herself upright.

"Jesus, woman," I hissed as I whipped back around and slid my arms beneath hers, "don't you ever wait for anything?"

"I hear that water running and I need to get into it," she damn near growled. "So, help me or get out of my way."

Cash reached around my body for her pain medication. "Just let me help you get it into her system, and then I'm gone."

"Fine," I grunted as I scooped Angel into my arms. "Bathroom, now."

Hearing her grunt and groan in pain was not my idea of a good time. Feeling her shiver in my arms as pain electrified her body wasn't my preferable way of spending an entire afternoon with her. I perched her delicate body on the edge of the bathroom countertop, making sure she had plenty of clearance. Her head fell to my shoulder, bleeding sweat against my shirt as I yanked my leather cut off my arms.

"Cash, get me her—"

"Here," he said as his hand came into view.

I stared down at the pill bottle before I took it. "All right, Angel. Think you can sit up for me?"

I felt her shake her head no.

I heard Cash rush out of the room before coming back and sticking a glass of lukewarm water in my face.

"How old is that?" I asked as I quirked an eyebrow.

"Does it matter when she's getting down medicine?" Cash asked with a blank expression.

"Jesus," Angel hissed. "I gotta take off these clothes. They smell."

I chuckled as I backed away a bit. "One thing at a time, gorgeous. Now, can you lift your head for me?"

She dangled it helplessly as I stood there with her pill in one hand and her glass of stale water in the other. I didn't like drinking stale water. I wanted that shit to be crisp, clear, and ice cold. But with the kind of pain she was in, lukewarm and stale was probably better.

"Angel," Cash said as he tried interjecting.

I shot him a look. "We're good."

He scoffed. "I want to make sure she can—"

"Cash, really," Angel said breathlessly as she tried picking up her head, "we've got this. I'll see you later today, okay?"

When she lifted her head to look at him, I thought we were sunk. Had she ever looked at me with that kind of swollen desperation behind those eyes of hers, and I would've never left her fucking side again. But instead of getting closer, instead of following his orders, Cash leaned toward her and kissed her forehead.

"See you in a few hours," he murmured.

Then, like a bolt of lightning, he was gone.

"And close the doors with you!" I exclaimed.

The bedroom door slammed with a thud, causing Angel to wince.

"Was that really necessary?" she mumbled as she peeked over at me.

I held the straw up to her lips. "Drink first, let it sit in your mouth, and we'll toss the pill into the water. See if that works better."

She grimaced. "What if it doesn't?"

I shrugged. "Well, you haven't heaved in a while, so there's that."

"Maybe I'll just heave all over you," she murmured as she took the glass of water out of my hands.

I grinned as I watched her take a long pull. She could be as stubborn as she wanted, but sometimes a distraction was all someone needed to help gain control of their body. She plucked that pill right out of my palm like a pro and tossed that shit back.

But when she went to swallow, her eyes widened.

"Mm-mm," she said as she shook her head.

"Angel," I warned.

Her eyes watered over. "Mm-mm. Mm-mm."

I slid my hands up and down her arms. "When you're ready, just swallow."

She whimpered softly. "Mm-mm."

Tears crested her eyes, and it killed me. I knew exactly how she felt. The second that shit hit her tongue, I knew she wanted to barf it right back up. I knew her body was fighting her on swallowing, and I grew worried. I wanted to help her, and I had no idea how the fuck to even begin doing that. But if one distraction helped out that much...

"Here," I said as I slid my hands up to her shoulders, "just concentrate on me. Lock your eyes with me."

Her fearful gaze held mine as my hands slowly explored. They rounded her shoulders as I stepped closer, her legs mindlessly parting for me. The heat of her pussy called to my cock, stiffening it against my jeans as my left hand slid back down to hers.

While my right hand slowly encircled her throat.

"Mmmmm?" she asked with a bit of an uptick to her voice at the end.

I wrapped my fingers around her throat, but not too tight. Not hard, just enough to get her curious.

Just enough to hook her focus.

"Now," I said gruffly as I held her gaze, "where were we?"

Her eyes darted between my own. "Mmm?"

I shook my head as I leaned in closer, tightening my grip just a tad. "Uh, uh, uuuuh. Gotta use those words, gorgeous."

Her lower lip quivered as her legs spread further, doing her damnedest to make way for my body. It took all I had to keep control. It took all I had to hover my lips over hers and not genuinely give into the urges coursing through my body. I wanted to fuck her right then and there. Right on that fucking bathroom countertop with the whole clubhouse listening in. I stroked my thumb along her pulse point, watching it quicken. I saw her skin flush, ready for my meaty bite.

Then, like the good girl I knew she was capable of being, she swallowed so she could speak.

Water, pain pill, and all.

"Baron?" she asked breathlessly.

I kept stroking her neck. "Yes, gorgeous?"

Her breath pulsed against my mouth. "I really need a shower. I smell like puke."

I chuckled as my hand migrated to the back of her head. I cupped the entire back of her skull against my palm, watching as she leaned back. Watching as her eyes closed. Watching as she sought comfort in me.

It had been a long time since I'd been able to bring anyone anything other than heartache and bloodshed.

"I can help with that," I said as I nuzzled my nose along her flushed cheek.

Before I pulled away and turned toward the shower.

"Hot, warm, or cool?" I asked.

"Private," Angel said.

I smirked to myself as I turned each water nozzle equally. "I'll be just outside if you need anything."

And I couldn't help but notice as I left her to engage in her private shower that she hadn't heaved yet.

21

———

CASH

"Knock, knock," I said as my knuckles rapped against Angel's bedroom door.

"Come on in, Cash!"

I smiled at how strong she sounded as I opened the door. "You're sounding better by the day."

"So," she said as she turned around in a t-shirt and a set of sweatpants that were much too big for her, "how do I look?"

I grinned as I leaned against the frame of the doorway. "Baron's clothes?"

Her arms flopped to her sides. "I'm drowning in them."

My grin morphed into a smile. "I'm just glad you're starting to feel better."

"God, me too," she said breathlessly as she turned to the mirror hanging on the wall. "There were a couple of days there where I honestly didn't think I'd make it to the finish line."

"The first week is rough. Everything from here on out should be smooth sailing."

She piled her hair onto her head and used a hair tie to secure it. "Hope Doc doesn't mind me dressing down."

I nodded toward the hallway. "Come on, he should already be here. Let's get you checked out."

"On it, boss!"

I chuckled to myself as she walked toward me. Even with Baron's baggy ass clothes on her, I saw those toned curves of hers just swishing with every movement.

"After you," I said as I ushered her out into the hallway with my hand.

"Such a gentleman," she said beneath a soft giggle.

It was a sound that I could get used to.

I followed her down the hallway, watching her try to navigate her surroundings. The couple of wrong turns that she took washed confusion over her face, and I enjoyed the way her nose wrinkled whenever she got lost in her train of thought.

The way she murmured to herself was precious, too.

"No, no, this way, I'm sure of it."

"Mmmm, I needed to take that right."

"Stairs! Finally."

I walked by her side as she turned the correct way to head toward the back of the clubhouse. "You're getting good at this."

She shrugged. "Hunter's been taking me on walks throughout the place to make sure clots don't form."

I nodded. "He's been keeping us updated on those, yes."

"This place is pretty big, though. I don't know how you guys managed to find a place like this."

"We didn't find it; we built it."

That stopped her in her tracks, and she looked up at me. "Wait, you guys just...bought the land and built this?"

"Is that my patient I hear?!" Doc called out from our patient room at the back of the clubhouse.

"Coming, Doc!" she called back.

"Yes," I said as I brushed past her and led the way to the door, "we bought the land and built it."

"There she is. And upright, I see," Doc chided as we came through the door. "Someone's been keeping up with her recovery walks."

I stood off in the corner and watched as Angel eased herself up onto the tabletop. "A surgical room and a doctor's office. Interesting."

Doc chuckled as he pulled on gloves. "All right, missy. Let me see those stitches."

I watched as Angel laid herself down, still wincing whenever her body broke that ninety-degree angle. I rushed toward her, cupping my hands beneath her head so that I could help her lying down. I eased her hair against the table and searched for a pillow. That surgical table had to feel like murder on her fucking back. But when I didn't find one in the room, I shrugged off my leather cut.

Before rolling it up and placing it beneath her head.

"Thanks, Cash," she said as she tilted her gaze back just enough to look at me upside down.

I tossed her a playful wink. "Lay still for Doc, all right?"

She nodded softly. "You got it, boss."

Doc pulled up her shirt and snapped on a pair of rubber gloves. Then, he poked, prodded, and studied her wound and her stitches while those glasses of his slid down the bridge of his nose. He hemmed and hawed to himself. I watched him jot down a few notes into her profile. But outside of a little bit of grunting from Angel whenever he pushed down, he didn't say much.

"So?" I asked.

Angel snickered. "Let the man work."

"Actually," Doc said as he popped his gloves off and tossed them into a trashcan, "things are looking really well."

"Yeah?" Angel and I asked in unison.

She propped herself up on her elbows. "I'm not gonna lie,

Doc, with the kind of pain I was in a few days ago, I honestly expected you to tell me you had to open me back up or something."

He chuckled as he jotted down a few more notes. "The pain from days three to five is something no one is ever prepared for. That's why I gave you those pain pills."

"Had a hard time keeping them down, though."

That caused Doc to slowly turn around. "But you kept them down?"

I interjected. "On day four she had some nausea from the pain that made keeping it down hard."

Doc turned to me, eyeing me carefully. "But you got her to keep it down?"

"Yes," Angel said, pulling Doc's attention back to her. "Baron helped me to keep it down. It was just particularly hard that day."

Doc studied her for a few seconds before he picked up a pen. He clicked it, yanked a pad out of his briefcase, and jotted something down. Angel looked up at me with a wary stare. I rubbed her hand up and down her spine, trying to quell the worry I knew she was beginning to feel.

It wasn't until Doc ripped the paper off the pad and handed it to her that I saw it was another prescription.

"You'll have to go into town to fill it; I don't carry stuff like that on me," Doc said as he clicked the pen and put it away. "But that's the liquid form of the same pain medication you've got right now. You should've run out of it—"

"This morning, yeah. I took my last pain pill."

Doc nodded. "You shouldn't need it. Not now. However, the second week can be a bit finicky. Some people are fine, others need an extra few days' worth of medicine. This prescription gives you four more days in liquid form, just in case."

Angel sighed with relief, and I had to admit, I wish one of us would've thought about that shit sooner.

"Thanks, Doc," she said as she placed the prescription into her sweatpants pocket. "I'll make sure to get it filled."

"Can one of us fill it on her behalf?" I asked as I stood behind her.

He shrugged. "Just send Hunter with it and we can fill it like we always do."

I wrapped my arm around Angel's body. "I can do that now, if you'd like."

Angel mindlessly put her hand into her pocket and pulled the prescription out for me. Just like that. Without so much as a fight or a look.

Huh.

"Thanks, Cash," she said as she released the piece of paper. "I really appreciate it."

I transferred it to my back pocket before I picked up my leather cut. "It's not a problem at all."

"Anything else I should know about?" Doc asked.

It didn't shock me that Angel damn near tripped over herself to answer him. "Just one thing."

Doc grinned. "You want to know when you can get back up on your feet and get back to work."

She nodded. "Just a tad."

Doc peered over the edge of his glasses at her. "I'm going to be back in one more week to make sure your healing is still on the right track. And if you're okay, I can clear you for minimal physical exertion."

"Define minimal?"

I couldn't help but curl my lips over my teeth. God, was she asking him what I thought she was?

"One step at a time," Doc said with a chuckle as he reached behind him and slid his briefcase off the stainless-steel countertop. "Just keep doing what you're doing. Take the pain medication when you need it. Rest, eat well, and stay hydrated. And in another week, when I come back, we can talk about what to do in terms of your mobility."

"But for now, business as usual?"

"I'm afraid so."

Angel sighed heavily. "Yep. Okay. Not like I haven't heard that a million other times from the guys at work."

She placed her hands on the edge of the table, ready to hop down. But I slid my arms beneath hers from behind and helped slide her to her feet.

"There you go," I said.

"I could've gotten it," she grumbled to herself.

I smirked. "You're cute when you're frustrated, you know that?"

"Yeah, well," she said as she turned to face me, "I'll be a lot cuter when I can shower for myself."

Even Doc laughed at that one before he ushered us out of the room. It felt so...weirdly domestic. Taking her to a doctor's appointment. Watching over her while the doctor examines her. Helping her down the hallway. Being proud as she made it up the stairs by herself. Watching her as she meandered into her room without a single ounce of directional help from me. It was almost like she lived there now. With us.

The thought alone tightened my chest.

"Home, sweet home," she said breathlessly as she slipped back beneath the covers of her bed.

My head swirled with all sorts of thoughts as I perched on the edge of the mattress. Could she ever call a place like this home? Could she ever see herself staying here with us? I wasn't sure about the other guys, but I had feelings for the woman. She was beautiful. Strong. Just the right amount of stubborn. She was intelligent and kind. She very obviously took care of that smoking hot body of—

"Cash?"

Her voice pulled me from my trance. "Yeah, Angel?"

She leaned back against her pillows. "Thanks for coming with me to that appointment."

I reached out and settled my hand on top of hers. "Anytime. It really wasn't a big deal."

"Well, it was to me. I've never liked doctors."

"Yeah?"

She shook her head. "They just...don't ever come during good times, you know?"

I wanted to press her on what she meant by that. I wanted to crack her open like a book and devour every single fucking page until her spine was arched like the crease of a book spine. But when her gaze ventured toward the wall, turning away from me, I decided not to push the issue.

I simply committed the little tidbit to memory.

"Can I get you anything before I head back out into the hallway?" I asked as I pushed the covers up her body a bit.

"Actually, could y—"

I tilted my head. "Could I what?"

Tears crested her eyes, and she blinked them away. "Nothing. It's okay."

"Angel."

"Cash, it's really nothing."

"Angel, look at me."

She sighed. "I'm just being dumb. It's fine."

I reached toward her, gripped her chin, and pulled her gaze to mine. "Angel."

Her eyes watered over again. "What?"

I smoothed my thumb along her lower lip. "What is it?"

Her gaze dropped to my mouth. "Nothing that I can have right now."

I swallowed hard as my dick pulsed to life. "Is there anything *else* I can get you? Something *else* you might need?"

Tears poured over onto her cheeks. "Could you just—"

I scooted closer to her. Fucking hell, I hated seeing her cry. "Just tell me. I know that's hard sometimes, but all you need to do is—"

"Will you lay down with me for a bit?"

I blinked as the words dawned on me. Was that it? She was upset over that?

She sighed and pulled the covers over her head. "Like I said, stupid."

I scooted the rest of the way up the bed and pulled the covers down so that I found the shell of her ear as she turned over onto her side. Then, I dipped my lips down and kissed it softly.

"Scooch over, little one," I whispered.

When she did just as I asked like the good little girl she was, I kicked my boots off, shrugged off my leather cut, and crawled into bed with her. Then, I pulled her magnificent body close. Her warmth overwhelmed me. The way the dips and peaks of her body melded to my muscles was a sensation I committed to memory almost immediately. She felt amazing in my grasp, like she had been carved out of the most beautiful rock just to fit the slats of my body.

I nuzzled my nose into her hair as she slid her leg in between mine.

"Just like that," she whispered as she wiggled that pert little ass of hers against my pelvis.

And as my arm locked around her waist, I knew then and there I'd never be able to let her leave. She'd never be able to call anywhere else home again except this clubhouse. Home would be this room. Home would be us. Home would be her, crooked against my body, wanting nothing more than my muscles blanketing her away from the world.

I'd convince her to do it, one way or another.

No matter what it cost me in the process.

"Why don't you like doctors?" I asked.

Her body tightened. "Just don't."

I traced mindless pictures against her body with my fingertips as we laid there. "Would it have anything to do with your brother, by any chance?"

"Cash," she groaned.

I squeezed her softly, scooting closer to her curves in bed. "If you really don't wanna talk about it, I won't make you. But it seems like it's weighing heavy, and you need all of the good feelings you can get to help you recuperate."

I honestly didn't think it was going to work. We laid there for a while in silence, with nothing but her body warmth to keep me company. She robbed me of her voice. She robbed me of her conversation. Fucking hell, I shouldn't have pried. I shouldn't have pushed her at all.

Then, she cleared her throat. "They just kept throwing him into the psych ward."

My ears perked up. "What was that?"

She sighed heavily. "The reason why I don't like doctors. It's because of my brother."

I figured as much, but I stayed quiet as she drew in a deep breath.

"There were a couple of times where I tried to interject. Where I did my best to help him. I was young, and I wasn't sure what to do. But I knew that doctors always helped, so when I found my brother face down in the bathroom for the first time with a needle in his arm, I called 911."

My grip tightened around her waist. "As you should have."

She shrugged softly. "But uh…they didn't help him. I mean, they revived him. Took him away. And then I didn't see him for a fucking month because the doctor in charge of him at the hospital stuck him in the psych ward instead of in a rehab facility."

I shook my head softly as she sniffled. I wanted to do nothing more than to take her pain away. I wanted to shoulder her burden just so I could stop the way she shivered in my grasp. The way she backed into me, as if she were trying to crawl into my body. She wiggled around in my arms. She twisted and turned herself over, grunting and wiping at the tears on her face as she settled her head my pillow.

I reached out and wiped a tear about to drip off the tip of her nose before her red gaze found mine. "It's more common than you think. Drug addicts go into the hospital and some nurse thinks they're having a mental breakdown."

Her lower lip quivered, and it broke my fucking heart. "They did it to him twice, Cash. That first time, and then again when I caught him shooting up in the closet in his room. I figured maybe since he wasn't passed out that time, that they'd know he needed rehab instead of being locked away. But—but they…they just…"

The tears fell effortlessly from her eyes, and all of a sudden, I realized why this case was so important to her. Even as a young child, she had tried her damnedest to protect her brother. To save him the only way she knew how. And now, all she had was wiping those fucking drugs off the street so they couldn't torture anybody else. It was her way of protecting the people around her from the thing that ruined her family.

She had a strong moral code, and that shit was attractive as fuck.

"Sorry," she whispered as she wiped at her face.

I shook my head and reached my knuckles up, catching her falling tears as we laid there in bed. "No need to be."

"Oh, God. My poor brother," she whimpered as her face wrinkled up.

And as she buried her face against my chest, I wrapped my arms around her. I pulled her trembling body on top of mine. I held her there, feeling her bury her wet face into the crook of my neck as her shoulders shook with her sobs.

"Get it all out," I whispered into her hair. "I'm right here, Angel."

I held her while she cried until she fell asleep on top of my body. Like a weighted blanket, shrouding me away from the harsh world outside.

I wanted us to lay like that forever.

After we helped her wipe those fucking drugs off our goddamn streets for good.

22

———

ANGEL

I hummed to myself as I stood at the sink, brushing and flossing my teeth. It felt good to get out of bed by myself. To not need help in and out of the shower. Lord knows that had gotten me into a fuckton of almost-trouble with the guys over the course of the last two weeks. But I felt good. I felt strong. And as I lifted my shirt to stare at my healing wound in the mirror, the only thing I saw was a massive scab that had formed over the rest of the wound.

A wound that wasn't even seeping any longer.

"Hell yeah, Angel," I said before I spit my toothpaste out in the sink. "You go, girl."

"Looks like someone's—"

"Ah!" I yelped the second I heard his voice. I whipped around to face Reid, who stood there in the entryway to the bathroom with his body propped against the wall. His hands folded over his chest. And his grin on display for me to see.

"Gotta little something here," he said as he lifted his finger to his chin.

I growled at him playfully before I turned back to the sink.

"You act like you've never seen someone brush their own teeth before."

"Well, for the past two weeks, this has been my job. So, can't blame a man for wanting to watch."

I rolled my eyes as I spit in the sink again. "Come to watch me foam at the mouth?"

I heard a familiar cadence of steps before Cash's voice sounded. "Hey, hey! Looks who's up and motoring around by herself."

"Motoring around, really?" Baron asked as his massive footfalls damn near shook the floor.

"She's got good color in her skin," Reid said as I rinsed my mouth out.

"I saw that she ate her breakfast," Cash said. "Was anyone up here to help her?"

"Just checked in with Hunter," Baron muttered. "He said she ate by herself."

I scrubbed my skin with facewash, then splashed some water on it to clean my skin. "I'm right here, you know? You could just, I don't know, ask me."

"Where would the fun be in that?" Reid asked.

I giggled to myself as I turned off the water and reached for my towel. But my hand couldn't land on it. Water dripped into my eyes, so I squeezed them shut to avoid any stinging. My hand darted around. My fingers kept unfurling, extending into the darkness as soap dripped to the tip of my nose.

"Here," Reid said plainly as the towel touched down against my palm, "you were close."

"Thanks," I said softly.

I dabbed my face off and wiped the stray water off my skin and the sink. God, it felt good to be alive. I could eat without my stomach swelling against angry stitches. My skin had its color back. My cheeks were flushed with life. They were right.

I looked great.

"You're impressive," Baron said gruffly, "I'll give you that."

I tossed him a playful wink. "Thanks, big guy."

Cash chuckled as Reid backed away from the door. He parted the guys like the Red Sea, and I waltzed through just as strong as ever on my feet. Walking didn't hurt. Climbing stairs didn't hurt. Getting back into bed didn't hurt. Moving around, turning my torso, stretching my body out as I raised my hands up and felt my back crack...

None of it hurt.

"Oh, thank fuck," I said breathlessly when I flopped back down into bed. "I didn't think I'd ever heal up."

"Bullet wounds are a bitch," Baron said as he stood at the foot of my bed.

"So," Cash said as he perched to my right, "Doc's gonna be here in less than half an hour."

It dawned on me. "Riiiiight, my two-week appointment."

"Yes," Reid said as he perched to my left, "your two-week appointment."

"We could do it here," Baron said. "If that's something you're interested in."

"Have Doc come to my room instead of me going down-stairs?" I asked.

He nodded. "If that's what you'd prefer."

I hunkered down beneath the covers. "I have to admit, this bed's pretty comfy."

"It is," Baron said.

Not asked, but stated.

I wondered if I'd ever be able to convince him to get back into it with me.

"Sure," I said with a shrug, "send him on up when he gets here."

Baron nodded to both of the guys. "I'll go keep an eye out. Make sure she's in something appropriate."

I furrowed my brow. "Appropriate?"

Cash slipped off the bed. "I can get her a pair of shorts from my room. Reid, you got any more shirts?"

"Yep," he said as he hopped off, not making a sound in the process.

I sat back up in bed and let Baron's shirt hang off my shoulder. "What's wrong with what I've got on?"

The way their eyes traced me made my skin tingle. The way Reid licked his lips as his eyes rounded down to my breasts made me shiver, even against the warmth of the bed itself. Cash just scoffed before he walked away, murmuring something about being right back. But it was Baron who pinned me with a look.

"You're not that stupid, Angel. Don't act like it. It's not a good look on you."

And with that, they exited my room.

"God, it feels good to be back," I said with a smile as I flopped back down onto the pillow.

After Cash brought me a pair of basketball shorts and Reid tossed me a slightly-better-fitting shirt, I wiggled beneath the covers and got changed. And it wasn't until I came up for air dressed in their clothes that I found they hadn't once turned their backs. I popped up from beneath the comforter to hungry eyes and a pair of tongues licking sets of lips that I wanted planted all over my body.

Yep. I'm definitely feeling better.

"Well, well, well, look at who's looking better," Doc said as he strolled in with his briefcase.

"Doc's here," Baron said as he lumbered in behind the man.

Cash and Reid took their positions up in corners of the room, staring like the hawks they were. Baron perched at the foot of the bed while Doc wrapped around to my right side, and I propped myself up with some pillows. He did all of the usual things: he checked my pulse, told me to open my mouth and say "ah." He checked my heart and my lungs. Felt along my lymph nodes.

Then, we got to the part I was anxious about.

"Ready for me to see that wound?" he asked.

I leaned back a bit and slipped my shirt up. "Ready when you are, Doc."

And when he pulled back the gauze taped to my skin, his smile told me everything. "Oh, yeah, that's looking a lot better."

"Yeah?" the three men asked in unison.

Doc slowly peeked over his shoulder at them. "Yes, it's looking a lot better."

"Any sign of infection?" Cash asked.

"How's the bounce back in her skin?" Reid asked.

"She gonna need anymore stitches?" Baron asked.

Doc slowly panned his gaze back to mine before he lowered his voice. "A bit anxious, I see."

I giggled softly. "They mean well."

He winked at me. "I know they do. Tell me, does this hurt?"

All eyes were on me as he pressed against my skin, working his way around the wound. And the entire time, nothing registered.

"Not even the smallest bit," I said.

Doc looked up at me for a second. "You sure? Not even if I do this?"

I winced a bit. "That was uncomfortable, but that's all it was. Uncomfortable."

His smile almost closed his eyes. "Great. That's fantastic. And all looks well, too. Those stitches have dissolved that I put on the inside of her body to help close things up a bit quicker, and the wound that's exposed is healing very nicely. Just let me clean it, put some fresh gauze on it, and you'll be good to go for the next couple of weeks."

I beamed with pride as the collective in the room seemed to release the breath that they were holding all together at once. I laid there while Doc did what he needed to do, and as I laid there, I couldn't help but clock the relief in their faces.

Had they really been that worried this entire time?

"All right," Doc said as he hiked up his leg and sat on the edge of my bed, "here are the rules for the next two weeks."

I groaned playfully. "All riiiiiiight. Hit me with it."

Doc smiled kindly. "You're still on restrictions, but mobility is fine now. No lifting anything over ten pounds, no heavy training of any sort, if you sweat then you need to immediately get your wound site clean, but that's it."

"That's it?"

"That's it, Miss Angel."

I tilted my head. "So, no heavy training means...I could at least go on walks? Or brisk runs?"

"Angel," Baron warned.

I shot him a look. "I'm just trying to find the line. That's all."

Doc nodded. "Fair enough. I wouldn't do a brisk run just yet. Brisk run is defined differently for people. I would stick with more stationary exercises. You know, having equipment to help you out and such. Walking on a treadmill you can stop at the drop of a hat and not have to worry about getting home. Weight benches, but don't go over ten pounds. Really, just don't do anything that engages your core too much. No ab workouts. No targeting exercises."

I couldn't get him to give me the kind of answer I was seeking, so I decided to simply blurt it out. After all, I knew I wasn't the only curious one in the room.

"What about sex?" I asked.

No one made a sound. Everything came to a grinding

fucking halt. And as I looked at Doc, he couldn't help but chuckle to himself.

"Like I said, no lifting more than ten pounds and no conditioning exercises for your core. Everything else, in moderation, is fine."

I nodded as if I were punctuating a sentence. "Okay. Thank you, Doctor."

He held out his hand, and I shook it. "The pleasure's all mine. I'll be back in a couple of weeks just to check in on you, but you should be fine in your recuperation from here on out. But as always—"

"If she develops anything out of the ordinary, you'll be our first call," Baron said as he walked over to Doc.

I couldn't help but be tempted by the bulge against his jeans.

Apparently, my question got someone's gears grinding.

"I'll walk you out, Doc," Baron said as he stood behind the man.

Doc packed up his briefcase and stood. "Until next time, Miss Angel."

I bowed my head softly at him. "Thank you again, Doctor."

And as Baron escorted Doc out of my bedroom, I watched him lean in and whisper something to Reid and then Cash. The two of them stared me down like hawks in a tree nest as Baron peered over his shoulder at me, and the grin on his face sizzled electricity down my spine. What the fuck had he told them? Why were they looking at me like that?

Nothing could have readied me for what happened the second Baron closed that bedroom door, though.

"Now," Reid said the second the door latched.

My eyes widened as he flew through the air. He pounced onto the bed, scurrying up it before I even had a chance to register what the fuck was happening. Cash wrapped his hands around my ankles, pulling my feet to the foot of the bed. And as Reid settled behind me, I felt him pick my head up and settle it in his lap.

"Cheeky little question you had for Doc," Cash said as he planted his hands on either side of my hips.

"I think you knew what you were doing when you asked, too," Reid said as he gathered my hair into a ponytail and set it off to the side.

My body came alive with curiosity and need. "What did Baron say to you guys?"

"Oh, nothing," Cash said as he perched on his knees in between my legs on top of the bed.

"Just to get you ready to watch," Reid said nonchalantly.

I furrowed my brow. "What—what does that mean?"

The second I asked the question, Cash grabbed the basketball shorts that he had given me and ripped them down my legs. I gasped, listening as stitches popped and fabric ripped. I tried to sit up, but Reid captured my shoulders. He eased me back down into his lap, where his girth grew against the back of my head.

Before those lumbering footfalls started back toward the bedroom door.

"Cash?" Reid asked.

His tongue dipped down to my thigh, and I groaned. "Oh, fuck."

"Mhmmmmm?" he hummed as he slid that tongue all the way up to my panties.

"Shit," I hissed.

"Better get on with the show," Reid said. "The big boy's expecting one."

And the second the doorknob turned, Cash pulled my panties off to the side and dove in.

"Oh, my Go—"

My exclamation was covered with Reid's hand. He wrapped his hand around my face, muffling my sounds as Cash's tongue immediately found my clit. He lapped against it, flattening his tongue as stars burst in my vision. I heard Baron in the room, but good God I couldn't see him. I smelled him, though. That musky scent with subtle hints of leather and dust.

"Well, well, well," Baron said as a surface creaked somewhere, "look at what we have here."

"She's beautiful, isn't she?" Reid asked.

My hips rolled against Cash's mouth. "Oh, shit. Oh, shit. Oh, shit."

"Filthy little mouth, too," Reid hissed as his hand clamped harder against my mouth.

"Mmmmmm, fuck. Cash. Please."

"Stop," Baron commanded.

And just like that, Cash pulled away.

"Wait, wait, wait, wait," I said breathlessly as I reached my hands down. Reid prevented me from looking down between my legs, but I didn't care. "Cash, please."

"Reid, your turn," Baron said.

Reid smirked down at me. "I'm not nearly as eager as he is."

The world swirled around me. "What?"

When Reid moved, I lobbed my head over in the direction of Baron, only to be met with the most amazing sight I'd ever seen. That mountainous man, with his stacked muscles and his brooding stare, sat there with his massive cock in his hand and his eyes pointed directly at my body. His skin, flushed with each pump of his callused hand. His tip, dripping wet.

I wanted to know what he tasted like.

"There there, little one," Cash said as he picked my head up and settled it into his lap.

"Cash," I whispered.

"Fucking hell, you smell amazing," Reid glowered as he dipped between my legs.

"Make her beg for it," Baron commanded.

"Baron," I whispered.

But when Reid kissed my ankle, I turned my gaze back down to him until Cash pulled me back down into his lap.

"No abdomen workouts, remember?" Cash asked.

I groaned as Reid's hot tongue slid up the inside of my calf. He kissed the crook of my knee, and goosebumps flew across my body. I felt as if I were on cloud nine. As if none of this was happening. I was dreaming, right? Doc had given me some medication, and I was fucking out of my mind.

I had to be.

Right?

"Reid, oh God," I groaned as he sucked at the skin on the inside of my thigh.

I bucked against him, but he pulled away. "So impatient."

Baron's voice was hot and demanding. "Eyes on me, Angel."

"Huh?" I asked as I lobbed my gaze over to him.

"Eyes. On. Me," Baron growled as he stroked his thick dick.

I licked my lips while I watched him. I gasped and groaned as Reid sucked hickies onto my thighs. My arousal dripped down my ass crack. Reid's long, dexterous fingers slid up and down my legs, then ventured over my hips and pinned me to the bed.

"You roll, I'm done. Understood?" Reid asked.

Baron chuckled. "Now the game's gettin' good."

I tried to turn my head to look down at Reid, but Cash caught my face in his palms. He guided my stare back to Baron, whose grin had grown wild with lust.

"Please," I said breathlessly, "please just—"

Baron tilted his head. "Just what, gorgeous?"

My lower lip quivered. "I just wanna feel him."

"How badly?" Reid asked.

Baron nodded to Reid. "He asked you a question, gorgeous."

I kicked my leg when Reid sucked one of my pussy lips into his mouth. My back arched before Cash brought me back down to the bed. Baron growled as I heard his hand stroking his dick with his own precum. Reid teased me, dipping his tongue in between my folds before pulling back out and kissing all the way to my hipbone.

If they wanted me to beg, then so fucking be it.

"Please, Reid," I groaned as I tried bucking my hips beneath his hands, "I can't take it. I can't—I've waited so long. I—I-I-I—oh, god, please."

"Please...what?" Cash asked before he bent forward and kissed my forehead.

I closed my eyes as my body came alive. "Please, let me come. It's all I want."

"Good girl," Cash growled.

Reid unleashed. He didn't even trace my sopping wet entrance with his finger to prepare me. He simply sank it in as his tongue slipped between my folds. My walls fluttered around his intrusion. I felt my slick clinging to him as his tongue softly worked my swollen mound. My body locked out and relaxed. Locked out and relaxed. That burning coil behind my gut tightened, threatening to pull me over the edge. Reid crooked his finger as Cash's hands slid down to my tits, and yet again, Baron's voice came alive from that chair.

"Get those things out so I can see them. I've wanted to see them for a while now," he glowered.

Reid licked up my slit and latched his mouth onto my clit just as Cash leaned me up. The angle gave me the leverage I needed to buck against Reid's face, but the moment didn't last for long. The second he got that shirt over my head, my body settled back down into his lap. Back down into the position that left me helpless to Reid's assault.

My tits bounced as my body chased its high.

"Yes, yes, yes. Reid. Oh, fuck. Right there. Right there. Right there. Just like that. Just like that. Oh, God, I'm gonna come. I'm gonna come."

"Ask nicely," Reid taunted.

"Please, please, please, please," I whimpered as my face contorted with pleasure. "Please, let me come. Reid, oh, fuck."

"Baron?" Cash asked. "Should we give in?"

"Ah, let her have it," he said as the pumping of his hand stopped. "We can always give her another one."

"Wait, what?" I asked breathlessly.

With one last deep lick of his rigid tongue, Reid pulled me over the edge. My eyes rolled back. Stars burst in my vision as my entire body locked out. My pussy fluttered around his finger as he pumped me, sending wet sounds sloshing all around the room. Baron growled as he pumped his thick cock. Cash massaged my tits, praising my body and tugging at my nipples. And as the high swirled around my head, holding me hostage in my own reverie, I collapsed against the bed.

Before I heard the clanking of a belt buckle.

"Huh?" I grunted.

"Now," Reid growled as he shoved his pants down and pulled his dick out, "you need to stay still for this one, Angel."

I looked over at Baron, but he nodded his head back to Reid. "Go on, look at him. Look at what he's about to do to you."

And when I panned my gaze back to him, I found him not between my legs, but perched on his knees with his long, veiny cock standing at attention. My eyes widened as he picked up my ankles. Cash bent forward and kissed the top of my head as he continued to play with my nipples. I groaned as Reid reached down and grabbed the base of his cock, sliding his thick head up and down my slit.

Then, Baron gave the command. "Now."

Reid stuffed me full, and it took every ounce of Cash keeping me steady to keep me from arching my back. My jaw unhinged with silent pleasure as Reid grunted, sinking every inch of himself into me in one fell swoop. His hands yanked my ankles upward. He tossed my legs over his shoulders. And as I laid there, helpless against their bodies, he pulled his dick back out and slammed it in.

"Oh, fuck!" I cried out.

"That's it," Baron growled. "Again."

Reid did as the man asked, and it rolled my eyes into the back of my head. "Oh, holy fuck."

"Again."

Thrust.

"Again."

Thrust.

"Oh, my fuck," I whimpered.

Baron snarled. "Again, Reid, and don't you fucking stop until she's screaming your name."

"It'll be my pleasure," Reid glowered.

The pounding of his hips against my own silenced my sounds. My jaw unhinged, but nothing came out as his assault against my body continued. There was no pain. No pressure. No anger. Just pleasure, lust, and all of the things that had been building between us for oh so long.

I'd never felt more wanted in all my life.

Reid's words shoved me closer to the edge. "Oh, fuck yeah. You like that, beautiful? You like how I fill you up? Oh, I wish you could see yourself from my perspective. So sweaty and spread open for me. Searching for words and finding none. Speechless really is a good look on you."

My hands found the sheets of the bed and my fingers twisted into it. Baron grunted rhythmically to my left while Cash whispered sweet nothings in my ear from above. Reid's cock jumped against my walls, sending my voice back up into my throat where I finally found my words.

Words that cried out instead of whispered.

"Reid, please!"

"Come for us," Baron growled.

My body unleashed. My legs locked out over Reid's shoulders as my walls clamped down around him. I milked him for all he had as his hips stuttered, then stopped. He fell to his hands, his sweaty forehead dancing against mine as those wispy tendrils of dirty blonde that looked browner with his sweat clung to my skin. My hands moved away from the sheets. I wrapped them around his forearms, feeling his muscles shiver and pulse. Feeling them race with the blood pumping through his body as he filled me up to the brim.

Before my pussy pulsed so hard that it spat him back out.

"Holy fuck," I said breathlessly as Reid tumbled off to the side.

I turned my head at just the right time, because the moment I did, I watched Baron's legs sprawl out. I watched his head fall back. His entire body jumped as threads of white arousal shot from the tip of his cock. I was mesmerized at the sight. I watched as his wasted cum shot up into the air and came charging back down to the ground. I watched it, again and again, as he tugged at his heavy balls. As his legs quivered with the exertion it took to pump his massive cock against his palm.

And when he collapsed, I rolled my head back into Cash's lap and stared up at him.

"What about you?" I asked hoarsely.

He smiled as he stroked my lower lip with his thumb. "How are you feeling?"

I swallowed thickly. "Alive."

"Good," Reid said as his hand fell haphazardly against my bare thigh.

"Curl up those legs for me," Baron said.

I wasn't sure who he was talking to, but when I felt his presence at the foot of the bed, I realized he had been talking to me. Gone was his girth, stuffed back into his pants as I heard his zipper create a barrier between us. He crawled into bed, motioning something with his head before Cash moved as well. My head hit the pillows, but it didn't stay there for long. Because as Cash wiggled his way down my right side, with Reid laying at my left side, Baron was the one to pick my head up and place it back in his lap.

Where we proceeded to run his fingers mindlessly through my hair.

"Wow," I whispered.

"Feeling better?" Baron asked with a grin.

I rolled my eyes. "Shut up, you liked it, too."

"We all did," Cash said.

"Yeah," was all Reid could manage.

His tired voice gave me pride. "Guess I'm not the only one that's worn out."

A yawn peeled through my lips, and it prompted someone to pull the comforter over my exposed body. I wasn't sure who did it, and I honestly didn't even care. All I wanted to do was soak up every ounce of this moment with the three of them surrounding me. Because it was the safest I had felt in a really long time. They had taken care of me. Respected me. Forced me to do what I needed to do when my body didn't cooperate. And not once had they bitched. Not once had it ever occurred to them to not clean up the mess that had dropped into their lap. They took responsibility. They took ownership of the situation, despite the innocence they preached. An innocence I was beginning to believe. And not only did I want to help them, but I wanted to stick around with them.

Loneliness no longer suited me.

Not after the world these men had shown me while at their side.

"Reid?" I asked as I closed my eyes.

"Uh huh?" he asked as his fingertips drew mindless faces along my thigh underneath the covers.

"Where is that footage you were talking about a little while back?"

Cash barked with laughter as Baron snickered, but it was Reid that turned over onto his side and propped himself up with his hand.

"Seriously?" he asked.

I blinked. "What?"

He scoffed. "You want to watch that footage now?"

"Do you ever stop to breathe, woman?" Baron asked.

I giggled as I peeked up at him upside down. "For two weeks, I haven't been able to breathe. And now, I can again."

Baron tilted his head as he massaged my scalp. It felt so good that I groaned as my eyes fell closed again, and I knew the answer coming before Reid even parted his lips to speak.

"In the morning, with coffee involved, we can talk," he said as he patted my thigh.

"But for now," Cash said as he curled up against me, "you still need rest."

I shook my head. "If you guys have proof of anything, I need to check in with Dee again and—"

Baron pressed his hands against my shoulders when I tried sitting up. "Lay down and go to sleep, or I'll tie you down until you sleep."

Exhaustion clouded my mind. "That a promise?"

"Jesus," Cash said with a chuckle.

"Ready for a round two already? Because I am," Reid said.

"No," Baron said as he went back to massaging my scalp, "she still needs rest. And when she wakes up, whenever that is, we can talk over food and coffee. Right?"

I was so relaxed that I almost didn't hear him, and before I knew it, Baron's massive hands engulfed my head and nodded it up and down for his own enjoyment.

"Exactly," Baron said, "good girl."

Cash barked with laughter, and it pulled a giggle from my lips. But he wasn't wrong. Even with just that little bit, I was worn the fuck out.

"Okay, maybe just a nap," I said as another yawn peeled its way from the back of my throat.

"And then I promise we'll talk," Reid said as he removed his hand from my thigh, only to find mine and lace our fingers together beneath the covers.

Like our little secret.

"Okay," I whispered as I smiled tiredly at him.

Before darkness pulled me under with each stroke of Baron's hands against my scalp.

23

———

ANGEL

The chirping of birds outside pulled me awake, and when I saw the heat of the sun streaking through the windows of my bedroom, I knew that I had slept the entire day away. I groaned as I rolled over, fully expecting to see at least one of the guys staring back at me.

But I found myself alone in that massive, gaping bed.

"Well, can't have everything, I suppose," I whispered to myself.

I threw off the covers, but it took me a second to raise myself up. I didn't feel pain, really. But there was tightness. I moved gingerly as I took myself to the bathroom. As I cleaned myself up and splashed some water in my face to wake me up. And as I stared at my reflection with water dripping down my features, I drew in a deep breath.

"Today's the day you get back to work, girl. Make it count."

After waking myself up, I walked back out into the bedroom to find a set of clothes waiting for me. Had those been there before? I peeked over at the bedroom door and found it cracked open, and that made me smile. I walked over to the clothes laid out for me. My washed and dried jeans without a hint of blood anywhere on them. There was a new top, though, which didn't shock me. Mine had been pretty much ruined with the fucking bullet that I took. But the size alone told me it was another one of Baron's t-shirts.

Guess I know what he likes now.

I pulled on my clothes and made my way out into the hallway. I noticed that Hunter wasn't out there, like usual, and at first it gave me pause. Was something wrong? Did I need to stay in my room?

Then, laughter bellowed up from downstairs.

"Did you see the look on that asshole's face when you started running?"

"Play that back again. I wanna watch it."

"All right, all right, but only one more time. If we keep laughing, we'll wake up Angel."

I kept my footsteps silent and cleared the stairs without so much as a creak. I eased down the hallway, making my way to the kitchen as the smell of coffee and the laughter of men tugged me closer still. Silence filled the space as shadows hovered just around the corner. I heard someone sipping a drink before an explosion boomed somewhere, and the guys fell apart again.

"Holy fuck! His face!"

"I can't wait to show her this. She's gonna be impressed."

"It's not to impress her," Baron said gruffly, "it's to prove to her that we're not the shitheads she's chasing."

I took my cue and stepped into the kitchen. "Guess you'll have to let me be the judge of that."

All eyes quickly whipped to me as I leaned against the doorway leading into the kitchen. My stomach growled, but I ignored it. My throat ached for coffee, but I stuffed the need down. The guys all looked at me and back at one another, all of them trying to figure out how to react.

But it was Reid who stood. "We didn't know you were awake."

I nodded. "I figured, judging by the laughter."

"Did we wake you up?" Cash asked.

I shook my head. "Nah. I didn't even hear the laughter until I got out into the hallway."

Baron nodded to an empty seat next to him. "Wanna come take a look?"

Cash stood to his feet. "I'll get her some coffee."

"You hungry?" Reid asked.

"Good to see you on your feet without help," Hunter said.

I smiled at him as I passed by, taking up residence next to Baron. "Good to be up on my feet without help."

"Here, fucking here," one of the guys whose name I didn't know yet said as he lifted his coffee mug into the air.

"Here, fucking here," the rest of the guys said before joining them.

And after they all took their long pulls from their mugs, Cash slipped a mug in front of me. "I hope cream and sugar's all right."

I smiled up at him. "It's great, thank you."

I took a generous gulp of the hot liquid before I growled softly as it worked its way down my throat. I shook my head, stomaching the burn as I went in for another sip. Dear God, I had missed coffee. The way it flushed energy through my veins. The way it brought me back to life every single morning.

I didn't realize I had finished the whole damn thing until I came up for air with my throat begging for a break.

"I'll...get you another one," Cash said as he plucked the mug from my hands.

I snickered. "Sorry."

"Hey, don't be sorry," Reid said with a shake of his head. "It's just good to see you up and about."

"You ready?" Baron asked as he handed me his phone.

I looked down at the paused video with a clear shot of the docks I had become all too familiar with in my research and studying of this place. I took the phone from him and tilted my head, hovering my thumb over the play button. I wasn't sure why I was so hesitant to press play; this was it. Supposedly, this was the proof I needed to point me in the right direction for my case. And if it was good enough, it might be footage I could even send back to Cap and Dee so that I could get outfitted with a team that could actually do something about the problem instead of babysitting me.

Because I knew that was what they had been doing. That was why they had bucked up against my orders. Why Dee always felt the need to talk over me. I had tasked them with a job, but my boss had probably tasked them with watching over me to make sure I didn't do anything stupid.

After all, being in bed for two weeks did give one time to think.

"You okay?" Cash asked as he sat my second mug of coffee on the table in front of me.

I drew in a deep breath and shook my head softly. "All right, Reid. You told me two weeks ago that you had this footage. That you guys could use my help. That this was proof that you guys weren't peddling the drugs that I thought you were."

The guys all looked around at one another as Reid stared me down. "Yes."

"And according to you, this is supposed to convince me to help you guys."

He nodded. "Yes. That's proof of who's really bringing those drugs into town. We've got footage of them unloading it at the docks. Proof—that's what you're holding. So, whenever you're ready."

Proof.

That one word sent my body into another shivering frenzy. Excitement coursed its way through my veins. My God, if they had found concrete proof of any of this, I didn't care about what it meant. I didn't care that it meant that they were right, and I was wrong. I didn't care that it meant that I had been chasing the wrong crew this entire time. I didn't care that it meant that I had been looking into the wrong people. I'd struggled to get proof to take to Cap ever since JonJon died. Ever since I knew there was a case that needed to be worked. And as all eyes were on me, that first mug of coffee rushed right through my system.

Jesus, I needed to pee.

I handed the phone back to Baron. "I'll be right back."

When I stood, everyone else stood with me. Including Baron. "You okay?"

I sighed heavily. "I have to pee, apparently. But I also just need a second to absorb all of this."

"Isn't this what you wanted?" Reid asked.

I looked up at Cash because I knew he'd understand. "This just changes everything, you know? I need to be prepared for that if you guys have what I think you do."

Cash nodded as his eyes filled with understanding. "Well, we do. So, take the time you need, okay?"

I pushed through the throng of men, making my way back to the stairs. "Reid, do me a favor and get it set up on a television or something, yeah? A bigger screen, so I can watch it as many times as I need to in order to take it all in. I need to go to the bathroom, but I promise it won't take me long."

"You got it," Reid said.

I rushed up the stairs as I tried to come to terms with what was happening. The night before bombarded my brain, swirling my thoughts with so many things that I didn't need to be thinking. Yes, they had taken care of me. Yes, in more ways than one. And yes, it was marvelous. But I was a federal officer and they were gray-area criminals, at best. There was no way in hell this was going to be anything other than what it was. Because if I found any shred of proof in that video that any of them had anything to do with any of this, I'd cuff them where they stood in their own fucking clubhouse. Because my loyalty would always lie with my brother. With my job. With the fire in my gut that told me that terrible people deserved terrible fates for hurting those around him.

Like my brother.

Who deserved justice.

I whistled to myself as I made my way into the bedroom. God, I felt great. Running up the stairs didn't hurt. Bending over the sink and splashing some water in my face didn't hurt. Even turning my back to crack it didn't hurt! I felt on top of the world. Sure, I wasn't one hundred percent. But I was a decent seventy, which was all I needed to help me focus.

Until a sound caught my ear. "I hear you this time, Reid. You stepped on that floorboard."

Silence echoed back at me.

"Reid?" I called out. "Is that you?"

A shadow moved just beyond the crook of the bathroom door, and I smiled. "All right, Baron. I know that you loom when you're protective, but you've gotta give a girl her privacy. I got up those stairs just fine."

The shadow stopped, and no voice returned back to me.

"Cash?"

Suddenly, the door ripped the rest of the way open. The shadow gave way to a tall, imposing figure whose face I immediately recognized.

"Scarface," I whispered.

That fucking bastard was in the clubhouse, in my fucking bedroom.

In a black leather jacket.

"BAROOOOON!" I roared as I leapt toward the only weapon I could peg in the moment, which was the stainless steel removable showerhead.

"Oh, no you don't," Scarface glowered.

"REID!" I yelped as he tried cornering me in the shower.

"Come here, bitch," he growled.

"Over my dead fucking body," I hissed.

I slung that fucking showerhead as hard as I could at that motherfucker's dome. I clocked him right in the temple, sending him stumbling backwards against the bathroom counter. It gave me just enough room to race out into the bedroom. And as I dove for the brass candlestick on my bedside table, I whipped around to find Scarface coming out of the bathroom. With his hand on his hip.

And instinct took over.

I leapt over the bed and grabbed the other candlestick off the opposing bedside table and threw it at that motherfucker's large ass forehead. It clinked against his face, and he groaned as he released the butt of his gun. I moved as quickly as I could, which wasn't fast, but faster than I had been. I grasped my bullet wound with one hand, trying to make sure I didn't do anything to bust that goddamn scab open while I wielded the other candlestick in my hand.

I had to get to that man's gun before he had a chance to draw it.

"CAAAAAAAAAAAAAAAASH!" I cried out. "Where the hell are you guys?!"

"You're mine, you little bitch," Scarface hissed.

"Ruuuuuuuun!" Baron roared over the cacophony unfolding. "Run, Angel, and don't look back! We'll find you!"

I should have known that my efforts would have been futile, however. Scarface reached for his gun again and I threw the other candlestick at his head, aiming straight for his forehead. If I could bust the skin, he'd bleed enough to cover his eyesight so that I could get out. But I didn't have a snowball's chance in hell of taking him head-on. Especially when I wasn't at full capacity with my body. Reid cried out for me. Cash bellowed over the noise. The sound of Baron roaring for me to run echoed off the corners of my brain as I watched Scarface cover his forehead with his hands as blood seeped through the slats of his fingers.

And in an instant, I allowed my instincts to run away from me. I lunged for that man's side, felt the cold hardened metal of his gun against my palm, and ripped it out of its holster. I needed a weapon with me to get out of this situation. I wasn't going to be caught without one like last time.

Until something came down against the nape of my neck.

"Oh, no you don't," a voice grunted.

Out of nowhere, my body slammed against the floor and was quickly flipped over. Pain streaked through my body, robbing me of a voice to cry out with. The man in the black leather jacket straddled me as he smiled down with his two golden front teeth. He stood there, with his feet on either side of my body, staring down at me from his perched position. Somehow, in all of the movement, he had wrestled the gun out of my hands. And as he held it at my head, he cocked the plunger back, aimed and ready to fire.

"Hell no. Not like this," I grunted.

I moved my hand as quickly as I could. I tangled my legs with his and tripped him up, taking him to the ground as I reached toward the back of his gun. I managed to find the button to pop the magazine out and tried to push the plunger forward, but before I could, a gunshot rang out. A gunshot so big and so bright that it rang my ears and shook my brain in my skull.

"ANGEEEEL!" Reid bellowed.

"Lights out for you," Scarface whispered against my ear before the barrel of his gun slammed against my temple.

Knocking me out cold.

24

───

REID

"BAROOOOOOOOOOOON!"

"What the fuck?" Baron glowered.

As if her scream was their entrance cue, the doors of our clubhouse blew wide the fuck open. Glass shattered, boots scurried along the floor, and within seconds, we were overwhelmed.

"Oh, no you don't," I growled as I pulled my gun off my hip.

"REID!" Angel yelped over our heads.

"Cash! Reid!" Baron yelled as our men started fighting off fuckers left and right. "Get to Angel! Now!"

I watched Baron reach for the phone that had the footage on it, but a bullet flew out of nowhere. I plugged the man on top of me with three bullets to the gut, then rolled him over so that his blood slicked the floor. I watched in horror as two bullets landed directly against Baron's phone, shattering it to bits.

Rendering it completely useless.

"No!" I exclaimed as I scrambled to get to my feet.

"Get to her now!" Baron exclaimed as he shoved me.

I used the blood to slide toward Cash and grabbed his arm. I yanked him out of the firefight, dipping us down as he slid with me. Bullets whizzed by our ears, barely missing our fucking skulls. And as we both made our way into the dining room, getting tripped up by the carpet, we whipped around and aimed down the sights of our guns.

Before I heard her again.

"CAAAAAAAAAAAASH! Where the hell are you guys?!"

"Not so fast," someone glowered behind us.

I whipped around like lightning and struck the man's gun out of his hand. Cash tackled him to the ground as I holstered my gun and trained the sunburned man's weapon against him.

"Too much sun this summer?" I asked.

The man gnashed his teeth together and I did the only thing that I knew to do. The second he tried shoving Cash off him, I put a bullet right between his fucking eyes.

Before skittering bootsteps rushed toward the stairs.

"Ruuuuuuun!" Baron bellowed from the kitchen. "Run, Angel, and don't look back! We'll find you!"

"We need more fire power," Cash said as he leapt up and grabbed my wrist. "Come on."

I pivoted on my feet and held my gun out as we moved from corner to corner. I wanted to get to Angel. I had to get to her. But we didn't stand a fucking chance with the men that poured through every orifice in our fucking clubhouse. Goddamn it, I should've left Angel with a fucking gun. It wasn't like she wasn't trained. She was a fucking federal goddamn agent, for crying out loud!

And if something happened to her again, I'd never forgive myself.

Cash and I turned down the hallway leading straight for the utility closet, but we ran over someone in the process. Holy fucking hell, how many men had gotten into the clubhouse? I flipped head over heels, landing on my back and staring up at the ceiling. Boots scrambled against the freshly waxed floors. I rolled over and shoved myself upright, jumping to my feet as the man in front of me pulled his gun off his hip with Cash pinned beneath him.

I was quicker than any of these fuckers, though. And a split second was all I needed to pull my mind away from Angel so that I could focus on getting my brothers out of this fucking mess. We had sat for too long. We had become sitting ducks while taking care of Angel, and this was our price.

This was our penance for thinking we could have more than we already did.

And before I knew it, while completely lost in thought, the man was bleeding from his chest as he sank to his knees.

"You good?" I asked as I walked over and held my hand out to Cash.

Gunshots rang out down the hallway as he clapped his hand against mine and heaved himself upright.

"Angel!" he roared as he stood to his feet. "Talk to us, girl!"

But there was nothing except fighting. Men growling. Bullets flying. Boots scuffing against the freshly-waxed floors.

"You, to the utility closet. We need to be armed up. I'm going upstairs to look for Angel," I said as I patted his shoulder.

"Then, take this to her," Cash said as he slid his gun into my other hand.

I shook my head. "No, you need—"

He grabbed my shoulders. "The utility closet is just down there. Now, go. Get her a fucking weapon and let her help us the way you know we need."

And he sure as fuck didn't have to tell me twice.

Down the hallway and up the stairs I went, closing the distance between my body and hers. If something had happened to her, they might as well throw me in her coffin and bury me alive. My feet scrambled against the carpet. Sweat permeated my brow as my stomach turned itself into knots. And seeing her bedroom door open did nothing for my worries.

Fucking hell, had someone gotten into her goddamn room?

I'm putting a fucking deadbolt on the inside of that fucking door.

"Angel!" I exclaimed as I skidded to a stop in the doorway.

"Huh?" a man covered with facial scars asked as he peered over his shoulder at me.

"Well," I said as I took stock of the scene; of Angel, lying there unconscious, and that man hovering over her with his gun taking aim, "at least I already have my weapon drawn."

I pulled the trigger, but the fucker was too quick and darted down the hallway. I was ready to chase after him but then my eyes caught Angel's unwavering form on the floor.

I crouched down and reached my hand out toward her neck. "Please be alive. Please be alive. Please be alive."

Feeling her pulse beating against my skin rushed relief through my system. So much relief, in fact, that I felt damn near nauseous from the dizziness of it. But it was soft. Thready. And I had been around Doc long enough to know that wasn't ever good. So, after clearing the rest of her room and realizing it was just her and I in there, I moved back out into the hallway and put on my best Baron impression.

"Kill that motherfucking woman when you find her!"

I glanced back at Angel still lying there helpless on the floor as footsteps fell hard against the stairs. So, that was their plan. Kill the DEA agent still in our possession and make it look like we killed her. I had to admit, it was efficient. And more than likely to do the job. Which was why I had to get Angel out of there. She needed a hospital, for crying out loud.

So, with my weapon in one hand, ready to fire in an instant, I reached for her with my free one and did my best to pick her up off the ground.

"Okay, come on," I grunted as I grabbed her wrist. "God, please don't get rug burn."

I slid her body, coated in blood, across the carpeted floor. The footsteps came closer, picking up in speed as voices I didn't recognize barked orders at one another. Not very efficient or stealthy, if anyone asked me about it. Pathetic, really. Cash would've had a damn field day taking those assholes out. They practically announced where they were! And yet, that didn't stop me from hiding Angel on the other side of the bed before I aimed my weapon over the edge of the mattress.

"She's in here," someone whispered beyond the door.

But when they inched it open, all they had was me staring back at them with a smile on my face.

"Sure about that?" I asked.

POP! POP!

Two bullets, two men, two more bodies racing one another to the ground. I watched them crumble into a pile of lifeless limbs as Angel laid there at my feet, still out cold. And where the hell was everyone? Why the hell were we being outnumbered in the fucking blitz attack?

Then, it dawned on me.

Patrols. You sent them out on patrols.

"Someone else is watching us," I muttered as I ripped my cell phone out of my pocket.

My fingers flew across the screen as I held my gun toward the doorway. If anyone I didn't recognize walked through that door before I got Angel out of there, they'd answer to the bullet in my gun's chamber. I sent out a crew-wide emergency text. One that I knew would get their attention. I tacked on the code at the end of the message that forced everyone's phone to make a sound, even if they had it on silent—courtesy of our prospect, Razor.

Then, I shot the text off and shoved my phone back into my pocket.

Me: All hands on deck at the clubhouse. We're under attack. Angel is out cold.

For the first time since I had pledged my loyalty to The Death Cheaters, I didn't know what to do. I was only one man, and I had a woman that needed more medical care than Doc would ever be able to give her in our place. Silence fell around us, hovering in the corners and lurking in the shadows that filled the darkness.

I had to abandon ship.

I had to get Angel to a hospital.

"All right," I grunted as I reached down for her body, "this isn't gonna be fun, Angel. But it'll do the job. Hang on, okay?"

I knew I had no right to be upset with my men. After all, even if they had been given orders, we sent the bulk of them out on patrol runs to help cover our asses from an attack. It wasn't like business completely stopped just because we were looking after Angel. We knew the liability she had become. We knew she'd be a target. So, we did what we do best: we prepared ourselves as best as we could while she recuperated.

Lot of good that fucking did us.

I situated Angel's body across my shoulder and silenced my footsteps, taking into account the lessons Cash had given all of us in keeping ourselves stealthy under pressure. I regulated my breathing. In through my nose, out through my mouth. I clung to Angel's form, taking great care to keep her body as still as possible. Her gaping head wound dripped blood down my back. For all I knew, she had a concussion. For all I knew, she had ripped that scab of hers wide open. She made no sound as I eased down the hallway, which only added to my worry that she was slipping further away from us.

"Just hold on, beautiful," I whispered.

I kept my head on a swivel as I listened out for any sounds that meant danger. Any sign that someone was lying in wait for us. At this point, I couldn't underestimate The Black Diamonds. I had to assume they were capable of anything and everything. They weren't the pathetic, idiotic crew that they had been years back when all of this started. No, they had become more organized. More ruthless. Hungrier for blood than I'd ever seen them. And when I came across one of our empty utility closets down one of the back hallways, I damn near pissed myself with relief.

"You'll be safe in here," I muttered as I swung the door open.

I took great care in placing Angel's body against the furthest wall. Even with the door slung wide open, the shadows cloaked her, which was what I needed. I peeked down at her shirt and felt a modicum of relief when I didn't see blood seeping through her shirt. But the blood trickling down her face warned me of a concussion.

"I'm coming back for you. I promise," I said.

Then I took a chance and placed a kiss against her cold, clammy cheek.

Before I locked the door from the inside and closed it behind me.

Then, I heard Baron's voice ignite. "Reid! You in here?!"

POP POP!

THUMP!

THWAK!

RATTATTATTATTA!

"REID?!" Baron bellowed.

I sprinted toward the sound of his voice. "I'm here! I'm fine! Where are you?!"

POP! "The fuck is going on?!"

Someone charged me from the left and I pivoted. I aimed my gun at the spindly man's chest, but my bloodlust got the better of me. The barrel of my gun dropped, aimed right for his knees as I took them out, one by one. He cried out in pain as he stumbled to the floor, his legs immobile as he grasped his knees and cried like a child wanting his mother.

I couldn't wait to torture that bastard for information.

It had been a while since I'd been allowed to flex those particular muscles.

Bikes roared and kicked up dust that filtered their way through any cracked orifice in the house. Baron continued to bark orders as gravel spewed everywhere outside. The rocks knocked against the windows and clamored for the porch, stacking themselves in little piles, ready to be swept back off and into position. Crimson leather jackets fluttered around corners, carrying with it men who were tired, hungry, and worn down. Dust clung to the air, making it hard to breathe. The smell of gunpowder filled my nostrils, choking off my ability to breathe. I didn't let that stop me, though.

I didn't let it stop me from mowing down every single black jacketed motherfucker that got in my way.

"Where is she?"

I heard his voice before I felt the force of his strength ripping me toward him. Cash yanked my arm, pulling me so fucking close that I couldn't pivot my eyes enough to see the entirety of his face.

"You gonna kiss me or something?" I asked with a grin.

Cash's eyes ignited with anger. "Where. Is she?"

"Answer him," Baron said as he came up behind me.

I shoved Cash off me and pointed my gun at a moving shadow behind him. "Don't move."

Cash girded himself. "Ready when you are."

I rested the barrel of my gun against his shoulder, steadying the metal even as my hand shook. We were fucked. If they were ambushing us, then we were royally and totally fucked.

"What are the chances they saw us at the dock?" I asked.

"Just shoot the fucker, Reid," Baron muttered.

With one pull of my trigger, my magazine emptied itself. And with it, the last of the Black Diamonds that had infiltrated the house lost his life. His blood trickled against the sparkling floors of the clubhouse as bikes raced around outside. Gravel knocked against the windows once more. Dust flew through the wide-open front door as my gaze lifted to take in the sight. The air smelled of blood and sweat. The sound of their retreating bikes was accompanied only by the sound of ours pursuing them.

"Slaughter every one of them that you get your hands on," Baron growled behind me.

Then, he grabbed my shoulder and turned me around.

"Where is she, Reid?"

I swallowed hard before I found my voice. "The empty tac closet upstairs. I locked the door from the inside before I put her in there."

"Good on you," Cash said as he whipped around and sprinted up the steps.

As Baron followed quickly in the man's footsteps, I stood there in the middle of the staircase, barely able to breathe. I slowly turned around, taking in the scourge of the waste around me. What the hell had just happened? The Black Diamonds had never attacked us before like that. Not so tactfully. Not so... personally.

It was as if they—

A distraction.

"Oh, my fucking God," I whispered to myself. "Baron! Cash!"

"What?!" they called out in unison.

I raced up the steps and found that Baron had already gotten Angel out of the closet. "A distraction."

"You're gonna have to be more specific than that," he said as he hoisted Angel over his shoulder.

"Is she awake yet?" I asked.

Cash blinked. "How long has she been out?"

I scoffed. "Does the gaping gash on her forehead not answer that question for you?"

"Reid!" Baron barked.

I shook my head quickly. "This was the distraction. Not the first time they rolled up; that was a warning. This was the distraction."

"Distraction *and* eradication?" Cash asked.

"That's pretty ballsy," Baron said as he walked by me, "even for them."

"So is pinning the murder of a DEA agent on us," I said as I pivoted with him to keep him in view. "But that didn't stop them from coming in here and making that their sole purpose."

Baron froze. "They what?"

"And you're sure about that?" Cash asked.

I glowered at Cash. "I walked in and found a man standing over her about to kill her. Are you gonna tell me that's not their plan?"

Cash's face reddened. "Tell me you plugged that motherfucker."

"Of course, I did! But I know without a shadow of a doubt that their goal today was to kill her, not us. We were just in the way when they stormed this place."

Cash vibrated with fury as we both turned to our president.

"So," Baron said before he drew in a deep breath, "pinning the drugs on us isn't going well, which means Plan B is pinning her murder on us."

"It's efficient," Cash said flatly.

"Exactly what I thought," I muttered beneath my breath.

Baron turned back toward the front door. "Which is why we need to get her to a hospital. She's no longer safe with us. Reid?"

"Yeah?"

"Call the guys."

I rolled my tongue up to the roof of my mouth and let out an ear-piercing whistle, ending with our men gathered in the foyer, stacked together like fucking sardines. And as Cash and Baron came down the stairs, Angel's unconscious body was dangled over his shoulder.

"All right, men, listen up!" Baron said as he continued to keep Angel's body still. "It's showtime. I need two groups of men on patrol, one immediately around here and one at the docks. Reid?"

"Yep?"

"What dock did you find them offloading shit at?"

I thumbed over my shoulder. "The one that's about ten or so miles to the south."

"Perfect," Baron said. "I need a group of men going in that direction toward the docks. I need as many cases of those drugs as we can steal."

"You what?" Cash asked.

"What for, Bossman?" Bic asked.

And that was when the feral look on Baron's face morphed into a grin that would have made any grown man nauseous.

"We're going to take a case of those drugs and place them right on the town's doorstep."

"What about her?" Pitchfork asked, pointing to Angel.

Still silent. Still hanging there. Still bleeding.

All the way down the back of Baron's jeans.

"She's coming with me," Cash said as he took Angel off Baron's shoulder and cradled her in her arms.

"Come on," I said as I held the front door open for him, "let's get her to a hospital."

And I sure as hell didn't wait for any of their reactions as I ushered them through, stepped outside, and closed the door behind me.

Angel had to pull through.

Otherwise, I wasn't going to be held responsible for what happened next.

25

CASH

I charged through the emergency room doors with Reid cradling Angel just behind me as we headed straight for the nursing desk. "Ma'am?"

The woman held up a finger at me as she talked away on the phone. "Yeah! That's what I told him!"

"Ma'am?"

She waggled her finger at me like I was a fucking two-year-old. "He did not. You've gotta be kidding me."

I didn't have the patience to wear down. "Nurse!"

She jumped at the sound of my voice. "Hold on a second, Linda."

The look she shot me would have gotten anyone else on any other given day strangled.

"Yes?" she asked curtly.

"Is there a doctor—"

"Cash?"

I spun around at the sound of Doc's voice. "Tell me you're on duty right now."

He walked up to me, took my arm, and pulled me off to the side. "What the hell did I tell you guys about coming to see me at the hospital? We have an emergency number for this exact reason."

I shook my head. "It's...a bit more complicated than that."

"Oh, my God," he murmured when Reid walked up with Angel in his arms. "What the hell happened?"

"She's been knocked unconscious, and her pulse is thready, at best."

"Nurse!" Doc barked. "I need a bed, a staff, and a possible O.R.!"

The nurse behind the desk flew from out of her seat as I stood there, watching the chaos unfold. Reid slipped Angel onto the hospital bed, but even I had underestimated how badly she had been hurt. Her skin had grown pale. Damn near translucent, with all of the blood she had lost. Blood that now stained not only her face and her neck, but also the torso of her shirt. Oh, no. No, no, no. We busted her wound open. Her eyelids didn't move. Didn't waver. Didn't crack open once. Those beautiful cocoa-colored eyes of hers, hidden away from a world she had no business being wrapped up with in the first place.

I'd never forgive myself if she didn't pull through.

"What happened?" Doc asked.

I shook my head. "Reid was the one that was there, but according to him, someone clocked her with the butt of a gun and knocked her out cold."

Doc shoved her shirt up and clocked the bleeding of her torso. "Shit."

Then, he grabbed my leather jacket and forced me to walk beside him as he jogged down the hallway with Reid on his other side. "Do you know how long she's been out?"

"No," we answered in unison

"Reid, does she have any medication allergies?"

"I don't know."

"Cash, has she ever had a concussion?"

"I don't know."

"Reid?"

"What?"

"Has she taken any of her pain medication today?"

"I-I-I—don't know."

"Cash?"

"Yeah, Doc?"

"Is there anything you guys *do* know?"

I pinned Doc with a look as a set of metal double doors eased open. "I know that she can't die. She's too precious for that."

He nodded. "We'll do our best."

"Dr. Henderson?"

Doc backed away from me and kept moving with the hospital bed. "Talk to me, Nurse Holliday."

"O.R. 2 is prepped and read—"

Baron stormed up. "Why hasn't she woken up yet, Doc? Why is it taking so long?"

Reid cleared his throat. "Will she wake up, Doc? Do we even know?"

"Shut the hell up with that shit," Baron hissed.

But Doc simply held up his hands as his nursing staff disappeared with Angel on that gurney while I stood there, shaking with fury.

"We have to get her stable and situated. Once we do, she can have visitors, and I'll have more answers than I've got right now."

Reid leaned against the painted cinderblock wall beside us. "Give it to us straight, then, how bad is this?"

For whatever reason, Doc looked at me when he answered. "She's lucky to be alive, judging by the amount of blood she's lost. We have to check and see how much head and neck damage that wound has caused. I'd bet my life on the fact that she's got a concuss—"

Baron held up his hand, thank fuck. "Do what you need to do and bill us what her insurance won't cover. We've got work to do."

Doc nodded. "I'll keep you guys updated. But—"

I snarled. "But what?"

Doc sighed as he shook his head. "Guys, I know a field agent when I see one. And if we discover that she is one? We'll have to contact her boss."

Baron and Reid looked over their shoulders at me, but I simply shrugged. What the fuck were we gonna do? Keep all this shit down on the low? I shrugged before I turned away from where they were taking Angel. Away from the woman that had cracked my sternum open and crawled inside, just so she could touch my heart. There was nothing more that we could do for her, and we had plenty to do back at the clubhouse.

War was coming.

And it would sink all of us if we didn't do something soon.

"Cash? You good?" Baron asked.

The smell of blood lingered heavily beneath my nostrils. "Yeah, yeah. I'm fine."

Reid placed his hand on my shoulder. "You don't look so good."

"Rockyyyyyy!"

"I'm fine," I said as I slid my hands down my face.

So much blood. There's so much blood. How do I get this blood back into Rocky?

"Cash? You need a minute?" Baron asked.

"Let's get him some water," Reid said.

"There's a chair over here; let's get him sitting down."

"Has he eaten today?"

"My blood is on your hands," Rocky said as I looked at my palms.

His blood dripped down my forearms as I knelt there, listening to him struggling to breathe. Listening to him begging for his life.

"I don't wanna die, Daddy. Help me."

"I've got you, sweet boy," I whispered as I scooped him into my arms, *"Daddy's right here."*

"Cash," Baron said as he tapped my cheek.

That snapped me out of it, and I jumped to my feet.

"Whoa, take it easy," Reid said as he held out his hands.

"Water?" one of the nurses asked as she held out a cup of water for me.

I searched all around for any sign of Doc. For any sign of Angel, really. To hear her voice one last time. To feel her touch one last time. Hell, to dip her to the floor and kiss the very life out of her, because surely that was a better way to die than this.

Than to die in a hospital surrounded by no one.

"You okay?" Reid asked.

I slowly turned my gaze to meet his stare. "Let's go. We've got bodies to drop."

"What?" the nurse asked.

"Delivery men," Baron said as he linked his arm with mine and glared down at me, "they really are a different breed. Come on, Cash. Let's go drop those *packages* off."

"Yeah," I said as I turned around and moved away from him, "packages."

The three of us charged through the hospital, making our way back toward the van, crawling into the back of that thing with Angel's blood still staining the floor made my stomach churn. But we couldn't focus on that. She was in the best place possible for someone in her predicament, and it was officially out of our hands.

But if they let her die, I'd kill every single person who wasn't capable of saving her life.

"So, what's next?" I asked.

Reid quirked an eyebrow. "You sure you're good to do this?"

"He's fine," Baron said. "Here's the plan: the three of us are heading to the docks. Bic and Pyre are already there scouting things out. They just messaged and said that a few of those crates are stacked in the northwestern warehouse by the junkyard, so it'll be easy enough to navigate in there without being seen."

"So, we're stealing the drugs we're not peddling?" I asked.

Reid snickered. "We're taking a crate or two and dumping that shit in Myrtle Beach's jurisdiction."

I blinked. "That's fucking brilliant."

"Kill anything that moves," Baron glowered. "But we aren't leaving without at least one of those fucking crates."

"You know what would make this even better?" I asked.

Reid couldn't help the grin that crossed his face. "If we left the cameras full of documentation along with the crates?"

I leaned against the wall of the van and closed my eyes. "Time to give those motherfuckers a taste of their own medicine."

"Hell yeah," Reid said.

"All right, now shut up so I can navigate this shit," Baron said as he eased us onto the highway, heading southward, straight for the docks.

26

BARON

Even with the open road in front of me—even with the promise of blood, death, and vengeance—I couldn't focus. My mind was elsewhere. It was back at the hospital, standing right outside that fucking O.R. while Doc and the hospital staff worked on Angel.

I wondered how alone she felt.

I wondered if she was in any pain.

I wondered if she was still alive.

First, a gunshot wound, and now a head wound? Death wasn't good enough for those motherfuckers. They touched what was mine. They hurt what was mine. And there was no place on the planet they'd be able to run where I wouldn't track their asses down in a heartbeat.

If Angel died, I'd spend my entire life making sure to ruin theirs. One by one.

Focus. Your lives depend on it.

"We're here," I said as I pulled off the road about half a mile away from the docks.

"We hiking the rest of the way?" Cash asked.

"Can't really go in making a fuckton of noise, now can we?"

"Especially since it's the middle of the night," Reid said.

I parked the van beneath the shade of a tree, right behind a massive red berry bush. I cut the engine and slid the keys out of the ignition, watching through the windshield as I peered out toward the dock. A pair of binoculars eased over my shoulder, and I quickly held them up to my face. Night had fallen heavily over Barbeau. Ocean waves lapped the shoreline, bobbing and weaving the few boats that were docked at the edge of the sea. I scanned the horizon, clocking anyone on the dock that may have looked suspicious. But there was hardly a soul around. There were barely any lights on in the warehouse we needed to scour. The guard hut boasted of one fat ass with his belt unbuckled as he shoveled ice cream into his face. And as I settled the binoculars into my lap, a smirk crossed my face.

"Piece of cake," I muttered as I unbuckled my seatbelt.

Until a motorcycle inched by the other side of the bush.

"Keep quiet," Cash whispered.

I ripped those binoculars back up to my face and saw none other than Jagger himself scooting by on his chromed-out motorcycle. The engine sputtered and roared, as if the fucking thing hadn't been cranked in years. I watched Jagger ease up to the front gate. He didn't even swipe a card before the gate opened for him. I panned the binoculars back to the guard hut, where the Ice Cream Monster seemed to smile and laugh as he held his hand up in the air.

Jagger eased by him, giving that fucker a high-five, and I wondered if he knew.

I wondered if he knew who had just touched him.

"Is that who I think it is?" Reid asked as he poked his head over my shoulder.

"Yep," I said, handing him the binoculars.

He held them up to his face before he scoffed. "I can't wait to hang those fucking lips of his on my wall."

I couldn't help but chuckle. "Let's go over the plan one more time."

Cash cleared his throat. "We're gonna sneak into that warehouse and come out with at least a crate each."

"Then what?" I asked.

"We're taking those crates into Myrtle Beach jurisdiction."

"Then what?" I asked.

"We're dropping them off at police headquarters in North Myrtle, along with the cameras, and booking it the fuck out of there," Cash said.

I turned myself around, popping my back in the process. "If anyone gets in your way—"

"We know, we know," Cash said as he waved his hand in the air. "Kill them."

"But quietly," Reid said.

I nodded. "No gunshots. No beating those fucker's faces in. Swift, quick, and efficient. We take them down with their own game so as to not draw attention to ourselves."

"You sure we don't need any sort of backup?" Cash asked.

I turned back toward the windshield. "We can't risk it with a last-minute plan. This has to work, and it has to work quickly. That means it's the three of us tonight, and no one else."

The van fell silent, and my thoughts were, once again, filled with Angel. God, that fucking hair of hers. I still felt its softness playing against the palm of my hand. I licked my lips, tasting her tangy nature on the tip of my tongue. How scared she must have been when we had left her in that room. I shook my head. Fucking hell, if that woman didn't pull through this—

I shook my head. I had to focus. We had to clean up one mess at a time. Once we put a bullet in the Black Diamonds for good, we could turn our attention back to her. Back to the strong, stubborn, valiant woman that had captured all three of us.

Until a ship horn damn near made me jump out of my fucking skin.

"You've gotta be kidding me," Reid murmured.

"Are they expecting another shipment tonight?" Cash asked.

I placed the binoculars before my eyes and saw Jagger swaggering down the dock where the boat was about to park.

"Looks like it," I said and handed the binoculars off to Reid.

"Well, at least we won't have to infiltrate the warehouse," Cash said.

"Jesus Christ, how many of them are there?" Reid asked.

I shrugged. "You're the one with the binoculars."

"You sure this is a good night for this?" Reid asked.

"Give me those," Cash hissed as he ripped the binoculars out of Reid's hand.

"We wait until they're done and they clear out," I said, folding my arms across my chest. "Then, we make our move."

"I'll keep a clock on where they take those crates," Cash said.

Reid snatched the binoculars back. "We both can."

I rolled my eyes. "Simmer down, kids, Daddy's tired. Now, let me have another look."

I got my hands on those binoculars again and, sure enough, those black jacketed assholes were unloading wooden crates stamped with that sun and moon logo on just about every side of the crate. They were tossed around like firewood, stacked on top of one another haphazardly like toddlers playing with fucking Legos. The more they unloaded, the more my jaw dropped open. How much of that drug did they need for our sleepy little oceanside town?

"Oh. My. God," I muttered.

"What?" Cash and Reid asked in unison.

The binoculars slowly slipped from my face. "They aren't just trying to move into our territory."

"What?" they said again in unison.

I handed the binoculars back to Reid. "Count those crates. How many do you see?"

He wasted no time in taking them and doing as I asked. "Jesus, there's at least fourteen of them."

"Let me see," Cash said as he yanked them from Reid's hands.

"Since when do you need fourteen crates of shit on top of the shit we've already seen them with just for a town that's got a few thousand people in it?" I asked.

"God damn," Cash murmured.

"You don't think...?" Reid asked.

I nodded slowly. "I don't think they're just trying to move into town."

"They're trying to distribute across the state," Cash said.

"Which means they're trying to make Barbeau their shipping home base," Reid said.

I unbuckled my seatbelt. "Come on, let's go."

"Now?!" Reid asked. "But they're still out there unloading—"

I threw open the van door. "Cash, you coming?"

"Hell yeah," he said as he threw open the back van doors.

"Baron," Reid said as he grabbed onto my leather jacket.

I peered over my shoulder. "These crates won't be any easier to snatch than right now. They're out in the open and everything."

"Yeah," Reid said with a nod of his head, "and so is half of their crew."

I scoffed. "There's six of them, at best. And I don't see any cops out here right now, do you?"

"Yeah, but we don't have backup because you said we didn't need any."

Cash chuckled as he came around to my side of the van. "Ready when you two are."

"Because we don't," I said as I shrugged off his touch. "Now, are you coming? Or are you gonna sit here and watch us have all the fun?"

This shit wasn't gonna stand. None of it. Not on my fucking watch. This was my hometown. This was my home state. That was my girl that I had claimed, and I had plans to claim her again, and again, and again, until she cried out for mercy and knew nothing but my name. I'd make her come for me until she smiled whenever I walked into a room.

No one fucked with what was mine.

Not even these assholes.

"Fall behind me. We stick to the shadows," I said as I lowered my voice.

Cash tapped my shoulder. "Behind you."

And when I heard Reid's voice, I damn near smiled. "Behind you."

Perfect.

Sticking to the shadows wasn't an issue. Cash had trained many of us well in that regard. But we still had a fence with barbed wire at the top that stood in between us and those crates. There were seven Black Diamond members there, including Jagger, helping to offload the shipment. They tossed crates to one another in a makeshift assembly line all the way down the dock. I ducked beside a bush that bucked right up to the fence. I watched that fat fuck of a security guard attempt to pick up a crate before one of the guys stopped him.

Then, I watched as one of those leather jacketed fucks picked up the crate.

"He's coming right toward us," Cash whispered.

"Hey, Jag!" the guy yelled as he turned around with the crate in his hands. "Where do you want this shipment?!"

Jagger shot the man a look before he waved his hand in the air, and I could tell the man was confused.

"I'll just set them right over here!"

"Shit," I hissed. "Get back, get back. Behind the bush, now."

We scrambled to get out of view before we all collectively held our breath. Sweat permeated my brow, dripping down the nape of my neck as my body wanted to force me to move. I refused, however. I kept my hawk eyes on that motherfucker as he walked straight toward us. He whistled through his puckered lips like some dumbass clocked in for a bird job—you know, 'cause you fly right through them to your paycheck? But nothing could have prepared me for how stupid that man would be when he set that crate behind the storage shed we faced.

Goddamn it, that crate was less than ten feet away from the fence line.

"Good hiding spot, Jag!" the man called out as he turned around and made his way back to the dock.

Reid inched out from behind the bush, but I grabbed his collar and yanked him back. "Not so fast."

He held out his hand. "It's right there!"

"Hello?" the man called out.

I slapped my palm against Reid's mouth and pinned him with a look. I'd break his neck myself if that fucker found us because he couldn't keep his fucking mouth shut.

"Hello?" the man asked again as he drew a weapon off his hip. "Anyone there?"

"Something wrong, Snapshot?!" Jagger called out.

"Not sure! Hold on!"

"Steady," I whispered. "Hold position."

Sweat trickled down my cheek as the clopping of Jagger's boots scuffed themselves up against the pavement. That bowlegged fuck sauntered up toward his man, his gaze peering beyond the fence and into the shadows. I swore to hell on high, he locked eyes with me. His stare, unwavering in its strength as he scanned the darkness.

I didn't even realize I was moving until I felt something clamp down against my wrist.

"Don't," Cash whispered.

I looked down and found my hand already on the butt of my gun. So, I quickly removed it.

Not without feeling disappointed, however.

"Idiot," Jagger muttered before he slapped his guy on the side of his head. "Get over here and help us instead of trying to find ways to get out of working for your keep."

"Jag, I swear, I thought I heard—"

Jagger grabbed the man's ear, causing him to yelp. "You questioning me?"

"Ah! No, Jag. Not a little bit. I really thought I'd heard—aaaa-AAAH!"

"Get back over there," Jagger growled as he tossed the man back toward the dock.

But not before he peered over his shoulder one last time and gave the darkness around us a good scan.

"Come on," Reid whispered, "just leave."

I slowly released the breath I held as Jagger turned his back and headed for the dock. I placed a knee on the ground, giving my back a fucking break as we watched those men unload two dozen of those fucking crates. Two dozen of them, stacked within ten feet from that fence. Jesus, they were comfortable.

"Do we have fence cutters?" Cash asked.

Reid grinned. "We've got something better. Look."

Jagger cupped his hands around his mouth and let out a high-pitched whistle, and like the good dogs they were, his men went running. They all gathered at the dock before Jagger's hands flailed everywhere, and even though we couldn't hear what the fuck he was saying, I realized why Reid had grown excited.

Jagger hadn't just gathered his men.

He had also gathered the dock hands.

"We won't get a better time than this," Reid murmured as he scrambled to his feet.

"Stay safe," Cash whispered.

"Reid," I said as I reached out and grabbed his wrist.

He crouched back down. "What is it, Bossman?"

I stared him down. "Three is ideal, but one will get the job done. Understood?"

He smiled so big that it closed his eyes. "Read ya loud and clear."

The second I released him, the spider monkey came out to play. He ripped his leather jacket off and took off his shirt before latching himself onto the fence. He scaled that thing like a fucking professional and didn't even so much as scuff up his skin as he lunged over the barbed wire. Even I didn't hear his boots plant themselves against the concrete as he steadied himself and slowly turned around.

Watching him inch toward those crates was the biggest thrill of my existence, and I wasn't even the one doing the work.

"He's got one," Cash said as he slipped out of the darkness.

"Here," Reid whispered, tossing it over.

Bending his knees, he caught the crate in his arms. Reid double-backed, snatching up another crate while Jagger continued to blow hot air into the atmosphere. But once he attempted to backtrack for a third, another ear-piercing whistle sounded in the air.

The group dispersed.

"Get back over the fence, Reid," I hissed.

I peeked around the shed shrouding us from view. "I think I can get the third one."

"Now," I spat.

And I sure as hell didn't have to tell him again.

He leapt onto the fence and threw his legs over it like a fucking pole vaulter. He dropped down to his feet, placing his hands on the ground as Cash tossed me a crate. I tucked it beneath my arm while Reid scooped up his clothes, and the three of us booked it back to the van.

"Take this and get in," I said, tossing the crate to Cash.

"Got it," he said and caught it in his arm.

"Should we test it to make sure?" Reid asked.

"Why?" I asked as I got behind the wheel of the car. "You jonesing or something?"

He shrugged. "They've been a step ahead of us the entire way. We should check and make sure this is the real stuff before dropping this shit forty minutes away with cameras that'll have our fingerprints all over it."

I cranked the engine and eased out from behind the bush. "Fine but make it quick. And don't make it a lot."

"Cash?" Reid asked.

I got us back on the road heading straight for North Myrtle Beach as wood snapped and nails popped. As I heard a small baggie unzip before something started squeaking.

"Oh, yeah," Reid said before he sputtered, "that's it right there."

"Good," I said as I merged onto the highway. "Now, put that shit up and stay quiet. We've still got to get the product where we want it. And Cash?"

"Yeah?"

"Do your best to wipe down those cameras."

27

REID

"Give'em here," I said as I held out my hand and wiggled my fingers to Cash.

"What?" he asked, wiping the cameras with his shirt. "Don't think I'm gonna do a decent enough job?"

I rolled my eyes and snatched it out of his hand. "Don't be like that. Not now."

"See how he treats me?" Cash asked with a smirk. "One dip and he's already barking orders."

"Just shut up and get it done," Baron said curtly.

"Anyone on our tail?" I asked as I pulled a microfiber cloth out of my pants.

"Where the fuck did you get that?" Cash asked.

"Just shut up and hand me the other camera," I hissed.

"No, you paranoid fuck, there's no one tailing us," Baron said.

I whipped my head up. "And you're sure about that?"

He craned his gaze over his shoulder. "Tuck it in, or I'm throwing you out. You're getting paranoid."

"Can you blame me?"

I still couldn't believe that we had gotten out of there scot-free. I honestly thought it was too good to be true. They had been a step ahead of us the entire time. Catching us by surprise. Ambushing us at the worst possible times. There had to be a tail on us. There was no way in hell they knew our movements that well.

Unless...

"Is there any chance that we've got a mole in our—"

Baron and Cash spoke together. "Shut up, Reid!"

I held up my hand. "Yep, yep. Read you loud and clear."

I did the best I could to work through the hazy high that filtered over my body. My muscles relaxed when I needed them to work. My mind raced when I needed it to stop. I leaned my head against the wall of the van, closing my eyes for a split second in an attempt to clear my mind.

But when I opened them back up, Baron and Cash were already heading back to the van.

"All right, I'm ready," I said with a grunt.

"Already done," Cash said as he hopped in and closed the van doors.

Baron clamored behind the steering wheel. "Planted and ready to go."

"You heard from Razor yet?"

"Got a text while we were hauling the boxes over to the corner."

I dug the heels of my hands into my eyes. "Wait, wait, wait, wait. What the fuck is going on?"

Cash chuckled. "You fell asleep, that's what the fuck is going on."

Baron cranked up the engine. "Don't worry, we've got everything covered."

I balked. "But I've only been out a few minutes!"

Cash snickered. "Try close to an hour."

Baron cranked his neck around. "I took the long way to North Myrtle just so your paranoid ass would go to bed."

I shot him a look. "You purposefully drove around to put me to sleep?"

"Yes," Cash and him said together.

I clicked my tongue. "Fair enough. But I want to see what you guys did."

Baron eased away from... wherever we were. "You can look out the window and see it as it passes by."

I scrambled to my feet and lunged toward the passenger's side window. I peered out long enough to see the three crates and two cameras stacked on a corner, right in front of North Myrtle's police headquarters.

"Can they see our license plate?" I asked.

Cash pulled it out of his inner jacket pocket. "What license plate?"

Baron chuckled. "We'll drive a few miles, tuck ourselves in an alley, and get it plated back on."

"Any other questions?" Cash asked as he tucked it back inside of his jacket.

I climbed into the passenger's seat. "Good work, guys. Very good work."

Baron barked with laughter and I turned my head in his direction. The smile that crossed his face was one for the books, and I couldn't help the way Cash's chuckling made me grin. We did it. Holy fuck, we had actually done it. I shook my head to clear the last of the cobwebs from my brain. I needed everything to jolt back to life. I needed my focus back.

I needed to see Angel.

"Hospital?" I asked.

Baron and Cash immediately stopped laughing.

"I'm game if you're game," Cash said.

"Baron?" I asked as I peeked over at him.

He dipped us into the first alley we came to. "Cash, get that plate back on the van. It's time to go see our girl."

"Hell yeah," he said as he threw the van doors open.

The clock ticked past one in the morning by the time we got to the hospital, and there was barely a car in the parking lot. Baron parked the van over by the dumpster, shrouded by as much darkness as possible. I needed to see her. I needed to lay eyes on her and know that she was still alive. That she was still breathing. But there was no way in hell that visiting hours were still going.

Not at a quarter past one in the morning.

"So, how are we gonna play this?" Cash asked as he stuck his head in between the two of us.

"Side entry?" Baron asked.

I shook my head. "Someone still has to get in there and open the door from that direction."

Cash shook his head. "Not if we wait for someone to come out on a smoke break.

Baron pointed. "You mean, like that?"

The three of us looked toward where he pointed and, sure enough, one of the doctors in his white-coated glory had stepped out to light one up. I grinned as I shoved my door open. Baron and Cash followed in stride as we made a beeline for that motherfucker.

But my gut clenched the second I realized who it was.

"Doc?" I asked as we approached him.

Baron quickly got in front of me and hovered over the man. "What are you still doing here?"

Doc took a long pull from his cigarette. "I take it you guys are here for Special Agent DeMarco."

"Who?" Cash asked.

Doc tossed his cigarette to the ground and stomped it out. "Angel. Her real name is Lonna DeMarco. She's a Special

Agent with the DEA."

The three of us looked around at one another. We were so used to calling her Angel, we forgot that was her real name.

"Don't get your panties in a bunch," Doc said as he turned around and ripped the side door open. "Everyone seems to calls her Angel. It was her mother's nickname, apparently."

I released the breath I didn't realize I had been holding. "I like Angel better."

He walked inside. "You know...It's amazing what else you can find out when you contact someone she actually knows."

Baron tried following him in stride, but Doc stopped him in his tracks.

"Where do you think you're going? Visiting hours are over. You'll have to come back in the morning."

Baron's temples pulsed. "No one keeps me from my girl. Now, where the fuck is she?"

Doc shook his head, though. "I can't. Not right now. We're still—"

Cash rushed him, wrapping his hand around the man's neck. "Nobody keeps us from her. Take us to her or get out of our way."

I simply slid my hands into the pockets of my leather jacket, though. "Just take us to her. We won't stay long."

I just wanted to hold her hand. I just wanted to lay eyes on her and know that she was still alive. That was all I wanted. And as Doc stared me down, I watched him relent.

"Let him go, Cash," I said. "He's fine."

He harrumphed as he dropped his hand. "So, what room?"

"*Please*," Baron said mockingly.

Doc scoffed as he rubbed his neck. "You owe me double for this."

"Whatever," Baron muttered, shoving his way past the man.

"Just spit it out already," Cash said as he stepped inside of the building.

"Thank you," I said, easing past Doc.

He just rolled his eyes, though. "She's on the I.C.U. floor. Room 433."

That whipped Baron back around. "I.C.U.?"

"The fuck did you do to her in that surgery?" Cash growled.

Doc shook his head as he pushed his way to the front of our makeshift pack. "Just stay with me and don't cause a ruckus. Let's go."

"Talk to us on the way," I said as I fell in line at his right side. "What's going on?"

Doc turned a sharp corner and slammed his hand into the elevator button. "I.C.U. rooms only allow one visitor at a time, so you'll have to take turns."

"Don't ignore his question," Baron warned.

"What's going on with her?" Cash asked.

The elevator doors dinged, and Doc stepped inside. "Come on, let's go."

I didn't like the fact that he wasn't answering us. I didn't like the fact that he was intentionally dodging our questions. I didn't know if he was trying to solidify control on his turf, or if things were really that bad with Angel. But once the elevator let us off on the fourth floor, the foul stench of disinfectant and death met my nostrils.

It prickled every hair on my body as Doc led us down the hallway.

"She's got a major gunshot wound that busted back open and a severe concussion. We're draining fluid off her brain via a catheter threaded into the base of her skull, but she's in a medically induced coma until the swelling of her brain goes down. So, yes, she's critical and needs an I.C.U. room until further notice."

He stopped just shy of a door, and I swore to hell on high, I couldn't get my lungs to draw in any air.

"Who's going first?" he asked as he held his hand out toward the door.

"How long will she be out?" Baron asked.

How long did the surgery take?" Cash asked.

"How many stitches did her gunshot wound need again?"

"How much blood did she lose?"

"Is she paralyzed?"

"Does she have any permanent damage?"

"Is anyone on their way to retrieve her?"

While the two of them talked Doc's fucking ear off, I slipped behind all of them. I grabbed the cold, unforgiving doorknob and twisted it open, then slipped inside without a second thought. The beeping of the machines arrested my heart. The tubes running in and out of her body at all angles made me sick to my stomach. Her pale, frail body laid there, spread out for the masses as machines registered every second of her unconscious life on paper.

"Oh, Angel," I whispered as my eyes watered.

It took all I had to go sit by her side. I hiked my leg up, perching my hip on the edge of her hospital bed. I looked down at her hands, her bloodied knuckles peering back up at me. A fighter to her core, and yet I couldn't help but grieve the life she had found in our presence.

"I'm so sorry," I murmured as I picked up her hand.

I brought every single knuckle to my lips to kiss. Every bruise was met with a healing kiss that I remembered my own mother giving me once upon a time. Back when life wasn't so... dirty.

"Something tells me you'd know what to do if you were here," I said with a soft snicker. "I mean, I know you're here, but I just—what I mean is—"

You're an idiot, Reid.

What did I talk about? Could she even hear me? I knew that my mother's homecare nurses encouraged me to talk with her as if things were normal. As if her condition hadn't completely eaten away at everything that made her, well, my mother. And if they encouraged talking during something like that, then maybe they'd give me the same advice. So, I did the only thing I knew to do.

I started talking.

"You know, I was in a room like this with Mom once," I said as I stroked my thumb along the top of her bruised hand. "She has dementia, you know. Full-time in-home care. I wanted to put her somewhere. Somewhere she'd be safe, where she'd be around people. But after trying to admit her somewhere, she became so combative that she fell and busted her head open. I didn't mean it, I swear, it just—all happened so fast. And before I knew it, she was in a room like this, and I just..."

My lower lip quivered, and it took me a second to get it under control.

"I guess disaster just follows me everywhere," I said.

Snap out of it, this isn't about you.

I cleared my throat. "But anyway. What I do know is that people leave this place. Mom left this place, and my grandfather left this place, and so will you. I know it doesn't feel like it right now. I know it might feel like hell inside of your body right now. But this place isn't forever. This condition of yours isn't forever. And when you wake up, I'm going to be right here. I swear it. Okay? On my mother's memories that her dementia has taken away from her, I will be here."

And as I brought her hand to my lips to kiss one last time, I prayed to a God I didn't believe in.

If you need a life, then take mine. But please, spare her this.

CASH

"How long will she be out?" Baron asked.

How long did the surgery take?" I asked.

Baron tilted his head. "How many stitches did her gunshot wound need again?"

I stepped closer to Doc. "How much blood did she lose?"

"Is she paralyzed?"

"Does she have any permanent damage?"

"Is anyone on their way to retrieve her?"

Doc held up his hand, stopping our barrage in its tracks. "She'll be out as long as it takes for her brain to heal. The surgery took around four hours, no hiccups but a lot of blood. I think we used four or five pints just to get her back to normal, and that isn't counting the ones we used in surgery."

"How many stitches?" Baron damn near growled.

Doc shot him a look. "Tuck it in, or you're gone. Got it? We're not in your clubhouse; we're in my place of work. You play by my rules here."

That straightened Baron's back as my voice grew harsh. "Then don't make us beg for these answers. Just give them to us."

Doc slowly turned his attention to me. "Her gunshot wound needed a fresh set of stitches, so I just redid them. She's not paralyzed, but any sort of damage that requires the brain to be in play won't be recognizable until we can bring her out of the medically induced coma. And yes, I had to notify her chain of command about her condition, so they're sending a team out here."

"A team?" Baron asked.

Doc nodded. "From the sounds of it, her partner and her boss are on their way."

"Oh, boy," I muttered.

"What is that?" Baron asked. "Where did Reid go?"

Doc thumbed over his shoulder. "He slipped inside. He's talking to her."

"She's awake?!" I asked a bit too quickly.

Doc's face sank. "I encourage people who have loved ones in the I.C.U. who are unconscious to talk with them. He's just... talking with her. Which is what you should all be doing right now."

Baron turned toward the closed door. "Can she hear us if we talk?"

Doc shrugged. "It's more possible with a medically induced coma, but the statistics still aren't sure. Maybe she can. Maybe it'll bring you guys some comfort to know she might be able to."

I watched Baron grab the doorknob. "You sure you wanna do that?"

He didn't stop moving as he inched the door open, however.

And the second I heard Reid sniffle, it stopped my heart in my chest.

"Jesus," Baron whispered.

I pivoted toward him and peered over his shoulder. "My God."

I watched as Reid held her lifeless hand. As he brought it to his lips to kiss. The tubes. The machines. All of them, working in tandem to keep her alive. I had to turn my back and close my eyes.

The anger welling within me was too much to bear.

"She's a fighter," Doc said as he placed his hand on my shoulder. "If anyone can make it out of here, it's her."

I swallowed hard. "Thanks, Doc."

"You want to go in behind him?" Baron asked.

"Only one visitor in there at a time," Doc said. "Let him finish, and then the two of you can have your turn."

Baron eased the door closed before we took a seat on either side of the door with my hands linked together in my lap and Baron stared at the nursing desk ahead. All of a sudden, we heard Reid's voice mounting.

"Please, Angel, just wake up. I'll beg you, if that's what it takes. Wake up so I can take you out to dinner. Wake up so that I can hold you the way you deserve. Please, Angel, just wake up. Just fight long enough to wake up, and I can do the rest."

My heart shattered at his words. At the broken boy lying in between the broken breaths. I looked over at Baron and found him staring at the ceiling with his eyes a bit glossier than normal. I found myself clenching my jaw so tight that a headache sprung up behind my head. Death Cheaters didn't beg. We stood tall and proud, and we got what we always wanted in the end.

"Please," Reid said with a soft sniffle, "just wake up for me. That's all I ask."

Except for now, anyway.

When the door popped open, I damn near knocked myself over leaping up out of that chair. I stood there, waiting to receive Reid—my brother and my best friend—in whatever shape he returned. The door eased open and there he stood, red, puffy eyes and all, and I wondered if he needed a hug.

Thank fuck, he flopped down into the chair I had just gotten up from.

"You next, Cash," Baron said.

"You sure?"

"Yep."

I peered into the room where Angel lay. "All right, then."

I eased my way inside and paused. But I couldn't stand to take another step toward her. She looked so...dead. Pale and fragile. I saw every vein snaking around beneath her skin. I watched her lungs move mechanically up and down while whirlybobs and doodads beeped and did whatever the fuck it was they were supposed to do. We were supposed to protect her. We were supposed to look after her. All women. All children. All the time. That was our moral code. Always keep them protected. Always keep them safe.

And we had failed her.

Twice.

"Don't be a puss," Baron said through the crack in the door. "She needs more than that right now."

Then, he closed the door with a thud.

Where I found the strength to move, I wasn't sure. But as if my legs had a mind of their own, I found myself gravitating toward her. Like always. She had this undeniable pull about her. This invisible string that latched onto anyone around her and reeled them in, like a fish on a line. I let her reel me in just like I had the first time. Just like I had so many other times before, like when I found her in that bedroom and didn't throw her out.

"Hey," I said as I sat on the edge of her bed.

I managed to pick up her hand, but watching it lay there in my palm kicked me in the gut.

"Jesus Christ," I whispered as I smoothed my thumb along her skin.

Even lying there in that bed, she was so soft. Soft, like her body when—

Get it together, Cash.

"My son would have loved you," I managed to choke out as I slid my thumb down the lengths of all of her fingers. "He always did enjoy people with charisma. Probably because he was so outgoing all the time."

Something wet leaked down my face and I drew in a deep breath.

"That sweet little boy came out of left field for me, you know," I said with a snicker. "A one-night stand halfway across the fucking country, and before I knew it, I had a three-week-old on my doorstep. His mother apparently died from complications in birth. I didn't—"

Shame overcame me as I closed my eyes. "I couldn't even remember her name."

I swallowed the knot overwhelming my throat as I laced our fingers together.

"It didn't stop me from stepping up to the plate, though. Responsibility. Above all else, that's what our crew is about. Taking responsibility and ownership over our life. And when I found that three-week-old little boy staring back at me with eyes the same color as mine, I just knew, you know? Fucking hell, there was even a time there where I thought about stepping away from the crew altogether. You know, before Rocky got sick."

The painful, horrendous memories came rushing back.

"It was just a lump on his shin, you know? It was bruised for a spell, so I figured he had just whapped himself really good on something. But even when the bruise faded, the lump just seemed to... grow, you know? So, took him to see Doc. Ran all the tests. Did all the things. And when Doc referred me to an oncologist? Well, doesn't take a genius to see where this story goes."

I closed my eyes and remembered how lovely my son's laughter sounded.

"God, all of those medications and all of that chemo. That—that poison rushing through his system. Amputation was the least of his worries most days. The doctors warned me about how bad it would be. How much of a toll it would take on his body. How aggressive the bone cancer was and how little of a shot we had. But Rocky wanted to fight."

The thought made me smile as I opened my eyes and looked back down at Angel.

"Rocky would've made Sylvester Stallone proud with how he fought. But the meds were just...just too much for his body. He was only ten, and one night, he screamed for me and I went running, I tell ya. I went running, Angel. And I found him just bleeding in bed. Every hole. Every exit. Everything just...just leaked with blood."

My chest jumped as I tried to control my emotions. "I begged him to hang on. That probably wasn't even fair to him. You know, his father's last words to him being words of tears. Words of begging. I wasn't ready to lose him, Angel. I wasn't ready to bury my son. And I'm not ready to bury you, do you hear me?"

I stood to my feet and released her hand. I hovered over her, cloaking her in my shadow as I inched my face toward hers.

"I'm not ready to bury you yet, so fight. Fight for me. Fight for Reid. Fight for Baron. And if you don't want to fight for us, then fight for Rocky. Fight for that ten-year-old little boy who will never know the joy of love, the pain of loss, the warmth of hot chocolate, the love of a mother, or the relief of vacation. Fight for that child inside all of us that still isn't ready to give up. That still isn't ready to give in. Because you've got Rocky levels of fight in you, Angel. He was all spunk, just like you. All fire and no ice. So, if you won't fight for us, and you won't fight for you, then fight for him."

God, she reminded me so much of him. The way she moved. The way she laughed. The way she threw herself in head first before thinking. Maybe that was why I had been so drawn to her. Maybe that was why I cared about her so fucking much.

I leaned forward and pressed the softest kiss to her lips before I moved my mouth to her ear.

"All you have to do is wake up," I whispered. "After that, we can do the rest."

29

BARON

I stood there with my hands clasped behind me. I stared at the closed hospital door, listening to the clock on the wall tick down the seconds. Reid sat in Cash's chair, staring forward. He hadn't moved since he sat, and I hadn't flinched since I told Cash to stop being a pussy and closed the door.

And when it opened back up, I found a red-faced Cash staring back at me.

"You're good," he said as he side-stepped me.

With all the strength I had left in my tired, old bones, I walked into her I.C.U. room. I reached out, flinging the door closed with my fingertips and watching to see if it made her move. The thump of the door made someone gasp on the other side. Reid grumbled something to himself, but what he said, I'd never know. Yet, as I stood there, searching for any sign of conscious life in her body, there were none.

Just a still form lying there, waiting.

I traced the lines of her tubes. I traced them back to the machines that beeped and took guesses as to what it monitored. Something trickled, and when my gaze fell to the floor, I found her piss bag filling up.

"'Atta, girl," I muttered.

But after those words left my mouth, I fell silent once more. I didn't know what to say, and that never happened. I didn't know what to do, and that feeling itself was foreign and unwanted. I'd never not known what to do. I'd never not known what to say. That was my purpose. That was what my men looked for me to do. To fill the silence. To answer the questions. To fill the gaps.

Just talk.

So, I drew in a short breath. "You're one tough broad, you know. Coming after us for the sake of your brother. We could use more good people like you in our crew."

My eye twitched as the words fell flat at my feet.

"Don't expect me to pour my heart out or nothin' like those two. They've always been wimps."

Hearing Cash and Reid snicker gave me hope.

Hope that we'd all actually make it out of this shit.

"Foster care was balls," I whispered.

I shook my head, trying to stop myself even as the words kept coming. "So, I ran away when I was young. Ran away from all that... that shit. And that abuse. The streets were always more welcoming than that hellhole, anyway."

I grinned at the thought of our former president.

"One day," I said as I approached her left side, "I was rooting around in the dumpster for some food for this cat I'd found on the corner. Just tossed into a box and left to die. And out of nowhere, I hear this thunderous voice that said, 'eat like shit, be like shit.'"

I grinned as I looked down at her lying there. "It was the first time I met Whicker. You know, our former president. He found this punk-ass little nineteen-year-old kid who had lived on the streets for four years, digging around in some trash for a fucking cat. God, what a sight I must've been."

I pressed my hands into her hospital bed and shifted myself a bit. "He offered me a place at his table. A place to eat. A place to rest. A place with friends, and family, and guys who watched each other's backs like brothers. I was only nineteen at the time, you know, when he offered me a spot in The Death Cheaters. No hope. No prospects. Nothing to offer anyone. And he just... gave me a life. Just handed it to me. Some punk ass kid with nothing to his name."

I raised my head and locked eyes with the wall. "I guess that's why I stood beside him all those years. Even when I knew he was headfirst into all those fucking drugs. Even when I knew his judgment was compromised."

I stood back to my feet, my body still unsure of what to do. My gaze caressed her, looking up and down for any signs of life. For any sign she was listening. But all I found were those precious little toes of hers peeking out from beneath a blanket that had fluttered off her legs.

I walked back to the foot of the bed and quickly tucked her feet back in.

"Has to be cold," I murmured before I cleared my throat. "Anyway, just get better, okay? Just...just get better. That's all we're asking. Okay, Angel?"

I wanted to go back and kiss her. Every fiber of my being wanted to plant my lips to hers and not leave until she woke up. I wanted to crawl under those covers with her, rip those tubes out of her body, and shove them into me. Maybe I could take the pain from her. Maybe I could ride it out for her.

Any single one of us deserved to be in that bed.

But not her.

"Just get better, all right?" I whispered as I patted her clothed feet.

And I knew if I kissed her—if I walked back toward her and planted my lips anywhere on her body—I'd want her to wake up. I'd beg her to wake up. And I knew that might not ever happen. She may never come back to me. To us. She may never get back to who she once was. She may wake up and not even remember a fucking thing.

The thought made me sick to my gut with anger. Those drugs took my president. They took my friend. They took the only father and the first person I ever really trusted. They took the man that saved my life, and now, they were about to take her.

I couldn't fucking stand it.

"Enough," I growled as I pivoted on the balls of my feet and charged out of the room.

"Baron?" Reid asked as he leapt up.

"What's wrong?" Cash asked.

I didn't even look at them. "Follow me."

"What's going on?" Reid asked as he fell in line to my left.

"Did something happen? Do we need to get a doctor?" Cash asked as he fell in line to my right.

"Shut the fuck up and follow me," I glowered.

"You guys done?" Doc asked as he stepped out of one of the rooms.

"Yep," I said, charging past him. "Elevator this way?"

"It is. I'll lead you guys out."

I felt their eyes on me the entire time as we rode the elevator back down to the main floor. Out the side exit we went, with Doc shooting off half-cocked promises of keeping us updated as much as he could. We knew that meant to stay away, though. Between the nursing staff giving us sideways looks and her boss from the DEA heading into town, we needed to keep our distance. And as me and my guys stepped outside, Doc's voice hardened.

"I'm very serious," he said.

I turned to face him. "About?"

He tilted his head and sighed. "This place is going to be crawling with agents. They're going to want answers that she can't currently provide."

I nodded. "I know."

Doc leveled his eyes with mine. "So, stay away. I will contact you as I feel it's necessary. But just know that no news from me is good news."

Reid licked his lips. "Understood."

"Hey, Doc?" Cash asked.

"What's up?"

"Thank you. For everything."

Doc drew in a deep breath. "You guys have saved my life not once, but twice. It's the least I can do. Keep your distance."

I playfully saluted him. "Loud and clear."

And as the side door thudded behind him, the three of us were alone.

Again.

"Sun's rising," Reid said as he stared off toward the horizon.

"Someone will be finding those crates any second," Cash muttered.

I turned and set my sights on our van. "Call up the guys. It's time for church."

"What's up?" Reid asked as he pulled out his phone.

"Any reason in particular?" Cash asked.

God, I loved it when a plan smacked me across the face.

"We're going to take a vote," I said, turning to face them.

"A vote on what?" Cash asked mindlessly as he typed away on his cell.

"Reid, how many cameras do we still have with footage on them?" I asked.

"Uh, at least three, minus the one that broke. Why?"

And as Cash sent off the text to his men guarding the clubhouse, a plan unfurled in my mind like an angry fist reaching for a weapon.

We were going to side ourselves with the DEA.

"We're going to vote on whether or not to turn over the cameras we still have to the DEA like good little informants."

30

ANGEL

His touch warmed me. The second he picked up my hand, all I wanted was to curl my fingers around his skin.

"I'm so sorry," Reid muttered.

Reid. I'm right here. I've got you.

"Something tells me you'd know what to do if you were here."

I'm right here, handsome. I promise. Just a bit... tired.

"I was in a room like this with Mom once."

With who? What happened?

"She has dementia, you know."

Come on, just squeeze his hand. You can do it.

"I guess disaster just follows me everywhere."

No, don't talk about yourself like that, handsome. It's okay. We all have our issues. Even me.

I heard him. He sounded so far away, but I heard him. I heard the tears in his voice that I wanted to wipe away. I heard the pain in his words whenever he mentioned his mother.

The way he squeezed my hand filled me with such painful delight.

I never wanted him to let go.

Wake up. Open your eyes. Your boys need you, Angel.

"What I do know is that people leave this place. Mom left this place, and my grandfather left this place, and so will you."

Will you be there when I leave?

"I know it doesn't feel like it right now. I know it might feel like hell inside of your..."

Goddamn it, why the hell am I so tired?

"And when you wake up, I'm going to be right here."

"My son would have loved you."

Hmmm? Jesus, I'm so tired.

"He always did enjoy people with charisma. Probably because he was so outgoing all the time."

Cash? Is that you?

"A one-night stand halfway across the fucking country, and before I knew it, I had a three-week-old on my doorstep."

Rocky? Cash, are you talking about Rocky? Because you don't have to talk about him. I promise, it's okay. I know it has to hurt.

Feeling him lace our fingers together brought me to life. Though, I wished that I could have opened my fucking eyes. How long had he been there? How long had he been sitting at my side?

Cash, I'm right here.

"... with the same color as mine, I just knew, you know?"

Same color what? What color? I bet it was a beautiful color.

"You know, before Rocky got sick."

I'm so tired. Why the hell am I so tired all the damn time? Goddamn it, Angel, stay awake! He's talking to you!

"It was just a bump on his shin, you know?"

I know, Cash. I know. I can't imagine what you must've

gone through. I'm so sorry. I'm so sorry for ever throwing him in your face.

"Well, doesn't take a genius to see where this story goes."

Tell me anyway. I'm always here to listen. Just talk to me, cutie.

"God, all of those medications and all of that chemo."

I'm so sorry, Cash. With my whole heart, I am so fucking sorry.

"Rocky would've made Sylvester Stallone proud with how he fought."

He's your son. I don't doubt that for a second.

"I wasn't ready to lose him, Angel. I wasn't ready to bury my son. And I'm not ready to bury you, do you hear me?"

I am, I swear. I know you can't hear me, but I can hear you.

"I'm not ready to bury you yet, so fight. Fight for me. Fight for Reid. Fight for Baron. And if you don't want to fight for us, then fight for Rocky."

Fucking hell, my eyes are so heavy.

"Fight for that ten-year-old little boy who will never know the joy of love, or the pain of loss, or the warmth of hot chocolate, or the love of a mother, or the relief of vacation."

Stay awake, he needs you. Cash! Talk louder! You're fading out!

"All you have to do is wake up. After that, we can do the rest."

"Foster care was balls."

Ah! Is someone there? Speak up! Who is it!?

"The streets were more welcoming than that hellhole, anyway."

Oh, my God. Baron. Baron! It's me! Can you hear me?!

"Eat like shit, be like shit."

What? The hell does that even mean? Baron, is everyone all right?

"It was the first time I met Whicker. You know, our former President."

God, why the fuck won't they wake me up? Wake me up, damn it!

"I was only nineteen at the time. You know, when he offered me a spot in The Death Cheaters."

I bet you were terrified. So young. You were so young, B.

"I guess that's why I stood beside him all those years. Even when I knew he was headfirst into all those fucking drugs."

Having someone that you love hooked on drugs is hard.

"Even when I knew his judgment was compromised."

I just want to hold them. Do you hear me? I just want to fucking hold them!

"That's all we're asking. Okay, Angel?"

What? What are you asking? What did I miss? Say it again, Baron. What did I miss?!

"Just get better, all right?"

I swear to God, guys, when I'm awake, I'll hold you again. On my life, I will hug you guys until you can't breathe. Right after my nap, okay? Just a little, tiny nap.

"Good morning, Miss DeMarco. And how are we this morning?"

Go away.

"Nurses say that your vital signs looked great overnight. You're doing really well here, you know."

Why do I recognize your voice? Who are you? State your name!

"If you haven't heard my name so far, I'm Doctor Henderson. Though, the guys once introduced me to you as Doc."

Doc! Oh, thank fuck. Doc, you've gotta get me out of here. My boys, they need me. Wake me up, okay? I just need to talk with them.

"You know, they're pretty rough around the edges."

You better watch your next set of words very carefully.

"But they're not terrible people."

Oh. Well, good, then.

"Don't get me wrong, they've gotten themselves into some terrible things because of their former president getting hooked on those drugs. But they've never peddled them, and I'd be willing to get on a stand and testify to that."

Shit! That's perfect. I just need some contact information on how to get in touch with you. You know, once you WAKE ME THE FUCK UP.

"You know, they'd probably fire me if they heard me talking to you about this, but it was actually their old president that tried to wrangle them into selling it. You know what they did instead?"

You can't tell me. I can't know. I can't know how they killed him.

"They dropped him at the Black Diamond's doorstep, that's what they did. Never heard from him again, to my knowledge. Though, they don't talk about it much."

Wait, what? I thought Baron—

"So, anyway. Whoever you're looking for right now? It's not them."

I already knew that, though. It was touching how Doc wanted to stand up for them. But the second that crew rolled up onto their clubhouse and unloaded bullets, I knew I had trained my sights on the wrong crew. They weren't who I was looking for, and yet somehow, they had become important to me.

More important than my career, apparently.

"Now, you get some rest," Doc said as exhaustion overtook my body, "and I'll come back around to check on you in a few hours."

Just wake me up. Just for a little bit.

"Sleep well, Miss DeMarco."

JUST WAKE ME UP ALREADY!

"Angel!"

If my body could have jolted, it would have.

"Oh, my God. Angel. What the hell have they done to you?"

Dee?

I felt someone stroking my hair. Holding my hand. Perched on my hospital bed. I wanted it to be them. I needed it to be them. Where had my boys gone?

Why hadn't they come back?

"Why the hell didn't you just get on that plane?" Dee whispered.

Because there's still a job to do. A job that you abandoned. A job that you promised to see through with me. Why did you break your promise, Dee?

"What in the high hell is going on in this room?!"

"Hello there, my name is Doctor Thomas Henderson. Why don't you come out here so we can—"

"Doctor. Perfect. Would you like to be the one to tell me why my agent is lying in an I.C.U. bed fighting for her fucking life!?"

Cap! Cut it out, he saved me. I'm just resting.

"Really, come outside and we can have a—"

"I'm not going anywhere, thank you very much. My name is

Captain Brandon Montgomery of the East Coast faction of the DEA. You have my agent lying in a bed, completely unconscious. You can answer my questions here."

"I really must insist that—"

Will everyone just shut up?!

"Can everyone shut it for a second?" Dee asked curtly.

Thank you. About damn time you showed back up, anyway.

The room fell silent, but I felt all eyes on me. Jesus Christ, what I wouldn't have given to open my eyes and address my boss directly. I could only imagine how infuriated he must have been to get that phone call. To get a call from some random doctor in South Carolina about how one of his agents is locked away in a hospital trying to recuperate.

When the hell would they be allowed to wake me up?

"Doctor Henderson," Cap said much too calmly.

"Yes, captain?"

"Would you kindly tell me, Special Agent DeMarco's partner, and everyone else in the room, how the hell one of my finest agents came to be in your possession this way?"

Finest agent?

He thought I was one of his finest agents?

"She was already unconscious when she came in," Doc said, "so I've got no idea how she got her wounds."

Good on you, Doc. Leave them out of this.

"I know how she got these wounds," Dee glowered.

Don't you fucking dare.

"It's those men. That...that crew she was chasing down."

Shut up, Dee.

"She was looking into them. Looking into the drugs, and she stumbled upon them. A crew that has a history with it. With this exact shit that's back out on the streets."

Shut the fuck up, Dee!

"They did this to her," he said as tears clouded his voice. "They did this, and they're gonna pay for what they've done."

Dee! Can it!

"She tracked them down like a wild dog, Cap. You would've been so proud of her. She tracked them to a bar in the area that they owned, and went undercover to try and get close. When that didn't work, she tailed them. Staked out their whole clubhouse. I mean, she was relentless, Cap. Willing to do anything to get the answers she needed."

No, they didn't do this to me. It's not them. It's that other crew. The Black Diamonds! They're the ones doing all of this!

"Tell me everything," Cap glowered.

"I'll leave you guys with some privacy, how does that sound?" Doc asked.

Don't you go anywhere, Doc. I'm not done with you yet!

"You know what I think?" Dee asked.

"What?" Cap asked.

Dee squeezed my hand a bit too hard. "I bet she got too close to the answer. The real answer. So, they tried taking her out."

HOW FUCKING DARE YOU!

Panic gripped my heart. My heart felt as if it had disconnected from my chest and slid into my stomach. No. Why was he saying such awful things? They weren't like that at all! Doc. He had to say something. He had to speak up. He had to tell them what he told me!

Tell them what you told me, Doc. Get back in here and tell them!

"What the hell is that noise?"

"Everyone, move out of the way!"

I felt lightheaded. Dizzy. As if the room around me tilted on its axis point. I struggled to breathe. I couldn't catch my breath. What was happening?

Am I dying?

"It's her heart monitor."

"Is it misfiring?"

Someone's cold fingers shoved their way against my neck while someone else touched my wrist.

"No, it's not misfiring. We have to give her a sedative."

"We can't give her anything else. She's already in a coma."

"A coma?!" Cap exclaimed.

"A medically induced one, yes."

"Do these monitors have a reset button?"

"Does she have a reset button?" Dee asked softly.

Everyone, just stop it!

And yet, I couldn't control it. My body operated as if I didn't exist. As if I weren't trapped in it, struggling to find a way out. I wasn't tired any longer. I wanted to get up and walk around. I wanted to shove my finger into my boss's face and tell him that he was wrong. That I was wrong. That we had all been wrong in our assumptions. It wasn't the Death Cheaters, and I had to wake up so that I could tell someone.

Anyone.

Someone willing to listen to me.

"She's still in there," Dee muttered, "she has to be. Angel, can you hear me?"

I hear you, Dee. I hear you!

"Everyone!" Cap barked. "I want patrols around this hospital, every hour, on the hour. I don't want a single nook and cranny to go unchecked. Those men are around here somewhere. The men that have done this to her. And we're not going to stop until we find them."

NO! PLEASE! YOU DON'T UNDERSTAND! THEY'RE HELPING ME! HELPING US!

I forced my body to move. Or at least I tried. I commanded my toes to wiggle and my head to lift. I prayed for my eyes to open. I begged for any religious life form willing to listen to just...listen. Just wake me up. That was all they had to do was wake me up. I wasn't in pain. I wasn't tired. If anything, I was ready to get up, get out of bed, and hunt down those Diamond fuckers until there were none left.

They killed my brother.

They deserved to die.

Wake up, Angel.

"We don't stop looking until we've rounded up every last one of them," Cap glowered.

Wake up, girl. Your men need you.

"We won't let them get away with this," Dee muttered against the shell of my ear.

"Now, get out there and find those motherfuckers!" Cap yelled out across my room.

STOP IT! PLEASE! YOU'VE GOT IT ALL WRONG!

"Looking for us?"

I froze. My heart froze. The monitors froze. The rapid beeping sounds dissipated into nothingness and everyone, even my boss, fell silent.

Baron?

"That's him. That's one of the guys," Dee said as he broke the silence.

God, what I wouldn't have given to slap that man across his face.

"Arrest him," Cap said hotly.

Dee squeezed my hand. "I guess it looks like they're gonna make it easy for us. God, what I wouldn't give for you to see this. You deserve to see it."

Just squeeze his hand. Just squeeze it.

I heard handcuffs unzipping and Baron grunting. I heard the satisfaction in Dee's voice while the anger in Cap's overtook his. I just had to squeeze Dee's hand. I just had to get his attention. Once I had it, I could explain everything.

Why the fuck can I not move, for fuck's sake!?

"Before you cart me off," Baron said as the shuffling came to a stop, "I really need you to look at something."

Cap scoffed. "And what might that be?"

Baron grunted again, and I swear to God, if he had any marks on him when I woke up, there would be hell to pay.

A smack for every scrape.

"Just tell me you'll watch it," Baron said gruffly. "Just tell me that you'll watch it before putting me in your blacked out SUV or whatever the fuck it is that carts you guys around."

"Why?" Cap asked. "Give me one good reason."

Dee, please. Do something. Say something. Just fucking watch it, for crying out loud.

Baron chuckled. "Because it's the footage Angel would have wanted to see if she were awake right now."

"Yeah, and who do you think is responsible for that?" Cap asked.

"Not us," Baron said as his voice stayed strong. "But if you watch the footage, you'll see who did it. Who's doing all of this, actually."

Yes, please. Watch the footage. Watch what they've brought you.

"Nah, I'm not in the mood today," my boss said.

CAP!

And just like that, my heart monitor blew through the fucking roof.

31

BARON

BEEP BEEP BEEP BEEP BEEP BEEP BEEP BEEP!

"What's happening? What's going on?" Dee asked as he continued to hold Angel's hand much too tightly for my liking.

"Do something, doctor!" the man in the suit in front of me barked.

The man behind me who held my wrists wrenched them up my back. "You stay put."

I snarled over my shoulder. "Like I'm fucking going anywhere."

"What's going on with her?!" Dee shouted.

"Well, from what I can see," Doc said as he kept his cool, "she can hear what's happening, and she's freaking out."

Almost immediately, her heart monitor stopped. Her face was lifeless. Her body, motionless. But that heart monitor had gone off twice already.

"She's really still in there. Angel!" I exclaimed.

Cap shoved his finger into my face. "Unless you want the maximum for all of the charges I'm gonna slap you with, I suggest you lower your voice."

"Watch the footage I've brought you, and we won't have any issues," I said as I held my head high.

"Is that a threat?" Cap snarled.

I shook my head. "I've come in peace. You're the one addressing me with hostility."

"Oh, you slimy little—"

"Let's just hear them out," Dee said breathlessly.

The room fell silent at his words before Cap spoke again. "What?"

I watched as her brokenhearted partner sank back down to the edge of the bed. The pain in his eyes was unmistakable. He cared about her. We all did.

I had to get them to listen to me, for all of our sakes.

Dee peered over his shoulder at his boss. "Let's watch whatever he's brought us. If they came down here, knowing they'd risk being arrested, they must have something worth seeing."

BEEP BEEP BEEP BEEP BEEP BEEP BEEP BEEP!

"That's it," I said as I leaned forward. "Fight, Angel. Fight for us!"

"You shut your fucking mouth," Cap growled.

"What is it that you want us to watch?" Dee asked as his gaze searched my face.

I locked my stare with Cap's. "You okay with this?"

The man's nostrils flared. "Don't really have a choice, now, do I?"

I grinned. "Angel has that effect on people."

Cap blinked. "My patience is wearing thin."

So, I took the hint and craned my head over my shoulder. "Reid! Get in here! They're willing to watch the footage!"

His silenced footsteps revealed his stature, and I grinned when Cap had to lean his head back to keep him in view. Reid was a tall son of a bitch. Taller than any of us. And watching that man's eyes widen, even if only for a split second, gave me enough pride to chew on for lunch as well as dinner.

"Here," Reid said, holding the camera out around my body.

"What's this?" Cap asked as he snatched it out of the man's hand.

"There are pictures and videos of those drug shipments she was tracking down," I said with a nod of my head. "She wasn't coming after us because we were suspects."

"Yeah, she was," Dee said.

I peeked over at him. "That's what she told you so that you'd come with her. But no, it's not the real reason why she was tracking us down."

Cap waved the camera in the air in front of him. "Then, why was she hunting you guys down like a pack of rabid dogs?"

It was Reid that answered him. "Because she knew we could help her in ways your teams couldn't."

That got his attention. "Explain."

"Cash?!" I barked.

His lumbering gait shoved him through the door and off to the side. "Our former president got addicted to that shit. Tried to get us to run it on the streets."

"It was a fucking nightmare," I said with a shake of my head.

Cash shrugged. "It was the Black Diamond's way of trying to establish an East Coast foothold in South Carolina for their growing cartel. Start with the tourists at the beaches and shit, and it filters through the rest of the state like wildfire."

"Uh huh," Cap said as he looked down at the camera he still clutched.

"She figured that out," I said as I looked over at Angel, still lying there in that fucking bed. "She figured out that we unseated our old president because of that shit. So, she figured we'd help her because of what happened to her brother."

Dee rushed in front of me, staring at me with widened eyes. "She told you that?"

Even Cap looked shocked. "She never tells anyone that."

Reid sighed. "We've got a couple other cameras filled with this kind of stuff. The one you're about to watch is the second shipment in as many days. So, whatever they're planning? It's big."

Cash folded his arms across his chest. "My best guess, because of what they did last time, is that they're gonna flood the streets with as much of it as they can. And that means overdoses."

"For starters," I murmured.

"And as of right now, there's no one in place to stop them," Reid said.

"Not with her in that bed, anyway," Cash said.

Cap started dicking around with the buttons on the camera as I cleared my throat. "You should know that we snuck in last night while they were offloading that second shipment."

Cap snapped his head back up. "Why?"

I looked over at Reid. "We wanted to get more footage. More proof, you know, for Angel. But what we ended up doing was taking a few crates of their merch and putting them near North Myrtle's police headquarters."

"Along with one of our cameras," Cash said plainly.

"You did, huh?" Dee asked.

Reid shrugged. "We didn't know what else to do. We didn't know how to get anyone else's attention without it making us look bad."

"It was the best we could come up with on the spot," I said flatly.

Cap's brows stitched themselves together before his gaze dropped back down to the camera. Dee reached over and pressed a couple of buttons, and then his eyes ignited with the light coming from the small screen in front of him. I stood there as my hands went numb. I stood there next to my men as the guy behind me slowly loosened his grip on my arms. And by the time Cap stopped the footage, his face had sunken into stone.

"Uncuff him," Dee said.

"Come again?" the guy behind me asked.

Cap slowly raised his head. "You heard the man."

"Thank you," I said.

"Now," Cap said hotly.

My arms quickly dropped, and I brought them to the front of my body. I rubbed at my wrists, trying to ignore the severe indentations against my skin. I hated cops. I hated them more than I hated those Black Diamond fucks. But with them on our side, there was no way in hell that those assholes were getting away with it.

I was proud of my men for voting to help instead of harm.

"I've done you a favor, and now you do me one," Cap said as he marched toward me.

He got into my face so close that, if it had been anyone else, I would've already knifed them to prove a point.

"You want to know how Angel got like she is now," I said.

Cap nodded. "You can start anytime you're ready."

I figured it was the least that I could do. "The first time she came by the clubhouse, we were ambushed. That was when she got shot in the gut. Doctor Henderson patched her up, but the Black Diamonds knew we'd be scrambling. So, they blitzed us while we weren't there."

"Beat her senseless," Reid spat with a scowl on his face.

Cap's face grew red with anger. "And you didn't have men posted with her. You just fucking left her there to fend for herself after a gunshot wound?"

"No," Reid said.

I watched him look over toward Angel's bed with pain in his eyes.

"I was there with her. I was—was left t—to—"

The moment his eyes glazed over, I reached out and placed my hand on his shoulder. "She's gonna be okay. This is all temporary, remember that."

"And how do you know that?" Dee spat.

I slowly panned my gaze toward him. "Because I know her, like you do."

He pointed his finger in my face. "You don't know shit about her."

"Are you guys still willing to help or not?" Cash asked.

"Depends," Dee said without hesitation. "Are you guys willing to help us? Or is this some sort of ploy to make yourselves look innocent?"

"None of this is your call," Cap said flatly.

Dee shrugged as he walked up to me. "I don't care whose call it is. All I care about is whether or not you and your men are willing to help."

I nodded without hesitation. "Of course."

Reid nodded. "Always."

Cash slid his hands into his pockets. "Just tell us where you need us."

Then, Dee turned toward a very angry Cap. "She asked for their help once, Cap. I mean, you saw what I just saw on that camera."

Cap chewed on the inside of his cheek. "Yep."

Dee took the camera from him and held it near his face. "We've got a camera full of evidence. According to them, there's more, too. More that not just we have, but another entire jurisdiction. Either way, someone is going to be looking into this now. We've got a chance to get ahead of it. To take everyone by surprise."

But I knew something that would get Cap on board.

"You should know," I said as I cracked my neck, "that some of those faces in the footage that we've got are cops."

The stone-cold look that dripped over Cap's face was one I'd never forget. "What?"

Reid drew in a deep breath. "It's true. Some of the police from our local precinct are seen in some of this footage helping them offload crates."

Cap tilted his head. "And you can prove this?"

I nodded. "Yeah, we can."

The man didn't hesitate to turn toward his agents standing outside of Angel's I.C.U. room.

"All right, everyone! Listen up! We've got a crew in the area who is familiar with the ins and outs of the people we're tracking! You listen to them! Educate yourself! And stay vigilant!"

"Does that mean you're helping?" I asked Dee as Cap shoved his way out the door.

Dee peered over his shoulder at Angel before he nodded. "Let's find a place to set up shop. She still needs her rest."

And as he looked over at her heart monitor for any sign of life, I found myself doing the same thing.

Anything to convince myself that she was still in there, fighting to get back to us.

32

CASH

"I want a full patrol around this hospital," Cap said as his voice echoed in through the waiting room outside. "I want security footage looked at by our professionals to make sure Special Agent DeMarco is safe and secure here at the hospital. I want to be shown anything that can be construed as a plausible threat."

I thumbed over my shoulder as I looked at Angel's partner. "He always like this?"

Dee snickered. "The next thing he'll want is a place to set up shop. Anywhere we can go that isn't here?"

Reid hooked his fingers into the pockets of his jeans. "We could set up shop at the clubhouse."

Baron slowly looked over at him with a killer stare.

"Or," Reid said as his eyebrows rose, "we could use one of our warehouses. They're mostly abandoned now. We use one of them as a mechanic shop for our bikes and vans. But it would be a good place to lay low."

I pointed at Reid. "That's not a half-bad idea, actually. Most of them are off the beaten path, so we'd hear people coming from at least a few miles away."

"Plus," Baron said as he drew in a deep breath through his

nose, "the warehouses provide more cover. More layers of protection between infiltration and location. The clubhouse is a target right now, anyway, so it's not the safest place we could be."

Dee licked his lips. "Then, one of the warehouses it is. You guys choose which one, and then we can get on the road."

Cap dipped his head back into the room. "Doc says only one person is allowed in the I.C.U. room at a time."

I grinned. "Guess we broke that rule a while back, huh?"

Dee snickered before he pushed through us. "Let's go get those drugs and those dirty fucking cops off the road."

I pointed at Baron as we walked out behind Dee. "What about the warehouse that—"

But it was Reid that held up his hand. "Cash makes a good point. We've got the perfect warehouse to lay low in if everyone wants to follow me."

Baron chuckled as he peeked over at me. "He's a good team lead, don't you think?"

I shot him a look. "Don't you go getting any funny ideas now."

He shrugged. "I'm just saying."

"Well, don't," I said flatly.

"You heard the man!" Cap barked. "Fall in line behind…"

"Reid," he said with a nod of his head.

"Reid!" Cap exclaimed. "His motorcycle is outside. It's…"

Reid smirked. "It's the red and silver one parked out by the dumpsters toward the side of the hospital."

One of the agents decked out in all black piped up. "The one with the chrome accents?"

Reid beamed with pride. "That's the one."

"I'm riding with him!" the agent shouted before he stepped out of the crowd.

That made me chuckle as I looked down at my boots.

"Everyone else!" Cap bellowed as he commanded his troops, "double up with a biker. We're riding tandem today, everyone!"

I had to admit, riding with a DEA agent on the back of my bike was a new one. Couldn't honestly say I enjoyed the feeling of some dude with his arms wrapped around me. But I sure as fuck wasn't gonna complain. We were out of hot water. At least, for that moment. And with Angel safe and sound back at the hospital, I knew we stood a chance.

We finally stood a chance at taking down the Black Diamonds.

"All right," Cap said as Baron stood next to him, "everyone has seen all of the footage on the cameras?"

The sea of black, helmeted heads nodded.

"Perfect," Cap said, placing his hands on the dusty, dirty table in front of him. "Now that we're all caught up on what's been happening, you should know that we reached out to Myrtle Beach Police before they had a chance to contact the local precinct. So, at least for now, they're in the dark."

"Hell yeah," I murmured as I stood in between two dinky looking agents.

"I gave them the rundown on everything we know so far," Dee said, stepping up to the plate, "and they're standing at the ready in case they're needed."

"Uh, guys?" the older man with the laptop asked.

"Say your peace," Cap said flatly.

The guy turned his laptop screen around. "There's another shipment coming into the dock tonight."

"You're fucking kidding me," Reid said.

I rushed toward the old man with the tech equipment. "Let me see that."

Cap quickly found his way over my shoulder. "What are you looking for?"

My eyes scanned the screen as I read the manifesto, and sure enough, I recognized the sign-off name.

"That," I said as I pointed.

"The signature?" the white-haired agent asked.

"Do you know that person?" Cap asked.

I tapped my finger against the screen. "That signature belongs to Detective Groundstone."

"Who?" Cap asked.

Reid leaned toward him. "The tall, lanky redheaded man in the videos that towers over everyone else."

"Ah, I see," Cap said.

"Good catch," I said as I patted the techy agent's shoulder, "and you're right. Looks like they're getting another shipment in tonight."

"What are the chances that it's a trap?" Dee asked.

Baron shrugged. "Not zero. But they've been scrambling lately. There's also as much of a chance that they don't know what's going on right now."

"If they're shipping in tonight and we can catch them red-handed, this case will be as open and shut as they come," Cap said.

I chuckled. "I like how that sounds."

"But," Cap said, pointing his finger into the air, "you guys won't be shooting your bullets. That's our job."

"Oh man," Reid said with a groan.

Baron shoved his elbow into Reid's ribcage. "Of course, captain."

Cap's face fell flat. "I'll just pretend I didn't hear that."

"Good idea," I said with a nod of my head.

"So, what are we helping with?" Baron asked. "Tell us what you need, and we'll provide."

Cap's back straightened. "We need your guys' help and prior knowledge to get us in and out without casualties. Help us navigate sticky situations in case someone does spot us."

"AKA," Dee said, "help us when we need heavier hands for help."

That damn near made me smile. "We can do that."

"But the important thing is that we do this by the book," Cap said as he clasped his hands behind his back. "If nothing else, because Special Agent DeMarco and her brother deserve that."

"Here, fucking here," I muttered.

"Seriously, though," Dee said as he leaned against the table, "what are the chances that there are three back-to-back shipments coming in at the same dock? If there's anything that smells like a trap, it's that."

I would have spoken, but Baron beat me to the punch. "We could go ahead. Scout things out. Me, Cash, and Reid are very familiar with how The Black Diamonds do things. We'll be able to know whether or not this is credible just by looking."

Cap leveled his gaze with Baron's. "You won't be going anywhere without my men in tow. At least one to each one of you."

I shrugged. "We wouldn't have it any other way."

"If we see any sign of those crates, you are our first call in," Reid said.

"Plus," Dee said as he came to stand by me, "I can go with them so that if we see the crates but we're a bit late, we've still got the manpower to rush them."

We all stood silent as Cap chewed on the inside of his cheek. His gaze fell to the laptop screen before he looked back up at me. His gaze volleyed around the room, almost as if he took the time to look each and every one of his agents in their eyes.

Almost as if to dare them to fuck this up.

"Sounds good to me," Cap finally said.

So, Baron raised his hand in the air and snapped his fingers. "Fall in line, guys!"

The crew moved steadily like a marching band. They formed a line along the outer perimeter of the warehouse room walls, staring inward at all of the DEA agents. Baron grinned with pride. I had to admit, it was a hell of a sight to behold. And as Cap smirked, he looked over at Dee.

"You take the three of them and two other men of ours. Load yourselves up, get down to the dock, and stay vigilant."

Dee didn't hesitate. "Browns. Vernon. You're with us."

"And if you see those crates?" Cap asked.

The entire room focused on him as his face turned red with fury.

"You end this," he glowered.

I saw why Angel enjoyed working for him.

The motorcycle vibrated between my legs. Every time the engine revved, it reminded me of Angel. God, what I wouldn't have given for her to be squeezing me around my waist instead of some dickhead named Vernon.

Who the hell hated their kid enough to name them Vernon anyway?

As our bikes soared toward the southernmost dock of the outskirts of Barbeau, I wondered how she was doing. Was she awake yet? Was she still stable? Maybe she had already opened her eyes? No, she couldn't do that. The coma was medically induced. The doctors put her under, and they were the only ones that could bring her out.

It killed me to think about it.

"Perch point," Baron said into the microphones we attached to our helmets.

I raised my hand to let him know that he had been heard, as did Cash. I was glad that none of our other men had been roped into this just yet because there was no telling what awaited us at the docks. I was thankful that Baron was taking this as seriously as it needed to be taken. The last thing we needed was yet more blood on our hands. So, a couple miles out from the docks, we took a sharp left that shot us up an embankment.

That led us to a hill that formed into a massive dune overlooking the whole of the coastline.

"Wow," Vernon said as we came to a stop at the cliffside, "it's beautiful up here."

I ripped my helmet off. "They're down below us on the dock. Or at least, they should be."

Vernon slipped off the back of my bike as Baron and Cash parked on either side of me. There was water as far as my eyes could see. White-capped waves, undulating out in the middle of the ocean. Highscape Dune was a local secret. A place we told tourists was blocked off due to mudslide and rockfall dangers. But really, it was just to keep their dirty, grimy hands off Barbeau's most decadent secret.

"So, we just sit here?" Cash asked. "Or do we need to help them out with something?"

Baron shook his head. "Stay back, just like we said we would. We've given them the vantage point. Now, it's up to them to find what they need."

The three DEA agents, dressed in all black and standing out against the watery horizon like a sore fucking thumb, crawled on their stomachs to the edge of the cliff. I watched with a tightly furrowed brow as they peeked their cameras over the edge, peering through the massive lenses and snapping pictures left and right.

God, how I wanted to plug those Diamond fuckers with bullets.

"She's in the best hands possible for getting out of this," Baron said as he settled his hand on my shoulder.

I drew in a deep breath through my nose. "That obvious, huh?"

Cash snickered. "You've always worn your emotions on your face."

Baron patted me. "She's gonna pull through just fine."

I shrugged off his touch, though. I didn't want to hear it. I was responsible for this. I left her in that room. I left her by herself to be attacked like an innocent animal feeding on lunch. I left her all alone, and now she was in a coma in the hospital when she should've been with us. On the backs of our bikes. Ending this with us for her brother.

I had to swallow the bile creeping up the back of my throat.

"I've got eyes on the package."

My ears perked up. "What did Vernon just say?"

I watched Dee scramble toward us. "We've got eyes on the package, guys. Good job."

Browns craned his head over his shoulder. "Eyes on the package. Triple confirmation. We need to get in there."

Baron shot Dee a look. "Phone your boss. It's time to do this."

Dee pulled his cell phone out of his pocket, dialed a number, and held it up to his ear. "Cap, it's me. Uh huh. Yep. All three of us. Triple confirmation, yes. Yep, we'll get into position. Uh huh. We can do that. Yep. Talk soon."

And when he hung up the phone, we all sat on pins and fucking needles.

"Well?" I asked.

Dee shoved his cell back into his pocket. "It's time to do this. Cap and the formation team are seven minutes out. We've been given strict instructions to stay up here and feed coordinated attacks to them through our earpieces. You know, eyes in the sky."

"Perfect," I said as I swung my leg off my bike. "What do you want us doing?"

"Reid," Baron said.

"What?" I asked. "It's a simple question."

Dee pinned me with a look, though. "You heard my boss. You guys watch from up here. From behind the scenes."

I shook my head. "Oh, no you don't. You guys aren't taking all the action from us. We deserve this."

"Reid," Baron said curtly.

"Seriously," I glowered as I got into Dee's face, "let us help."

"I can't," Dee said, shaking his head.

"He's right, you know," Cash said.

I slowly peered over my shoulder. "You'll have to be more specific than that."

But when Cash looked at me, I knew exactly who he was talking about.

"Oh, come on," I glowered. "Not you, too."

"I know you feel responsible, but now isn't the time to let your guilt speak for you," Cash said as he leaned back on his bike. "If we go in there, it makes their case sloppy, at best. We have to stay behind on this one and let them do what they do best. If anything, so it holds up in court."

I scoffed and looked over at Baron. "You can't be serious. We're just gonna sit this one out? After what they did to her?!"

It was Dee who grabbed my arm and swung me back around to face him. "Do you know which one beat her like that? Which one, exactly?"

I nodded without hesitation. "Yeah, I do."

"Show me."

"Reid," Baron warned.

I shot him a look. "We help by providing support and answering their questions, right?"

He didn't answer. He simply continued to stare me down, as if that would get me to stop.

"Show. Me," Dee commanded.

So, I grabbed his wrist and led him to the edge of the cliff.

"See the one over there? The one with the sort of gray and blondish hair?"

Dee pulled a gun scope out of his back pocket and held it up to his face. "The one with all of the pocked zit scars on his face?"

"That's the one."

He slowly lowered the scope. "That's who beat her like that?"

I licked my lips. "Yep."

He tucked the scope back in his pocket. "Let us do this the way we need to for our court case, and I won't question whatever the fuck has happened between the three of you and Angel. Deal?"

I peered over my shoulder at Baron. "What do you think?"

Cash snickered. "Fine by me."

"I wasn't asking you," I said flatly.

Baron ground his teeth together before he relented. "Deal. Just plug that scarface son of a bitch for us."

Dee pulled his gun off his hip and checked the magazine. "That's a deal I'll always be able to make."

Maybe Angel's partner wasn't so bad after all.

"They're here," Vernon said.

Dee placed his finger to his earpiece. "Yep, read you loud and clear."

"What is he saying?" Baron asked.

Dee drew in a deep breath. "They're here and getting into position. On Cap's count, they're going in."

"You guys wanna come and see?" Browns asked.

"Hell yeah," Cash said as he walked to the edge of the cliff.

"Get down. Yeah, like that. Just crouch down and become one with the cliff's edge," Browns said.

"Don't mind if I do," Baron muttered as he took up a perched point beside Cash.

But I didn't move as I looked over at Dee. "You ready for this?"

He gazed out over the blue horizon. "I wish she were here to see this."

I nodded mindlessly. "Me, too."

Dee quickly placed his finger back to his earpiece. "They're heading in. Let's go."

"What would Angel be doing right now if she were with us?"

Dee ripped the scope out of his back pocket once more and attached it to his gun. "Wanna know why we call her Angel?"

"Because it was once her mother's nickname?"

Dee's eyebrows rose. "She really does open up to you guys, doesn't she?"

I decided to keep my secrets to myself. "Something like that."

He cocked his gun and crouched down at the edge of the cliff. "We call her 'Angel' because she's our angel eyes. She's the master at calling out positions from above."

I smiled as I crouched next to him. "Well, let's do her justice then."

"In position," Dee said.

And not three seconds later, sirens whirred from out of nowhere as a massive SUV crashed through the dock gates.

"This is the DEA! Everyone! Put down your weapons!"

34

ANGEL

"Oh, my God, Angel. You should've seen the looks on their faces," Reid said as he roared with laughter.

"You would've been proud of Dee, too. There wasn't a motherfucker he set his scope on that he didn't pluck from all the way up on that dune," Cash said with pride.

"Don't let Reid fool you, either," Baron said as he perched himself on the edge of my bedside. "He called out those positions as everyone scattered like a pro."

"I think I could have a career in it, honestly," Reid said.

Cash sputtered as he laughed. "Over your dead body, asshole."

There were my boys. My excited, accomplished boys. All of them, in that room with me, breaking rules the way God intended them to be broken. I hated that I still couldn't move. That I still couldn't open my eyes. That I couldn't be there when they rushed those motherfucks on the dock and arrested them one by one.

But having them all in my room while they filled me in on things was enough.

"I have to admit, that partner of yours is a spitfire," Baron said.

"You should know," Reid said as he bent his lips to my ear, "that he had a very special bullet for a very special someone with scars on his face."

"Don't tell her that," Cash muttered.

"Don't tell me you think she won't like it," Baron said playfully.

"That man is never touching you again. Dee and I made sure of that," Reid whispered.

God, what I wouldn't have given to throw my arms around his neck and crash our lips together. I knew Dee would get along with them. Given enough time to push past facades and stereotypes, Dee was more like them than most.

How many did you get? Did you catch them red handed? Is everyone okay?

BEEP BEEP BEEP BEEP BEEP BEEP BEEP BEEP!

"Whoa, whoa, whoa, whoa," Baron said as he took my hand, "settle down, sweet girl. Everyone's okay. Everyone made it out just fine. No one got hurt. Shh, shh, shh."

BEEP BEEP BEEP BEEP BE--... BEEP BEEP BEEP... BEEP BEEP... BEEP... BEEP BEEP.

"That's a good girl," Baron whispered.

"We got 'em," Cash said as he picked up my foot and massaged it. "Reid called out those positions as they scattered, and one by one, they were picked off."

"I've never seen so many arrests in my entire life," Baron murmured.

"We caught them with the crates, too," Reid said as he perched on the other side of me. "We caught them right in the middle of unloading them."

"And those dirty cops we saw?" Cash asked. "Already being charged."

"Seems that our cameras with all of their footage came in very handy with your boss," Baron said.

God, I bet Cap had a field day. If there was one thing he couldn't stand, it was a cop that went back on his word. Cap started out as a beat cop in his local town way back in the day. He took that shit very, very seriously. He always dedicated himself to the right cause, even if he did walk around like he had a stick shoved up his asshole.

I wish I could have been there with you guys.

Reid snickered. "I mean, between hijacking those crates that we did, putting them in Myrtle Beach territory, and working with the DEA? We could damn near be informants at this point."

"Don't tempt me. I had way too much fun watching those idiots go down," Baron said.

"You know what was awesome, though?" Cash asked.

What? Tell me, cutie pie, what was so brand-spanking awesome?

Cash leaned down into my ear, as if he were whispering a secret. "Watching Baron negotiate the terms of our innocence with your boss would've made you wet as hell."

"Cash," Baron warned.

"What?" he asked as he rose back up. "It would have."

Oh, trust me. It did.

I couldn't wait to tell him that myself, too.

Baron chuckled. "Anyway, the DEA has the real assholes in custody, and we've helped to clear our names by helping to clear our hometown's streets."

"We have you to thank for that, too," Cash said as he ran his fingers through my hair.

"So, when you wake up, you'll be free to go home," Baron said mindlessly.

"We hope you don't go, though," Reid said.

"Reid," Cash hissed.

"What?!" he asked as his voice grew high-pitched.

"It's her decision," Baron said. "It's always been her decision, and hers alone."

"Well, I'm not lying to her, even if we aren't sure that she can hear us," Reid said.

"Oh, she can hear us, all right," Cash said. "She'll come back to us, too. She's too strong not to."

My heart grew three sizes that day. One for each man I had somehow managed to grow to care about. I didn't know how it happened. I wasn't sure what I'd tell them once I finally woke up. Once I was finally allowed out of my skin prison. But I had.

I cared for all three of them.

And I wasn't leaving them unless I absolutely had to.

"Your brother's been avenged," Baron said as he laced our fingers together.

"You did it," Reid said as he took my other hand and laced our fingers together as well.

Cash picked up my other foot and massaged it, too. "Just rest so you can come back to us sooner, okay? That's all we ask."

My God, we did it.

My brother could finally rest in peace.

Tears brewed behind my eyes. Even though my chest didn't jump. Even though my heart monitor crept back up, I couldn't help myself. The overwhelming happiness was too much. My yearning for them was too strong. And as a tear slid out from beneath my crusted eyelid, it slipped down my cheek, I felt a pair of lips press against it.

"We knew you were in there," Reid whispered against my skin.

I will always be here. Always.

I tried my best to stay awake. I did my best to stay up while they chattered on happily about the DEA sting. It all sounded so amazing, so wonderful. The culmination of so much hard work on everyone's part. But I couldn't. My body simply wouldn't allow me to stay awake. Their voices faded in and out until darkness overcame me, and every time I felt myself rising to the surface, I was met with the sounds of silence.

Beeping, unrestrained silence.

God, this fucking sucks.

Days passed by in a blur. Sometimes, I swore I heard my boys laughing. Sometimes, I swore I felt Dee's hand grasping mine. Hell, at one point in time, I would have bet my life on the fact that Cap had talked with me. But my body was too tired. It all came back in snippets. Little mindless snapshots of a life passing me by while I wasted away in a hospital bed. Being turned by nursing staff. Being sponge-bathed by people I didn't know. Listening to Doc prattle on about medications and how wounds were healing well. How the drain catheter was close to being removed.

And sometimes, I woke up to someone stroking my hair.

"My sweet girl."

Or someone reading me a book.

"Oh, you're gonna like this part, princess."

Or someone holding my hand and crying.

"You've got this, princess. Just stay strong a little longer for us."

I'd never felt so cherished in all my life, and all I wanted was to tell them just how much all of them being there meant to me. Taking time out of their daily lives to come sit with me. Talking with me, hoping I heard them. Giving me something to wake up to. Something to look forward to.

Something to remind me that all of it was real.

That they were real.

JonJon, you'd be so fucking proud of them right now.

"He'd be so proud of you right now, Angel."

Dee squeezed my hand before his forehead touched down against my own.

"He would be so, so fucking proud of you," he whispered.

How's Cap? Is he doing okay?

"I won't take up much of your time, I know you're resting," Cap said as he patted my arm. "But, uh, the guys send their regards. You know, Vernon. Browns. McTavish."

How's Mrs. McTavish? Has she had her baby yet?

"When you wake up, all I want you to focus on is getting better," Cap said as my hospital bed bowed to his seated position.

Seriously, did she have the baby yet?

"And, uh, I just want you to know that when you wake up—when you, uh, when you come home—there's a team lead job waiting for you."

Wait, what?

Cap snickered. "I don't know why I never recommended you for it in the first place, because you're perfect for the job. You're resourceful. Tenacious. Stubborn as hell."

You're damn right.

"I need someone like that heading up my coastal lead teams."

JonJon, I did it. Did you hear that? I did it!

"How long did you say it would take again, Doc?"

Huh?

"It depends on the person, really. Could take twenty-four hours. Could take up to three days."

"Well, it's already been two," Cash said. "Shouldn't she have woken up by now?"

Where did Cap g—Wait, what did he say?

Doc sighed. "It's not a formal art, you guys. It takes time. I can give you a roundabout timeframe, but it's all up to her body and what it feels is right."

How long has it been? What day is it? Is Cap still here?

"When do we know she's coming out of it?" Reid asked.

When I start doing this.

I bared down as hard as I could. Granted, it wasn't much. But when I felt my stomach muscles contract, the pain that shot through my body soared my heart through the roof. Grunts tried to bubble up the back of my throat as I commanded my legs to move. As I willed my hands to flex. And as pain rushed through every vein of my body, I fought.

I fought harder than I ever had in my entire life.

"When that starts happening," Doc said before he cried out. "I need a nurse!"

"Angel!" Baron bellowed.

"Angel, open those eyes for us," Reid said.

"Squeeze my hand," Cash said as he slid his roughed-up palm against mine. "If you can hear me, just squeeze my hand."

Come on, you've been under long enough. Let's open these eyes.

"Back up," Doc said as Cash's hand slipped out of mine. "You can't all be in here, anyway. Nurses! Get them out."

"Over my dead body," Baron glowered.

"Angel!" Reid exclaimed.

"Open those eyes for us, princess!" Cash cried out.

"Come on," Doc muttered as both of my hands grew eerily cold. "Wake up. Open those eyes for us. I know it's hard, but you can do this. You've come this far. Bring it home for us."

"Angel!" Baron bellowed.

I didn't know if it was his voice, the desperation in their pleas, or the way the pain coursing through my body seemed to remind me that I was alive. But when my eyes snapped open, I gasped for air. Spit dribbled down my lips, inching closer to my neck as tears flooded my gaze. My arms shot into the air. I wiggled my toes for the first time in what seemed like years.

And as tears flooded my cheeks, threatening to drown out my body, I saw them. Three blurry shadows, looming over me. Cloaking me in their shadow.

My boys.

"What did she say?" Baron asked. "Doc! She's trying to talk."

Oh, my boys.

Doc appeared in my vision. "Hold still, we have to remove your breathing tube. On the count of three, exhale as hard as you can for me. All right?"

I nodded my head as tears rushed my neck.

"All right," he said as he grasped the tube. "Three. Two. One. Exhale!"

I girded my stomach and bared down on my lungs. I choked and slobbered on myself as the pipe worked its way out of my body. My eyes rolled back. My stomach jumped. Nausea washed over me, threatening to ruin my entire world as the pipe emerged from my lungs and exited through my mouth.

And when I gasped for fresh air for the very first time since blacking out, kisses peppered my face.

"We knew you could do it."

"There's my good girl."

"Hey there, princess. Can you hear me?"

"Looking more gorgeous than ever, if you ask me."

"My boys," I choked out.

I raised my shaking hands into the air and cupped their cheeks. Felt their tears. Slid my fingertips over their smiles and relished their warmth. My body felt so cold. So empty. So useless for so fucking long. Yet, as their lips coated my face, warmth encompassed me.

I was finally back.

"Oh, my God. My boys," I choked out.

"We have to start unhooking her from the machines. We've got tests we need to run," Doc said.

"Just a few more seconds, Doc," Baron said.

"We'll move in a bit, we promise," Cash said breathlessly.

"You are so strong," Reid said as he pressed a kiss to my forehead, "so very, very strong."

I snickered. "Ain't gotta tell me that twice."

"All right," Doc said, "I've given you all the time that I can. Angel?"

"Yeah, Doc?" I asked groggily.

"We're going to perform some preliminary tests before I get a nurse in here to draw blood and schedule scans. You good with that?"

I lobbed my head toward his voice. "Fucking hell, it feels good to move."

He smiled. "I bet it does."

I swallowed hard. "Yeah, yeah, that all sounds great. But when can I get out of here?"

Baron chuckled. "Shocker."

"Let's take this one step at a time, okay?" Cash asked.

"Well, it's a good question," Reid said. "When can she at least be moved to a regular room?"

Doc flashed a harsh light in my eyes. "Good dilation. Means the draining catheter worked for your concussion. How's your head feeling?"

I shrugged. "A bit weird."

"Weird, how?" Doc asked.

I shook it softly. "Empty. Or maybe just swimmy?"

"No pain?" he asked.

I shook it again. "Not even in my neck. Is that good?"

Doc grinned from ear to ear. "That's very good, Angel. Very, very good."

"Ha-HA!" Cash exclaimed as he clapped his hands. "She did it! I knew she could do it."

Baron smiled. For the first time, I saw him smile. And it stopped my heart in its tracks.

"'Atta, girl. I knew you could do it."

Reid couldn't help himself as he placed another kiss on my forehead. "We'll have you out of here in no time, okay? Just you wait."

"What is it?" Cash asked.

I hadn't even realized that I'd been staring at him. But I couldn't help myself. I was so relieved that they were there, and so fucking happy to be alert and coherent and moving. However, I had things I wanted to say to them.

Private, important things.

"Doc, can you give us all a second?" I asked.

He thumbed over his shoulder. "I'll go ahead and get those scans scheduled before I send the nurses in."

"Thanks."

And it wasn't until he exited the room, leaving the door cracked behind him, that I reached out and took Cash's hand.

"I heard it. I heard all of it."

Cash's smile fell from his face. "What?"

I squeezed his hand. "I heard what you said. I heard all of you, really. And there are things I want to say, okay? So, let me get them out."

Cash tilted his head. "Of course."

I slid my thumb up and down the knuckles of his fingers. "I don't care what you think about yourself, you're an amazing father. You did right by that boy until the very end. Not many men would have done what you did, making the choices you made. And I know you feel like you failed him. But if you ask me? He got the exact father he needed for the life he was destined to live. He got you, and I know he had a life well-lived because of it."

Cash's eyes were so wide that I thought they'd pop out of his head. "Thank you."

I moved my hand up to Reid's face and cupped his cheek. "Tell me your memories, and I will help keep them alive for you. Tell me all of them, and then we can talk about them so they aren't gone any longer. Anything you want. Any memory, any time, any place. And we can talk about them for as long as you'd like. Okay?"

Tears crept into his eyes. "Okay. Yeah, I—I can do that."

Then, I lobbed my head back over and placed my other hand on Baron's forearm. "It hurts the most when ones we love betray us. But you and I both know how absolutely terrible drugs are. It can change a person, right down to their core. Change them into someone we don't even recognize. I watched them devour my brother like you watched them devour Whicker. And whenever you're ready to talk about it, know that I get it. I understand, Baron. And I am always ready and willing to listen."

"Goddamn it, you beautiful woman," he growled.

He dipped down and crashed his lips to mine.

The moan that escaped from my mouth was swallowed down the back of his throat. His tongue commanded respect as it raked across the roof of my mouth, and my heart monitor fluttered wildly in the wind. My body came alive. My spirit soared into the heavens. Everything warmed, from my toes to my nose, as his hand slipped beneath my head.

I love this man.

"I love you, too," Baron muttered.

"Wait, what?" I asked against his lips.

He pulled back softly. Just enough to gaze into my eyes. "You said that out loud, sweet girl."

I blushed furiously. "I—I did?"

He grinned. "You did."

I slid my fingers into his thick salt and pepper hair. "Well, I do."

He captured my lips one more time softly. "I love you, too, Angel."

Then, someone bumped Baron out of the way before Cash appeared in my field of vision. "My turn."

He didn't crash his lips to mine, but instead settled them softly against my tired, cracked pout. His tongue slid along my lips, almost as if he were licking my wounds clean. I cupped the back of his head and pulled myself upright against him. His arms cloaked me, pulling me into his strength as someone propped pillows up behind my back.

And as our lips parted, he settled me against their softness.

"I love you, too, Cash," I whispered.

He nuzzled his nose against mine. "I love you, too, Angel."

"Angel?" Reid asked.

My gaze searched for him. "Yeah, Reid?"

He slowly came into view. "Can I ask you something?"

I reached out and ran my fingers through his hair. "Of course."

His forehead softly came down against mine. "Don't kiss me yet."

My brow furrowed together. "Why not?"

He picked up his head and gazed deeply into my eyes. "Because I love you. I love you with everything that I am. But I want our kiss to happen when the time is right. Not out of desperation, sadness, or a craving. But when it's really, actually right."

I smiled softly. "Who would've thought that Reid would've been the softie romantic?"

"Me," Baron and Cash said together.

Reid rolled his eyes. "Fuck you both."

I winked at him. "Nah, just me. Though, I'm sure they wouldn't mind watching."

"Wait," Baron said, "does that mean *you* don't mind us watching?"

"Yeah, I'm not gonna ask about that one."

I gasped. "Dee!"

He laughed as he came into the room, parting the guys like the red fucking sea. "Come here, girl."

"Dee! You're still here!" I exclaimed.

I didn't have enough strength to sit up, but I didn't have to, because the instant he threw himself at me, I wrapped him up and refused to let him go.

"You gonna start believing me a little more now?" I muttered against the crook of his neck.

He cackled as he held me close. "I won't have a choice since you're about to be my boss."

"If you take the job, that is," Cap said.

I smiled at him over Dee's shoulder. "We do have much to discuss."

Cap held up his hand, though. "When you're better and not in the hospital. For now, focus on getting out of here. Then, we can talk about your very bright future at the DEA."

I nodded. "Thank you, sir."

"All right, everyone," Cap said as he clapped his hands together. "Show's over. Nothing to see here. Everyone, back to the plane! We board in two hours' time!"

"Does that mean you, too?" I asked Dee.

He released me and tucked a strand of hair behind my ear. "I've got the okay to stay through the weekend. But you know bad guys and their drugs."

I smiled. "They never stay down for long."

"Exactly."

"I hate to break things up," Doc said as he closed the door behind him, blocking out the cacophony skittering around in the hallway. "But it's blood test time."

"I've come to suck your blood," I said mockingly.

Doc smiled as he came up to my side. "I see your strength is returning."

I gave him a thumbs up. "Slowly, but surely."

"Good," Dee said as he stood up and patted the top of my hand, "means we can get you out of here quicker."

"One step at a time," my boys said in unison.

My boys.

I really enjoyed the way that sounded bouncing around in my head.

Four Weeks Later

The salted air wafted beneath my nose as a cool breeze kicked up. I leaned against the railing, holding my arms out as the blanket Baron picked up for me in town the other day fluttered around my body. I had been back at the clubhouse for three weeks since my discharge, and they hadn't let me out of their sight. Everywhere I went, there they were. Every meal. Every need. Every whim indulged.

I almost didn't want to go back to the real world.

Listening to them talk about how they bum-rushed the Black Diamonds down at the dock never ceased to make me jealous. Oh, what I would have given to have been a fly on the wall for their arrest. Still, as I drew in a deep breath of fresh air, I found myself appreciative of the efforts of my coworkers.

Of my partner.

Of my boys.

"You don't have to, you know," Baron said as he came up behind me.

I smiled when he threaded his arms around my waist. "I don't have to what?"

He kissed the top of my head. "Go back to work. You know we wouldn't make you if you didn't want to. We'd understand."

I smiled brighter than ever before. "I love what I do for work, though."

He buried his nose into my hair. "Then, do what makes you happy."

"I do that already."

"I think that statement requires a bit of proof," Cash said as he came and slid his hand into mine, "don't you think?"

I cackled at his comment before Reid slid his hand into my other one. "Seeing you upright is nice."

I peeked over at him as I threaded our fingers together. "You say that every day."

Reid leaned in and kissed my temple. "I'll never stop saying it, either."

Cash squeezed my hand. "I'd rather have her on her back, if we're being honest."

I snickered. "We can make that happen, you know. The bed's just upstairs."

I expected laughter. Or chuckling. Hell, even a bit of a snicker. Anything to tell me that they had caught my joke, or that I hadn't overstepped a line. They had been so overprotective of me. Helping me in and out of the bathtub. Out of the shower. Off the fucking toilet, for crying out loud.

I had no privacy around these men.

I wasn't sure I wanted it, though.

"How are you feeling, sweet girl?" Baron asked.

I released their hands and turned around in his arms so I could look up into his face when I answered.

"I've never felt better, actually. Why?"

Reid clicked his tongue. "She did have a good check up with Doc yesterday."

Cash slid his hand along the nape of my neck before threading his fingers through my hair. "She's also eating better now."

I closed my eyes at the feel of his touch. "Mmmm, not my fault Baron can cook up a storm."

His knee slipped between my thighs. "She does act like she's got her strength back."

Cash pulled my head back, looking at me upside down. "And we have waited so very, very long."

Goddamn it, I was ready to melt in a puddle at their feet. "Kiss me, Cash."

He grinned. "Ain't gotta tell me twice."

When his lips descended to mine, I was transported. Baron's knee worked its way softly against my clothed pussy as Cash's tongue slid down the back of my throat. I lost my hands in his hair. I pulled him closer, wanting more of him as Baron's hands gripped my waist. His fingertips curled into my excess, holding me against the railing as the sea breeze wrapped around all of us.

Then, Reid yanked me away and tossed me over his shoulder.

"Oh!" I squealed.

He spanked my ass. "I'll take her upstairs. You two, follow me."

I giggled all the way back into the house. I waved at the guys being rushed out the door by Baron, and all they did was cackle as Cash rushed me up the stairs. Before I knew it, my body bounced against a soft mattress. Pillows fell to the floor. My blanket fluttered into the corner as Cash grabbed my ankles, pulling me to the edge of the bed.

His hardened dick bulged against his jeans.

"Oh, we're gonna have a field day with you," he growled as he reached down for something.

My nipples puckered at the sound of his voice. "God, I hope so."

Chains rattled and snaps popped before someone rolled me over. My clothes were stripped off my body as my boys pulled me in all different directions. Off came my shirt. My bra. My skirt. Even my toes were bared for them as someone damn near ripped my socks to shreds getting them off my feet. My body was naked for them. I felt their heated, unforgiving stares along my back. And as Cash gripped my hips, something wrapped itself around my ankles.

"Make sure she can't go anywhere," Baron glowered.

And when I peeked around my body, I found Reid securing leather restraints around my ankles.

"Where did you get those?" I asked breathlessly.

Cash gripped my ass cheeks and pulled them apart. "God damn it, am I gonna have fun with you."

"Hey, be careful with that hole now," I said jokingly. "Not all of them have been used."

"Jesus Christ, please tell me you're not joking," Reid growled.

My eyes widened. I'd never heard him like that before. Feral and hungry. Ready for action. I swallowed hard as I gazed up at him. Something dropped against my asshole before it dripped down my crack. My toes curled. My head laid itself against the bed as I locked my eyes with Reid. And as he stood there, pulling his thick dick out of his pants, my jaw unhinged at the sheer girth of his cock.

"Dear God," I whispered.

He stroked himself right in front of me. "I think she wants to taste Baron first."

"What?" I asked mindlessly.

"Let's see what you taste like, hmm?" Cash asked.

The second his tongue touched down against my asshole, my entire body relaxed. I groaned with my cheek against the comforter as Cash spanked my ass. I jumped at his assault. My eyes rolled back as he shoved his tongue into my virginal, puckered hole. And as Reid stroked himself, all I wanted was to taste him. All I wanted was to lick that precum off the tip of his cock.

But Baron stepped into my field of vision and bounced his dick off my lips. "Open wide and be a good girl for me."

And oh, how good I wanted to be for him.

My jaw unhinged and he slipped against my tongue, marking whatever his cock touched. My eyes rolled into the back of my head as Cash lapped up my asshole, dipping down so far that he managed to tickle my entrance. My legs bucked. My ass slammed back against his face. Baron grunted as he wrapped his hand into my tangled hair, holding me steady as my throat expanded for him.

Before something thick tickled my entrance.

"Mmmm, mm, oh, fuck," I groaned around Baron's length.

Cash growled as he spanked both of my ass cheeks at once. "Time to stuff that pussy."

"Yes, yes, yes, yes, OH FUCK!"

"Goddamn it, sweet girl. Open that throat for me," Baron growled.

Cash buried himself into my depths, raking against my swollen walls as Baron forced his way down the back of my throat. I gagged and bucked back, my body trying to scurry away as Baron held me steady. My pussy collapsed around Cash, pulling sounds from his body that sounded otherworldly. I lost myself in them. In the rhythmic thumping of Cash's balls on my clit. In the fevered pitches of Baron's growls and grunts as his cock grew thicker against the back of my throat. My eyes rolled back. I heard Reid hissing and cursing beneath his breath, a hungry sound that tightened that coil behind my gut. I dug my hands into the mattress. I bucked ravenously back against Cash's dick. I felt him stuttering. I felt him slipping. And as Baron pinned my cheek to the mattress, all of us stilled.

As our orgasms crashed over us at once.

"Holy fucking Christ," Cash grunted.

"Good girl. Such a good fucking girl for me," Baron hissed.

And all I could do was lay there as my eyes fluttered closed and my body locked out.

I couldn't move. I couldn't breathe. My pussy pushed Cash's cock out. Baron eased his dick from my mouth, with my spit mixed with his arousal trickling from the corner of my mouth. He moved just long enough for me to see Reid in all his flushed glory. His dick, spewing threads of cum to the floor as I watched him fall back against the wall.

I'd never felt more cherished in all my life.

"Wrists," Cash commanded.

"Can do," Baron said gruffly.

I couldn't open my eyes, though. They were much too heavy with the force of the pleasure that had crashed over me. My body shivered. It quaked against the comforter as my body leaked with them. The restraints fell away from my ankles, but they were replaced by shackles upon my wrists. I lifted my head long enough to watch Baron latch the last one around me. His smirk, cockeyed and tired, and fucking hell, I took way too much pride in that.

Until Baron pulled a knife from his pocket and flipped it open.

"Huh?" I asked, my head still in a daze.

"I think I want that mouth next," Reid said as he stepped up to the side of the bed.

"Perfect," Baron said as he touched the blunt end of the blade against the top of my spine.

"Baron," I said breathlessly.

He removed the knife, grabbed my hair, yanked my head up, and pinned me with a look. "I suggest you stay very, very still, sweet girl."

I nodded quickly. "Okay."

He kissed my cheek. "Very still."

As he shoved my head back down to the bed, I damn near held my breath as he slid the knife down my spine. My toes curled as goosebumps of anticipation fled across my body. He teased that blade against me, parting my legs and pressing its blunt end into the excess of my inner thighs. My jaw quivered as Cash flopped into a chair in my field of vision, his dick still stiff as he stroked himself slowly.

"Like what you see, princess?" he asked with a grin.

But Reid quickly slipped into my field of vision. "Why don't you show me that tongue of yours?"

My eyes fluttered closed. "Huh?"

Baron spanked my ass so hard that it made me yelp.

"Ah!"

"Do as he says," Baron commanded.

I quickly stuck my tongue out and watched Reid settle his heavy dick onto the comforter. My mouth watered at the veins bulging at its tip. I was hungry for him. Hungry for all of them. And as Baron slid that knife between my legs, I felt the sharp edge of it slip between my pussy folds.

"Baron?" I asked quickly.

"Hold very, very still," he growled.

Reid inched his dick along my tongue, creeping it closer to my lips. Baron slid that sharp knife along my pussy folds, and I felt hair falling against my thigh. With every inch that tucked itself inside of my mouth, chunks of hair fell from my pussy. One stroke, one shave, one patch free of the confines my body had grown to protect itself in the hospital.

I felt free with every stroke of Baron's knife as Reid bottomed out against my face.

"God fucking damn it," he grunted.

"Almost there," Baron murmured.

I hollowed out my cheeks, teasing Reid's dick with the tip of my tongue as the last of my overgrown pussy hairs fell toward the bed. I felt something shifting beneath me before a hand cupped my newly-shaved folds, and I swear I knew nothing but the pleasure they shot through the marrow of my bones. Reid grabbed my hair, pumping my head as he fucked my face. Baron kept fondling my body, massaging my pussy folds until my juices ran down the expanse of my stomach.

"Baron, please," I whimpered.

Reid growled. "That's it. Vibrate that dick. Say my name."

"Reid," I groaned.

"Again."

My head bobbed quicker as he moved me how he wanted me. "Oh, Reid."

Baron slid his thick girth between my pussy folds. "One more time for me, sweet girl."

"Fucking Christ," Reid growled as he fucked my throat.

"Baron!" I cried out.

When he sank into me, the world faded into nothingness. Cash cheered me on as Reid stuffed my throat full and Baron pounded into me. The headboard of the bed bashed into the wall. The plaster cracked and gave way as Baron's fingertips curled heavily into my excess, his fingernails leaving marks as his fingerprints forever etched themselves into my skin. Every time he bucked me forward, it sank me deeper onto Reid's dick until the whole of me was taken up by them.

"I'm gonna come. I'm gonna come."

Reid yanked my head off his cock. "What was that, my little cum dumpster?"

I gasped for air. "So close. Please, don't stop. Baron, oh my God."

Reid cackled. "That's what I thought."

He shoved my head back down onto his dick, except this time, he held it there. My throat collapsed around him as I cried out Baron's name, his girth overwhelming me with its motions. Holes drilled into the walls. Cash chanted my name. Reid snarled, his cock stiffening as it pulsed with each and every load it blew down the back of my throat.

And when Baron's movements ceased, I felt his length filling me to the brim.

"Oooooh, my Goooood," I groaned.

"That's it," Reid hissed, "there's my gorgeous girl. So good for us. So obedient."

Baron collapsed, sending my stomach plummeting to the bed just before he caught himself on the mattress with his hands. The evidence of our love for one another seeped from between my thighs, soaking the bed beneath my stomach as someone removed the restraints from my wrists.

"Flip her over," Reid demanded. "It's time for me to have a turn."

I didn't know who rolled me over, but someone did, a smile overtook my face as I gazed up at the ceiling. With my body spent and my heart full, the bed moved with Reid's movements. He crawled up my body, on the prowl, like a lion in heat. He hovered over me, my legs spread for him as his massive dick cradled itself between my swollen, drenched pussy lips.

"Look at me," he said.

I forced myself to focus on him. "Reid."

He smiled softly before he bent down and kissed my nose. "I love you, Angel."

Tears rushed my eyes as my heart took flight. "You—you do?"

He searched my gaze. "More than I've ever loved anyone."

My lower lip quivered. "I love you too, Reid. I love you so—oh, my fuck! Oh!"

With one lurch of his hips, he stuffed my pussy full of him. My eyes rolled back. The world tilted over onto itself. But he didn't move. He sank our hips together. His cock filled my cunt. But as our hips sat together, all he did was lean back onto his haunches.

He gripped my hips and brought me with him.

"Mm, mm, mm," he said as he licked his lips, "I'm going to take my time with you."

"Reid," I said through my panting.

He stroked my slit before his thumb sank down to my clit. "I bet I can make you shake for me without my dick even moving."

"I-I-I-I—I—uh—"

He chuckled. "What? Cat got your tongue?"

The second he flicked his thumb over my swollen nub, my legs jumped. My walls throbbed. My pussy warmed. He swirled his thumb slowly. Deftly. Tenderly, around my swollen mound, as my jaw unhinged in silent pleasure. My hands tangled themselves in the damp comforter beneath me. My toes danced along the soft sheets as my knees wrapped around behind him.

His touch was so soft.

"Reid," I whispered.

"Oh, you'll be screaming my name by the time I'm done with you," he glowered.

His thumb moved quicker, swirling around my clit before he flicked it across its tip. My eyes snapped open as my back arched, and I found my body fucking itself against his dick.

"That's it," he hissed, "take what you want, my little whore. Milk my dick for all its worth."

"Reid," I choked out. "Oh, fuck."

He moved his thumb faster, applying a bit of pressure that

damn near blew me through the fucking roof. "That's it. Coat me in your mark. Drip down my balls, gorgeous. Oh, what a mess you are for me. I knew I wouldn't have to move. So horny for me. I bet you'll do all the fucking work just to fall apart, won't you?"

"Yes."

"Won't you?"

My eyes rolled back. "Oh fuck, yes."

"Then come for me, my little slut."

"Reid!" I cried out.

"There it is! I told you, gorgeous!"

I didn't even care. I didn't care how desperate I looked or what kind of a mess I made. I shoved myself onto his dick. I raked that protrusion against my walls as I ground myself against his thumb. I shivered in his wake. My pussy quaked with his movements. My body rolled and my back arched as I locked my legs around him.

Holding him close.

Never letting him go.

Then, I felt it.

"Yes, yes, yes, yes!" I cried out. "I'm coming. I'm coming. I'm coming."

"There it is," Reid growled.

"Goddamn it, Reid," I snarled.

"That's it," Baron said as he rushed to my side. "Be a good girl and open that mouth for me."

I lobbed my head over to look at him, but I didn't move quickly enough.

So, Reid spanked my clit. "Do as the nice man asks, my little cum slut."

I rested my cheek on the bed and unhinged my jaw for Baron.

"Good girl," he said as he sank his fingers into my hair.

"Looks like a reward is in order, then," Reid said, slowly moving his dick.

So fucking slowly that it was torturous.

"Fucking hell," I groaned.

Baron hissed. "Won't take long if you keep doing that."

I hollowed out my cheeks as Reid slowly inched his way back in. He pulled himself all the way out. All the way to the tip. Then, eased himself back in. Taking his sweet, precious time as my pussy juices dripped down my ass crack. Reid's thumb found my clit once more. He stroked it, languidly, matching the lazy movements of his cock as Baron claimed my throat.

"Fuck—yes—oh, my God. Angel. Such a good girl for us."

"Mmmmmmmmmmm."

I hummed around his dick as he exploded down my throat once again. He stumbled, his body falling to the bed as his shoulder slammed into the headboard. I felt him shifting as Reid teased my oversensitive nub. His dick, swelling my walls until I couldn't take it a second longer. Baron picked up my head and placed it in his lap. He panted for air as he stroked his fingers through my hair.

Then, Reid snapped his fingers. "Cash? You want another ride?"

I heard him stand before a chuckle fell from his lips. "Always."

Reid ushered his free hand toward me, as if I were nothing but a carnival ride. "By all means, step up to the plate."

"Fuck," I whispered.

Baron helped me turn my head. "Let's see that pretty little tongue of yours again. And Reid?"

"Yeah, Bossman?"

"Hand me her ankles."

My eyes widened. "Hand me her wh—amghmblgh."

Cash slid his cock into my watering mouth, but it was Reid who lifted my legs. He bent them across my stomach, toward my chest, where Baron then reached up and wrapped his massive hands around the entirety of my ankles. They folded me in half, my body pinned for them as I tilted my head back. Cash threaded his fingers into my hair, cocking my head at an angle that didn't hurt as he swiveled his hips.

"We have the best princess," Cash said as he smiled down at me.

But it was Reid who teased my asshole. "There's no toy in the world that can beat this view."

"I wonder what these taste like," Baron said as he brought my feet closer to his mouth.

I tried talking around Cash's girth. "I don't know if you wanna---mmmmmmmm my Gooooood."

Cash fucked my throat. "That's it. I can't handle it. Your throat is too good for me to hold still."

Reid pulled out and slammed himself back into my body. "Now you know how I feel about this tight little pussy."

"Mm, mm, mm," Baron said as he swirled his tongue around my ticklish toes, "you like that, don't you?"

I whimpered around Cash's dick as he tilted my chin up. It opened my throat, allowing the last inch or so of his intrusion to slide into place. Electricity overwhelmed me. My pussy clamped down around Reid's dick with every stroke of Baron's tongue. Never in my life had I felt so much at once. So full. So used. So beautiful. So...breathtaking. I didn't know whether to cry or come. I didn't know whether to moan or groan. And as they invaded the whole of my body, it transported me to another dimension.

One where nothing mattered except the four of us.

"Such a good girl," Baron growled with my big toe in his mouth.

"Does my princess want her stomach filled?" Cash asked.

I nodded quickly. "Mhm. Mhm. Mhm. Mhm."

Reid leaned onto the backs of my legs, pounding into my body as he stared down at my face. "Keep your eyes on me, gorgeous. Don't you dare close them. Not even once. Understood?"

My stare widened as I nodded. "Uh huh. Uh huh."

"Oh, fuck. So close," Cash hissed.

I reached out and curled my hands into the sheets of the bed. I kept my gaze locked on Reid, whose face contorted into monumental pleasure. My curves jumped with his assault. My tits threatened to smack me in the face as Cash unloaded, pouring his arousal down my throat. I swallowed every droplet of him. I swirled my tongue around the tip of his dick, feeling him shiver before he stumbled back. He collapsed into the chair in the corner before his head fell back against the wall.

His dick dwindled, hanging there, completely spent.

"Good fucking God," Cash managed to choke out.

"I love you," Reid growled. "God damn it, gorgeous, you're the only one for me."

"I love you," I said breathlessly.

"I love you," Baron said.

"I love you," Cash whispered.

"Mine," Reid snarled as he gnashed his teeth together.

I bucked my hips as Baron continued to hold my ankles at bay. My pussy dripped with their threads of arousal. My head swirled with their sounds. And as Reid's hips finally stuttered, Baron released my legs. They fell lifeless over Reid's shoulders as his lips dropped to mine, kissing me so deeply that I couldn't breathe. The world swirled around me. My lungs cried out for air. And yet, as he slammed into me one last time, our bodies unleashed together.

As if nothing else in the room existed.

"Oh, Angel," Reid growled down the back of my throat.

I wrapped my arms and legs around him, locking him against me as my body quaked uncontrollably.

"Reid," I said before I gasped for air, "oh, Reid. Don't move. Don't you dare move."

He sucked on my lower lip. "I'm going nowhere, gorgeous. Never, ever."

I wanted to make that same promise. I wanted to tell them that I was going nowhere. That I'd live with them. Love with them. Live my life with them for as long as they'd have me. My lungs burned as Reid and I collapsed. I gasped and panted, feeling life rush back through my muscles. The world swirled around and around, falling apart in exploding colors only to piece themselves back together again.

But Reid did the honors for me.

"You're not going anywhere, do you hear me?" he asked as his cock continued to fill me up.

I nodded. "Yes."

He picked his head up and gazed into my eyes. "You're living with us. You're staying with us. You'll find work with the DEA from here. But you're not going anywhere. Understood?"

I almost went cross-eyed from how lovely it sounded. "Understood."

He bent forward and kissed the tip of my nose. "Good."

"You mean that, right?" I asked quickly.

Reid paused his movements. "Every single fucking bit of it."

My eyes watered over. "Yeah?"

He pulled his hips back, removing his dick from between my legs as a gush of warm wetness poured from between my thighs.

"Yeah, gorgeous," he said as he settled softly on top of me, "I meant every syllable."

"He meant it for us, too," Baron said.

"Mhm," Cash hummed from his dilapidated position in the chair.

"I love you, Reid."

He smiled. "I love you, too, Angel."

I tilted my head back a bit. "I love you, Baron."

He bent forward and kissed my forehead. "I love you, too, Angel."

"Cash?" I asked.

"Hmmm?"

I giggled softly. "I love you."

He dug deep and found his strength. "I love you, too, princess."

And as I laid there, staring up at the ceiling of what was probably my new bedroom, I knew that whatever career move I made, I'd do it with them in mind. I knew that whatever decision I made, they'd be at the forefront of my considerations. My life was there with them. In some ways, it always had been, it had just taken me a while to figure it out. They were perfect for me. All of them. My boys. My men.

My knights in leather-clad armor atop their shining horses.

My men saved me. They helped me. They took down the cartel that killed my brother. That killed their president. All of us were bound before we ever met. Bound by a singular evil that needed to be snuffed out. Destined to meet and fueled by the same righteous rage.

I'd never felt more at home in my entire life.

"Welcome home," I whispered to myself.

"Welcome home," my boys said in unison.

ABOUT THE AUTHOR

Savannah Rylan is a romance writer that spends most of her time writing and reading. When not writing about sexy bikers and the women that love them, you can find her chasing around her toddler and two fur babies with her husband. She used to live in warm sunny California but has since moved to the East Coast where she has to deal with snow now, which she isn't too pleased about.

You can join her mailing list here!
Check out her website!

Box Sets

The Bad Disciples MC Box Set
The Road Rebels MC Box Set
Marked Skulls MC Box Set
Dead Souls MC Complete Collection
Black Hornets MC Box Set
The Lost Boys MC: The Complete Collection
The Callaghan Mafia Box Set
The Black Cobras MC
Dragon Riders MC
Dirty Misfits MC
Steel Scorpions MC

Series

Twisted Metal
Twisted Glass
Twisted Hearts
Twisted Flames

Bender (Steel Scorpions MC #1)
Angel (Steel Scorpions MC #2)
Goose (Steel Scorpions MC #3)
Viper (Steel Scorpions MC #4)
Reaper (Steel Scorpions MC #5)
Fangs (Steel Scorpions MC #6)

Brooks (Dirty Misfits MC #1)
Porter (Dirty Misfits MC #2)
Asher (Dirty Misfits MC #3)
Cole (Dirty Misfits MC #4)
Tanner (Dirty Misfits MC #5)
Finn (Dirty Misfits MC #6)

Link (Dragon Riders MC #1)
Bowser (Dragon Riders MC #2)
Ash (Dragon Riders MC #3)
Knuckles (Dragon Riders MC #4)
Sly (Dragon Riders MC #5)

Declan (The Callaghan Mafia #1)
Brody (The Callaghan Mafia #2)
Gael (The Callaghan Mafia #3)
Flynn (The Callaghan Mafia #4)

Cage (Dead Souls MC: Prospects #1)
Bear (Dead Souls MC: Prospects #2)
Saint (Dead Souls MC: Prospects #3)
Ryker (Dead Souls MC: Prospects #4)
Toxin (Dead Souls MC: Prospects #5)

Texas (The Lost Boys MC #1)
Stone (The Lost Boys MC #2)

Bronx (The Lost Boys MC #3)
Notch (The Lost Boys MC #4)
Diego (The Lost Boys MC #5)
Puck (The Lost Boys MC #6)
Frost (The Lost Boys MC #7)
West (The Lost Boys MC #8)

Jace (The Black Hornets MC #1)
Maverick (The Black Hornets MC #2)
Duke (The Black Hornets MC #3)
Colt (The Black Hornets MC #4)
Thor (The Black Hornets MC #5)
Jagger (The Black Hornets MC #6)

Knox (Dead Souls MC #1)
Grave (Dead Souls MC #2)
Brewer (Dead Souls MC #3)
Rock (Dead Souls MC #4)
Diesel (Deal Souls MC #5)

Girth (Marked Skulls MC #1)
Rodeo (Marked Skulls MC #2)
Abe (Marked Skulls MC #3)
Oz (Marked Skulls MC #4)
Dash (Marked Skulls MC #5)

Hawk (The Road Rebels MC #1)
Talon (The Road Rebels MC #2)
Snake (The Road Rebels MC #3)
Fox (The Road Rebels MC #4)

Gunner (The Bad Disciples MC #1)